For Douglas,
who got interested

THE
MAN
WHO
WAS
AFRAID

Part
I

1

Actually, we're all afraid, but I'm honest enough to admit it. I'm going to admit it as it's never been admitted before. Others have their moments of honesty, but I'll clobber my fears, one and all, with a book, and it won't be the Bible, which Elmer Gantry used on roaches. I'm going to run them ragged, those fears, so they'll drop panting, with their flickering tongues out, out like a light, a red light. I'll exercise them and exorcise them. Bell, book, and candle. I want to put it all down before I die. I'll have to hurry—I don't expect I have much time. I had my first dizzy spell this morning.

I was lying on my back when I woke up, which is the corpse-on-a-slab position that invariably scares me into quickly doing something—such as twitching my left hand—to ascertain if I'm paralyzed. Being forty-seven, and in a hectic profession, and having been born in Manhattan, to which I am compelled for business purposes to return, I have no reason to believe that I shall get through any particular night without a stroke. (*That* started when I was forced to recite, "If I should die before I wake—") My friends are popping all around me, and as for the movie stars of my childhood, who bounded and slapped and dueled, they're gone, totally gone.

After last night I woke up all too soon, as usual, and yet necessarily, to break a nightmare that I don't even want to talk about. I mean I can't talk about it just now—I'm not being inconsistent, I'll get around to it, but right now I have to talk about how the room was spinning around. It had never done that before. I don't drink because I'm afraid of how I'll act when I'm drunk. The wall and ceiling spun from right to left, fast, fast, fast, like a pinwheel. If it had been really (reelly) outside of me

I'd have enjoyed it, as at a circus or a fair. You know, you gape at the latest trick—Lord, what wonders engineers and acrobats perform. But of course I knew this was subjective because I hadn't paid for a cyclorama. I turned my head on my pillow to the left, and a weight shifted in my cerebellum, and the room spun faster. I closed my eyes, and *they* seemed to rotate.

It passed. Everything does. That's what's so good—and so bad. In a way it would be better if it were still going on, for then I wouldn't have to be waiting for it to return. In three minutes or so I was able to sit up tentatively and make out, by the dawn's early light, the relevant print in my Merck Manual, which I keep on the night table for just such an emergency. Probably you are unacquainted with the *Merck Manual of Diagnosis and Therapy*, which I'm sure the American Medical Association wants to keep out of the hands of the laity. It's a trade secret. You recall how, after the doctor has made his preliminary examination at your bedside, got you to stick out your tongue, has made you gag, and has inserted his thermometer—he asks to go to the bathroom (or finds his way there unaided), making the excuse that he wants to wash his hands. When I was a child I used to wonder whether he quietly puked, or peeed (what an interesting past tense!), but now I know what he does. Behind the closed door he takes out of his black bag—I believe it's always called his *little* black bag—the Merck Manual and looks up your symptoms. Then he runs his finger down the prescription section, for obviously it's a rare mind that can keep straight all those details about grams and grains. The subtitle admits, "A Source of Ready Reference for the Physician." I don't use it for self-treatment. I use it to know the worst. Then I go to the doctor, who won't tell me the truth. Actually the AMA should put this book into all our hands, for it would drum up a lot of trade, as we get a line on things that might be wrong with us that we never even thought of before, the appalling possibilities, fifteen hundred pages of them.

My copy is the 1950 edition, which throws light on how far

back what some sneeringly call my hypochondria dates. I am not a hypochondriac. I merely face up to things, while most people, ostriches, hide, and don't know what they are hiding from or even that they are hiding. It takes courage to be afraid. I always know exactly what I'm afraid of. Nothing is going to take *me* by surprise.

An old hand, I didn't search the index for such a puerile and unscientific word as "dizziness." I turned to "vertigo" (see p. 968). That's what Swift had in his last years—those who say he was insane are just maligning him because he maligned them. I saw that the affliction could be otogenic or psychogenic, but my trembling forefinger hovered, for the etiology, over Category 5— or 8:

(5) *Cardiovascular:* Hypertension, arteriosclerosis, postural hypotension, overactive carotid sinus reflex, cardiac failure. . . . (8) *Neoplastic:* Tumors of the cerebrum, cerebellum, cerebellopontine angle, 8th nerve, and labyrinth.

I put my hand over my heart. It seemed to skip a beat (cardiac arrhythmia)—or be about to skip. You laugh at me, but admit you laugh uneasily. Can you swear you have never been afraid of a heart attack? If so, it is because you are certain you are going to die of cancer, which, as a matter of fact, is statistically less likely, though likely enough. This is what I mean by being honest. I'm going to voice all your fears for you, and inject some new ones, because while I want to deal with the fears of ordinary civilian life (thank God, I was 4-F in the draft), one of my fears is that of being ordinary (which alternates with the fear of being abnormal). In the days when I was afraid of the draft, that was settled at the medical when my chart was marked "PN." I took that to be short for "pneumonic," but some of my best friends argued it stood for "psychoneurotic."

The neat thing about a heart attack is that being terrified of one brings it on.

I doubt if a heart transplant would work. Am I big-hearted? They have a lot of trouble with sizes. I feel I could do with a brain transplant—I'm beginning to lose my memory, which is another reason for frantic note-taking. My brain cells are dying. Two days ago I called the boss "Harvey," whose name is Garvey. In the first grade there was a boy who punched me in the stomach, and *his* name was Harvey (was it his first name or his last?), but of course I didn't bother Garvey with an explanation. I know a psychoanalyst would make a great deal of this *lapsus linguae,* but a neurologist would say the old synapses just aren't what they used to be. You can't beat a neurologist for gloom. And now vertigo. There have been other lapses. All I can look forward to in that area, for whatever future there is, is that my memory will get so bad that I won't even remember the lapses anymore. Like Swift's Struldbrugs, those senile drivelers, or my great-aunt Francine.

I'm also losing my hair, as if that were part of the cerebral degeneration. The last time I looked into a mirror I palpated my cheeks with a distinct feeling of disaster. The upper part, at the cheekbone, showed middle-age bulge. Below was sagging. Wrinkles and flabbiness and emaciation come from the metabolic loss of subcutaneous fat. So there I was—and it's going to be a while before I venture another peek (I don't have to look to electric-shave or even to comb)—there I was, by looks and by touch, simultaneously—within an area of just a few centimeters—too fat and too thin. I shook my head to see if my cheeks flapped. It was hard to tell. I think they did. After a few shakes a headache nailed in, which meant another bad day, as I'm chary of aspirin, which makes me sweat.

Speaking of brains leads directly to Merck Category 8. I could be developing a nice little glioma. They say you have to be really brainy to grow a brain tumor: it's the product of high activity in lively overcharged soil. I'm smarter than I thought I was when I nearly funked out (not flunked out) of Dartmouth. It's not at all unlikely that I've got something that's reached the stage of pressure on the optic nerve or on the semicircular canals. I could have started it with that fall I had on the bike at eight, the bike I didn't want. I slammed into the lamppost.

An innocent little bump. A bump that your mother pooh-poohs. "It's nothing, my crybaby," she said, but I knew better. I wasn't yelling my head off for nothing. I had a prescience of what had started then and there in my head, what I would hear from forty years later if I survived that long. A cell had been jolted into abnormality. I'm not going to make fifty. Apart from the question of whether I want to. Following the room-spinnings will come extension tremors, staggering, deafness, blindness, and an end that no drugs can dull. They'll have to cut my spinal cord or something. A literally head-splitting end. Sometimes it sprouts right out of the cranium like a tulip bulb, and you have to wear a hat, and a high hat at that.

I have an aphorism that I didn't get from La Rochefoucauld: *Those who are afraid are always justified, eventually if not immediately.* And there's a corollary that mothers should learn: *No child cries for nothing.* Everyone used to bear down on me with the accusation that I blubbered easily and excessively, but I had excellent reasons.

In two hours and thirty-seven minutes I'm supposed to leap up to get ready to go to work. If I get up I'll fall down. And even if I groped to the car, how could I drive? I'd just slam into another lamppost. "Men are but children of a larger growth," a larger brain growth. I'll risk losing my job and my paltry income before I'll risk becoming a red-and-white splotch—or if I diet, splatch—on the highway, one of this year's 56,000. It's no use being even a good driver anymore, because some fool is sure to crash into you sooner or later. Of the fatal so-called accidents, I'm convinced that half of them are suicides. Have *you* any other explanation for veering across a lane in broad daylight for a head-on collision? Personally I think disturbed people should stay in bed, and that's exactly what I'm going to do.

Besides my present just fear of getting up, I have a thousand others, equally just, that I suppose, with this enforced and sickening leisure that has dropped upon me, I could present, in Mercky textbook style, by classification, such as the fear of open places, closed places, high places, icy places. But it will yield more of a story if I proceed chronologically, with the very first wail.

Far from being a blubberer, when I was born I had to be slapped three times on the gluteals before I would cry. I seriously considered not taking that first breath. What was being offered that I should bother to open my bleary blue eyes that didn't focus? I strongly preferred my previous situation of floating inertia, of amniotic security. I have been trying to get back into the womb ever since, by symbolic action. That's why I'm a great copulator, a great knocker at the door. At night, as the best method of coaxing Sleep (Death's brother), I curl up in the prenatal position.

I do not profess, with Dali, to offer anything in the way of recollections of the womb. But you don't have to be an obstetrician to know it's a great place. It was my mother's second parturition, and she participated undimmedly in it, in those old-fashioned days, looking on without shots and pills, and without a mirror and without a husband. What she saw, she insisted (she did not always spare my sensibilities), was "a scrawny little thing." I promptly asked if my sister had been scrawny too. "No, she was sort of chubby." Clichés like that add fuel to sibling rivalry, as do the early photos; I only wish my sister and I had both been as simple as my mother thought we were, and as she was. To a neighbor fretting over a first pregnancy, I overheard her give the assurance, "It's nothing—it's like getting rid of a football." I have always loathed football, a rough and bewildering exploitation of the young by those who wish they still were. It is almost as boring as baseball, which is dangerous also and should be called beanball.

"Sport is an unfailing cause of ill will." (George Orwell)

I must have been afraid of a great many things that I no

longer remember, including darkness, noises, falling out of the crib, and anything that came toward my now focusing eyes too fast. There must have been times when I had no faith that I would be fed. Then there was the foul damp cling of the diaper, which embraced your lower half like the dirty Old Man of the Slimy Sea (seaweed still carries me back to old infantile filth). It slubbered and sewered and chafed, this parasite, taking liberties like an incubus with a sleeping virgin. Frankly, shockingly, at first you didn't mind stewing in what you didn't know was your own juice. We are blessed with a high tolerance for our own juices: true love is being able to have the same attitude toward someone else's. Anyway, babies sleep through a great deal, and I wish I did. After a time discomfort passed from the obscure to the definite, and you were in full crying possession of the fact that you needed again to be released from the Old Man of the Slimy Sea. If you then weren't, if the operation was delayed by the incalculable carelessness of those in attendance, you got panicky and writhed your extremities like a boa-constricted pig.

I pass over diaper-pin-pricks and the colic and other infantile disorders, mercifully forgotten. I have an excruciatingly low threshold of pain. Hot glasses and plates that pretendedly delicate women can hold I drop. A woman once dropped me because I dropped her mother's Sèvres teapot. I wasn't supposed to be there anyway, and I was trying to latch on to her hand when she bounced up and said, "Let's have tea—you can help!" It is only fair to report that this nubile young thing held the precious object round its pale blue belly, proffering me the handle, but even that—making due allowance for the fact that tea was not what flustered I had come for—was too hot. It was the end of a promising relation, and there must have been a deal of patching up to do with her mother, but I was soon able to look back with equanimity, for who wants to be stroked by leathery hands? Women being tougher than men, it becomes them to conceal it. I don't take soup in company, since everybody else has usually finished before I can start, it being vulgar to blow. Burns out the alimentary canal, anyway. To paraphrase Dr. Johnson, a man who doesn't have a decent regard for his mucous membranes won't care about anything else either. I also avoid spices.

My two earliest distinct memories must have conditioned me to expect the worst. I nearly died on both occasions, and I don't see why I didn't expire of fright, if nothing else. In fact, I shouldn't be thinking of this, in my condition. People with memories—mine falters only for what's recent—die a thousand deaths. I sip those two deaths over and over, a slow sweet poison.

The first occasion had all the externals of malign innocence. You know, it's on the sunny days, not the foul ones, that people fling themselves off the Golden Gate Bridge. The gods—or the bosses—tend to smile just before they strike you down: indeed the smiling is the first part of the blow. It was a fine spring morning, the peeping crocuses were purpling the suburban lawns, and my sister, plump, superficially jolly, had wheedled permission from Mother to push me down the street in my carriage. Around the corner, safely out of sight of the house, she thought it would be a good idea to change my diapers. That's what she claims: she says she felt that I was wet: I've gone over this with her again and again without succeeding in pinning her down as to what she meant by *felt*: whether she felt *me*, or whether she just had a subjective conviction. Seven years older than I, she decided to perform the service that she had often seen rendered but had never had the opportunity to do herself. Live and learn. Or rather, learn, but not live. It was sheer sisterly motherliness, so she claims. Personally I'm not convinced I was wet, and as for her real motive—it would be a bit flattering to both of us to surmise she was seized with an inexhaustible voyeurism—judge from the event.

Operating from the bottom, she untucked my blanket and threw the lower part of it over my face, preparatory to a leisurely search for the pins. And that was it, that was very nearly it, as we said in World War II. The sun went out—I lay in muffled darkness. I didn't even know that I couldn't breathe. I have the impression that I held my breath rather than pumping for the air that wasn't there. Half in love with easeful death, as the poet says. It was soft and easeful like some new kind of reverse bonnet: nothing but the end of a spring day, just another surprising fact of life at that period of surprises. I mean I felt that this was normal too. Oh, I was a resigned baby. Conscious fear had to wait to grow up.

What happened next was a passerby, an old geezer out with his dog, who snatched the smothery-mothery blanket away and saw, I am told, a purple face, crocus-croak. I didn't feel purple then, but I've made up for lost feelings since. One consequence is that I can't sleep with my head under the covers, even though it's cold and my nose is frosty. Another consequence is that I could never be persuaded to see Paul Robeson or Laurence Olivier or anyone else smother Desdemona: the feigning is too real, like the time a hand crushed my mouth and nostrils in Central Park and I was mugged.

I will tell more of (on) my sister later. She always said I was a tattletale. On one occasion that should have made her blush—but nothing made her blush—I gave the perfect answer: "You're the tattletail!" I doubt if she remembers. Whenever I'm witty it turns out I'm the only one who remembers.

Then there is the white fear of hospitals, a peculiar blessing of our civilization. I had a tonsillectomy at three. I was stretched out on a slab and something enveloped my face again. ("Cover her face; mine eyes dazzle; she died young.") The anesthetist probably began as a candle-snuffer before he went on to higher things. He smiled and smiled as he prepared to extinguish me. The surgeon smiled too as he sharpened his knife. He made a preliminary visit to the hospital cot to soften me up. "So how's our young man. Tomorrow is ice cream day." The thing that descended on my face seemed to be metallic—it certainly felt so—like those covers that waiters put over helpless, palpitatingly hot dishes, with a hole in the middle for the thumb. I saw something through an aperture before I saw nothing. Sniff-snuff.

And the night after that morning did bring ice cream, my favorite vanilla (favorite doubtless from its association with milk, which my full-breasted mother denied me: I was the up-to-date formula baby). (I have mixed feelings about not having had the motherly—but also, like the pram blanket, smothery—breast.) But the vanilla, when I choked on it and painfully gargled it out, had a strawberry sauce that turned out to be my own blood. HEM-ORRHAGE.

The white attendants at cotside mitosed from one to four, with that sudden bustle of attention that you may have to pay for with your life, but it's flattering while it lasts. Finally you have become interesting. I don't know what was done to stanch me: needle and thread? cauterization? But here I am with only a few scars, including the ones I open my mouth to study occasionally in my magnifying shaving mirror, the one I bought when I suspected cancer of the gums. (My gums bleed very easily.) Had I been born ten years later, when that operation had gone out of fashion, my tonsils would never have been raped, my tender mucous membranes left unbled. I think my tonsils have been growng back, anyway, unless those lumps are neoplasms.

As an ectomorph I am prone to diseases of the upper respiratory tract. I have more than the usual number of sore throats and colds. A stuffy nose brings back the trauma of the past, the panicky knowledge that I am half asphyxiated already, since I have to breathe through my mouth (and how can I eat—or drop my jaw in sleep?). When I see a woman with a slender throat—which the damnfool poets praise—I don't envy her her narrow trachea.

I have never set foot in a hospital since, not even for a visit (except for once). I'd as soon cross the threshold of a funeral parlor, which is what I'll be doing the next time. Born and bled there—that's enough. Which is why I haven't called a doctor, provided I could reach the phone. They wear white at hospitals because they should wear black, since—the great modern discovery—we are all the opposite of what we seem. That must include me. I keep thinking if I appear unhealthy it's a sign I'll reach eighty-seven. I even exaggerate my unhealth in the hope of tricking the opposite reality to a similar exaggeration. You know, pretend you're dying, when in fact you're only going mad.

It follows that if I strike others as cowardly, it's because I'm brave. As I said.

2

What are little boys afraid of? It can have something to do with what they are told they are made of. "Snips 'n' snails 'n' puppy-dogs' tails." The "puppy-dogs' tails" is a transparent allusion to what boys have that girls don't. The whole jingle is as vicious a piece of sexual propaganda as *Alice in Wonderland*, with its flamingo croquet, whose author frankly admitted, "I am fond of children—except boys." This rhymed contrast that my dear sister kept mouthing at me—it was one form of her oral aggression—obviously originated with a girl or old maid in the throes of penis envy. "Sugar 'n' spice 'n' everything nice," forsooth! Coming from my sister, that was very, very funny. Spice isn't nice anyway, as I've already explained: it just sears. But, hearing it so often and no matter how incredulous I managed to be, I was decoyed into a good deal of childish speculation over what the statement about my alleged composition meant. With precocious *ben trovato* I groped my way toward a connection between "tails" and the dangler I had that was also tender and that would elicit a yelp from me if anyone managed to step on it (which wouldn't be easy). This, mind you, was forty years before I read the first part of Bertrand Russell's autobiography, in which he relates how he ignominiously fell down and injured his penis and had to spend days sitting in a hot tub. This center of worry was established early, especially as I wet my bed till I was seven.

The adult, pondering "snails," associates not only with phallic protrusions but also slime, white semen (seamen, heh, heh, those sexy sailors, ramming into every port!): in other words, our old maid rhymster's fear of—but at the same time longing for—intercourse and impregnation. Naturally, accidentally, I stepped on snails when we went to the shore, and the crushed remains on my bare feet were disgusting, as was the slime living snails left behind. I wouldn't want to be made of *that*: though it takes getting used to that I was made of semen. Once, when I was munching a hamburger, and went into slow motion on account of something gritty, Sis said she had put a snail in it. I didn't stop retching even when, after watching me for a while, she added that she was just joking and hadn't done anything. I never inspected for the truth. My eyes were closed for about an hour. I wouldn't get up until they said they would send for an ambulance if I didn't (which was probably another lie).

"Snips" was a puzzler. Some versions have it as "snaps." Would it not be dogs snipping or snapping at? Little boys are made of dog-bites and tails and crunchy snails. I went through a period of being scared of all the suburban hounds. From "snip-snap" I leaped to Jack Sprat in my junior year at college, when, in preparation for a term paper on Swift, I had to deal with his poem "A Description of a City Shower," which ends in typical vein:

Sweepings from butchers' stalls, dung, guts, and blood,
Drowned puppies, stinking sprats, all drenched in mud,
Dead cats and turnip-tops come tumbling down the flood.

There are the puppies and there are other disgusting things: there is a fuller list of the ingredients of nasty boys, right up to the turnip-top, which refers to red hair, the nastiest type of nasty boy (see Renard's *Poil de Carotte*). It so happens that I have red hair, or had until it started clumping out. Red hair means coarse hair, an apparently unavoidable nickname (I fail to see why—brown-haired people aren't called "Brown," unless that's their name), sunburn, freckles, and emotional sensitivity (called by enemies "temper"). If you don't relish being called "Red" (I don't even relish relish), wait till you're bald or gray, then only your old friends will keep up the habit, often with a smile, and if you can't stand that, move.

While being literary, or subliterary, let me mention another thing that pushes you into the abyss: the reading you are early exposed to. My sister lost forever the homicidal opportunity to change my diapers, although I continued to be swaddled in rubber at night. As the years passed, they tried various devices to break me of the bed-wetting habit. Dry supper, no matter how thirsty. One contrivance around my waist rang a buzzer at the first trickle. Another was meant to sting me—send me yelping to the john—but fortunately malfunctioned, and every morning in answer to the invariable question and, all too often, even more humiliating unswathing and uncovering, I proved soaked and unstung. Stubborn child. "He loves his own pee." To which I might have replied that I preferred it to anyone else's. When are you going to stop being a baby? Sheety-shame! To get even, but in the guise of entertainment and admonition, my sister took to keeping me awake with intonations from Grimm's *Fairy Tales* (grim indeed) and from a hideous book of verse entitled *The Golden Staircase*. It should have been called *The Slopes of Hell*.

Do you suck your thumb? *The Golden Staircase* had something to reduce that small problem.

> The great tall sailor always comes
> To little boys who suck their thumbs;
> And ere they dream what he's about,
> He takes the great sharp scissors out
> And cuts their thumbs clean off—and then,
> You know, they never grow again.

Little Conrad failed to heed his Mamma. When she was out, he went on sucking. The bloody-red sailor giant strode through the door. "Snip! Snap! Snip!" (there's *that* again).

> Mamma comes home; there Conrad stands,
> And looks quite sad, and shows his hands—

"Ah!" said Mamma, "I knew he'd come
To naughty little Suck-a-Thumb."

So this is when Freud, little Sigmund, began to worry about castration, having already been circumcised, which is bad enough. I'm not joking—the author, Heinrich Hoffmann, was a nineteenth-century German, like the brothers Grimm (which is enough to make one afraid of Germans). Someone thought it only fair that English-speaking children be traumatized too, and rendered also into English, in plenty of time for Sis and me, Hoffmann's "The Story of Augustus Who Would Not Have Any Soup" and "The Dreadful Story About Harriet and the Matches." Augustus, like me, did not always care to finish his soup. In fact,

one cold winter's day,
He screamed out—"Take the soup away!
O take the nasty soup away!
I won't have any soup today."

Each day he got weaker, but stubbornly refused the soup, even as I stubbornly pee-souped the sheets.

The third day comes; O what a sin
To make himself so pale and thin.
Yet, when the soup is put on table,
He screams, as loud as he is able,—
"Not any soup for me, I say:
O take the nasty soup away!
I won't have any soup today."

Look at him, now the fourth day's come!
He scarcely weighs a sugar plum;
He's like a little bit of thread,
And on the fifth day, he was—dead!

As for Harriet, the pyromaniac (not to be confused with The Little Match Girl of Hans Christian Andersen), sugar-'n'-spice

Harriet, with her joy in matches, burnt down the house and herself, leaving only—boo-hoo!—her little scarlet shoes and some pussies that screeched for help in vain:

> Make haste, make haste, me-ow, me-o,
> She'll burn to death, we told her so.

I have to be fair to myself: I have never derived a sexual thrill from fires. I was an unburnt child that feared the fire, even as I was an unbitten boy that feared dogs. I did slice my pinky on a carving-knife, at five, in my curiosity to open a package that wasn't even for me, nearly lost that digit (three stitches), which would have ended my flashy right-hand octaves at the piano before they began, and of course the residuum is that I never carve. When asked to, I display my scar, and if they presume to argue, "Come, now, Kenneth, aren't you being a little pathological?" I tell them that I'm left-handed (*gauche, linkisch*), which is also true.

Taking part in, being forced to take part in, what Durkheim would denominate "the collective superexcitation" of Grimm's *Fairy Tales* was enough to wet anyone's pants. These generated consuming worries. Whom did I resemble in that cast of monsters, and was the outside world that they expected me to face like this? Did it consist of wicked skinny hags and mean pacts that were horrible to keep and dreadful to break? Take that blatantly sexual tale, "The Frog-King." The frog insisted on turning up at the princess's table and eating from her golden plate, and he wasn't just going to stay on the floor, either, when she went to bed. The odious thing, pop-eyed and slimy, was determined to hop right on her and stick out in her direction his fly-catching tongue. And he had this right, well, like a husband, really. He *became* her husband: the happy ending averred that he was a king's son who had been wickedly transformed, but that now the evil spell was broken. But what guarantee was there, I wanted to know, that the princess wouldn't wake up one night and find that she was sharing her sheets with a frog again? What had happened once could happen twice. Her first awareness might be slime under her nighty. I went off on a parable of marriage. After the honeymoon, the princess discovers she's married a frog. Or he was a man, but she's rolled over and crushed him, and now he's not a man but something squashed and with not even much ooze.

I felt the princess's disgust, but I felt the frog's plight. I took too many sides in all the stories, and was miserable. The hero's triumph was always soiled with the taste of someone else's defeat. "Then Gretel gave her a push that drove her far into it, and shut the iron door, and fastened the bolt. Oh! then she began to howl quite horribly, but Gretel ran away, and the godless witch was miserably burnt to death." I stayed behind in the oven, while the story lurched blithely onward to a reunion of brother and sister (who wants that?). I lingered over disasters like an ambulance-chaser. How was the witch's burning different, as pain and therefore as point, from Harriet's, and if the lesson of Augustus and the soup was to eat what was put before you, isn't that what the witch planned to do with Hänsel and Gretel? Even witches have to eat, and this happened to be a carnivorous witch that didn't care for gingerbread any more than I do.

I can see that I narrowly escaped becoming a social worker, who has an explanation—always away from personal responsibility—for everything. Conrad sucked his thumb because he didn't get enough of his mother's milk. His mother didn't have enough milk on account of poor diet. Her diet was poor because, for reasons beyond her control, Conrad's father had left her. He had left her for reasons beyond *his* control, and in fact he was the product of a pattern, since *he* had been abandoned as an infant—also for quite impersonal reasons—by *his* father, who also sucked his thumb, etc. (if you know whose thumb I mean).

As we get older, darkness may denote an awful absence—total oblivion, perpetual night, the coffin. For a little child it means an awful presence or potential presence. He is afraid that something is there or is on the way. Furniture shapes into monsters, with head and threatening arms—and what's in the closet? He listens for it. Light will keep it away. Even fifteen watts will. I pleaded for the smallest bulb. Failing that, leave my door open and the upstairs hall light on. Failing that, the downstairs light, which sent some faint reassurance upward. But adults are so careless, when they aren't mean. A switch would be turned off, and I'd scream. Or I'd wake up to darkness. They had *said* they would leave the hall light on all night, but they would say anything and not mean it. Was my door closed too? It smelt closed. What nameless thing was breathing toward my throat?

My sister learned to look cross-eyed. She had no trouble finding out that this scared me. Anything with the eyes scared me. I encountered a man with the largest milk-blue eyes I have ever seen, wide open (a little too wide, with too much white—like egg-white), clicking the pavement with an aluminum cane. He was young and blond and there didn't seem to be anything wrong with his legs. He walked straight ahead as if he would walk over you or anything in his path. You stopped pulling your tricycle along and stared at him, and you were not sure whether he was staring back or not. He seemed to be staring back. Afterward you were told he wasn't. He almost tapped your shoe. I asked if he was a zombie or, in his Palm Beach suit, a ghost. Ghosts walked right through you.

This become compounded with a movie involving a woman who walked in her sleep. In scene after scene she would slowly sit up in her bed, eyes open, switch sideways with military or automaton precision, arise to her full height, stick her arms out, and march. She marched all over the house, doing she didn't know what, and it was supposed to be funny, but I didn't laugh. To tell the truth, I wet my pants a little. Some comedians, the Marx brothers or their equivalent, would dart under her outstretched arms, put ridiculous hats on her, and joke with her the next day, when she was awake. But every time she marched around at night, with the eyes that didn't see anything, I felt personally threatened. She looked like a walking corpse to me (not that I knew anything about corpses apart from hearsay). She kept advancing upon me, even after I fled to another seat. I looked for her afterward in my closet. She and the blind man mixed together in nightmares. I, so to speak, married them, and they marched down the aisle, arm-in-arm, intoning, "We are such stuff as dreams are made on."

I couldn't face a fried egg sunny-side up on account of its resemblance to an eye. The German for "egg" is "Ei," which proves it.

It amused Sis to extinguish the light and tell me, in pitch darkness, that she was looking cross-eyed at me. This was always good for a yelp.

Do we have to like our relatives? We are brought up to believe that we must. But why? We didn't pick them. We get the friends we deserve, maybe even the face we deserve, but I'm no Southerner when it comes to Sis, or, for that matter, Dad. There is no memory of my ever kissing him or him kissing me. He would have deemed that unmanly. Sis was about as kissable as a big fat pumpkin. She got fatter and I got thinner: cause and effect. She stood between me and my dear mother, enacted the stepmother of the fairy tales. I naturally concluded "stepmother" had something to do with *stepping on* the little one.

Dad was in the wood-pulp business, home very little. He would go to Oregon to look at trees. Mother was a socialite or socializer, out a lot. I was left alone with the surrogate parent, who slammed me around when she got back from school and, later, when I did. Even if both parents were home, and it was night and I wanted to sleep (I worried already then about not getting enough sleep), or I had a headache in the afternoon and wanted quiet, Sis's portable or radio would blast me from her room next to mine. She had (and still has) the most deplorable taste, not for real jazz, but for the hit of the week, and was evidently hard of hearing, to boot. I was already picking out tunes on the upright piano, with the aid of *The Book of Knowl-*

29

edge (you know, "Betty" B. Flat meets "George" G. Natural and they get together in a chord), and was begging for lessons, and liked—I know it sounds priggish—symphonies, as accidentally encountered on the console downstairs. I don't mean I was a little Mozart. I may just have been reacting to Sis, that blessing in disguise. If her idea of the utmost in sound was "A Little Hut in Hoboken," then I wanted the palaces of the past.

Bang on the wall. Beat with your little fists until she heeds. "Lower that. I can't sleep."

"Well, isn't that just too bad. Little piss-in-bed wants sleepy-sleepy. Go to the toilet."

"I'll tell Mom."

"Tittle-tattle. Shut your door, runt!"

"You know I can't sleep with the door shut."

"And I can't hear with the radio off. Isn't that funny?"

"I didn't say off. I said low."

"This is my room. Another squeak from you and I'll come in and fix your wagon, good. I'm going to come in, and I'm coming cross-eyed."

I went through the same thing, as an adult, with electronic torture from neighboring apartments in Manhattan. You know the famous story of the wife who asked her husband the time, and the man next door said, "Twenty to nine." The eaves-dropping opportunities are tremendous, the peeping can be good too, but I moved to New Jersey, where I bang on the piano instead of on paper-thin walls.

The bigger people are always trying to get you to do something you're not ready for. Own a car, and you're contemptuous of the dangers of a bike. Own a bike, and you look down upon the tricycle. But the Latinate synonym for the latter vehicle, *velocipede*, is testimony to its manifold perils, of which I became—and remain—richly aware. It is indeed *swift of foot* when you've lost control going down the slope before your house and the pedals rotate so fast that your little feet lose all contact with them. You are churning toward what you are certain is your end. You swerve to avoid a lamppost (the same lamppost that four years later received you and your bike), and of course you keel over, and the left handlebar, on which you just happen to have lost the rubber, rips through your shirt and into your rib like a piece of shrapnel. So this, blood-red, is what you're supposed to leap for joy at when it's found under the merry Christmas tree. Santa brought it, who watched whether you were good. Why did he give it me, since I still wet the bed and even took a bite at Sis three days ago (to prove what boys are made of)? The most I wanted to do was lead it around, the way I led the quacking duck the year before. I never wanted to go anywhere on it, especially after I gave it an experimental kick down that hill and saw what happened to it with nobody on it. Oh, I was wise beyond my years—"Kenneth" has "ken" in it, doesn't it?—and it was my rib that had to be plastered, not Sis's (cushioned in fat) or Dad's.

For my seventh birthday I asked for a first-aid kit. I played doctor with the girl next door, who was two years my senior, little Agnes Rooney with the sea-green eyes and honey hair. She had that nice hay smell inherent in girls her age, preferable, in my opinion, to anything you buy at the drugstore. You will snicker at the probability that "playing doctor" meant that sex reared its diminutive head. It is true that Agnes kept trying to pull my pants down to apply bandages in areas where I denied needing them. She was an only child. But, though my accident was now years behind me, I was fixated on the region above the waist: nothing had ever happened to me below it. I drew up her dress and her slip to her nonexistent breasts and plastered her there, covering the milkless nipples, and allowed her to mend my ribs.

At the shore she wore a two-piece suit, which was literally pointless. It was there, a little later, that I experienced a timid awakening. Agnes and I romped a good deal, and I had begun to get interested in wrestling—preferably with smaller boys—on the mat in gym. It was obviously less injurious than boxing, and one needed some sort of self-defense, since bawling was even less effectual at school than at home. I took it into my head to practice with Agnes on the sands. I would show her how to get a person down with a necklock. But in the midst of the demonstration, about which she was not at all cooperative, something went wrong—maybe I hadn't allowed for her greater weight—and it was I who tripped and went down. She sat astride me as I lay on my back breathlessly contemplating her soggy bra, which sagged meaninglessly as she bent forward to pinion my arms. I looked around for help, but there was nobody near. Her naked knees clasped my thighs. I was in a real bind. It was humiliating. I heaved my trunk in an effort to throw her off. She just gave a preoccupied smile and rode tightly the bucking bronco. After two thrusts against her soft crotch I stopped, conscious of a new embarrassment. I looked into her face and there was just the tail end of a smile now. I didn't dare glance down to where the trouble was. We seriously studied each other's eyes. If she dismounted now, my first erection—at least my first in company—would be poker-plain under my bathing trunks. I must keep her to me until normalcy and calm returned. My heart pounded. Could she see it rattling? Did she realize—could she feel, the change down there? The terror of something that was part of me but that I was helpless to control exceeded the incidental pressure-pleasure. I had but lately stopped wetting the bed, and now I had a distinct, trickly, overriding feeling that I wanted to wet Agnes.

"I'll bet you can't stay on me for five minutes."

So I cunningly gained time, my petty lust passed, and I don't know to this day what Agnes was or was not aware of. Was I not suitable for masturbation, seeing what girls do with railings? Agnes just sat comfortably, in Van de Velde's Position IV. But, as with bed-wetting, here was worry over the involuntary again. Didn't St. Augustine declare that to be the sign of the fall of man? Adam before could control his penis; afterward it controlled him. It sure bosses me. Sometimes I worry because it's up; other times I worry because it isn't.

I also was conditioned to connect sex with struggle, with conflict. We tear our pleasures with rough strife. At some unknown time I woke to stifled groans coming from my mother's room across the hall. She—the voice was unrecognizable, but it must have been she—was in pain. She was crying softly, "No, no—stop—wait." Somebody was hurting her, there in the double bed, behind the closed door. I naturally suspected Sis, but as I groped bravely to my open door, I heard *her* snoring. Dad was home. Dad was hurting Mommy. What could I do? Get the operator, call the police? I took another brave step, toward the newel, the floor creaked under my bare foot, and suddenly there was quiet from that room. I tiptoed back to mine. Was she dead? Be sensible. He's rough—you know how rough he can be, he was in the Army, but he just couldn't, he just wouldn't. I lay pondering, but, secretive, in the morning I asked no questions.

That evening, in true adult, escapist fashion, I announced that I would sleep with my door closed—for the first time in my life. "Sis snores too loud." Maybe it had been some sort of nightmare, or a Joan-of-Arc experience: had she not heard voices? Now that disturbances were coming from the outside, the rational thing to do was to shut them out, after searching my room carefully, under the bed and in the closet.

If all masochists turn out to be sadists, surely there is no cause to be surprised at a switch from claustrophobia to agoraphobia, the one being, as it were, the inside of the other.

I had a crisis about whether to turn the latch—I'd be blocking danger but also locking out help. This was settled by my mother's forbidding it.

"Do you lock *your* door?" I asked.

She answered no, and I took in my breath to say more, but didn't. Only, they saw I was going to say something, and waited. She and Dad looked at me, there in the lighted hallway, and

33

then they looked at each other. Significantly? "What's come over the boy?"

"*You've* come over her"—that's what I might have said years later, "and I don't like it one tittle, not one tit-tittle!" Which reminds me of the Jewish joke about Mrs. Schwartz and Mrs. Hirsch meeting at the shopping center, the latter looking very worried and explaining that her little Herb had been told by the teacher to go to the psychiatrist, who discovered that he had an Oedipus complex. Mrs. Schwartz comforts with, "Oy, oy, Oedipus or Schmoedipus, I wouldn't worry, as long as he's a good boy and loves his mamma."

I went through a phase of dirty words, later than Gesell said I should. I have reason to remember the time when, at the dining table, just after I had munched on a drumstick, I uncontrollably came out with, "Two balls and a bat." "What's that?" inquired my mother. Dad didn't say anything. "Two balls and a bat," I repeated, then cast my eyes down at my plate. It welled up from the unconscious, for no identifiable reason. Everybody was aware of my lack of interest in baseball, which I understand is played, anyway, with only one ball. Cricket would also have been ruled out. It is true that I had started my long career with ping-pong, the only game I have ever cared for (except horseshoes) and we were always losing the balls, but why *two* in particular—and besides, the other thing is called a paddle. My mother was baffled. Dad, it turned out, was not. Early next morning, before going to work, he strode into my room. "Come into the bathroom." There he applied Ivory to my washcloth and vigorously soaped my mouth, inside and out, the teeth, the gums. I was all one foam, tearful but undiluted. "Perhaps you will have a cleaner mouth from now on."

My sister, who hasn't lost any weight, reminds me that not all the violence came from others. "You had a lousy temper, Red," she says. She claims I tried to dispose of her, once and for all, in the Long Island Sound. I recall the episode to which she refers, which I feel was one of panic and grasping at any straw.

34

As regards swimming, I alternated between underconfidence and overconfidence. It is so terrible to go under that one becomes positively eager to learn not to. The eventual result was a pretty strong, if plodding, Australian crawl. One afternoon I was tumbled by a wave. I grabbed for the only person nearby, who seemed to be enjoying firm bottom. But Sis was over her head too and went down with me clutching her at the shoulders. I rode aloft, elated monarch of all I surveyed, including air. I felt nine feet tall—in a way I was, but there was frantic motion in my lower depths. Well, the lifeguard rushed out in his boat and pulled me off, and soon had Sis stretched on the beach, where he gave her artificial respiration, kneading of the ribs (no kissing in those days). Certainly this was not a conscious attempt on my part to return one blue face for another, though I have always been alive to the advantages of having my mother all to myself.

Sis more or less disposed of herself soon after. She went to two of Westchester's best boarding schools, was expelled from both, never graduated, and eloped at seventeen with a clerk at the A&P, after being caught on the porch glider *in flagrante delicto* with a marine. There *are* men that go for these cushiony types.

3

You may think there's nothing to be afraid of in playing the piano. Then you've never given a performance in public and been smitten with stage fright. My second teacher—for at last they gave me teachers—had been the pupil of one with a Russian or Polish name (you have to be Russian or Polish to be a great pianist, just as you have to be Jewish to be a violinist) who, my teacher solemnly told me, was the greatest pianist alive, but the public never knew it, for he had to be tranquilized with drugs before he could emerge from the wings, and his hands either shook or were half-paralyzed, and after a number of nervous breakdowns in public he gave up and confined himself to teaching. But in the privacy of his living room or in a few collectors' rarities of records, if he could forget or did not know that anyone was listening, he let himself go and soared to unreachable heights. Famous rivals used to sneak in and put their heads to his door when he was practicing. That, at least, was the legend, and I empathized with both the positive and the negative sides of it, remembering what happened to me when my first teacher had a get-together of her pupils and their parents.

This was at an early stage, during Duvernoy ("The School of Mechanism") and before Czerny ("The School of Velocity"). All that was expected of me, when my turn came to go to the piano (a shaky upright—I was never sure it wouldn't topple over on me), was to get through Beethoven's Minuet in G. You could scarcely ask for less than that. I had a liking that came close to a crush for young Miss Ellis, whose main working hours were spent at the dime store playing sheet music. "Have you a sweetheart, Miss Ellis?" "You'll be my sweetheart, if you get this right." She had red hair too (self-love!) and a wide friendly mouth that drew me like raspberry cream. I would visually lick her freckled profile as she demonstrated a passage. I scarcely knew which I wanted to do more—caress the keys or her. Not having read the Henry Miller novel in which the boy crudely seduces his piano teacher, I settled for the keys, but the happy union was when our hands touched at the keyboard, as they often, perforce, did. "This way, Ken, wrists up, and don't forget, as soon as you've struck the C, to stick your thumb under to have it ready for the F." Gosh, as I look back, and think where I should have wanted to stick my thumbs, but probably didn't want to then—this is just grown-up lust. I was an unprecocious eight, or if precocious, only in a certain manual dexterity at the keyboard and at the ping-pong table.

Still, such skills may be of use to the lover. I must, if I get a chance, try out a touch typist. Looking at pictures of Casanova, who had 116 mistresses, I wondered what women could have seen in that gangling, swarthy, hawk-nosed man. Then I came upon a picture that revealed his hands, those exquisite, highly dextrous hands—and he knew exactly what to do with them, went right to the point. In short—which Casanova *wasn't*—handsome is as handsome does.

To get back to the Minuet in G, I longed with all my heart to please Miss Ellis, which is why I quelled my forebodings and strode to the sacrificial altar, but there were all those people sitting expectant, staring now at me and no one else, and I had been preceded by older pupils who had performed harder things with hateful aplomb. Nervously I accelerated the tempo, the minuet turned into a polka, and on reaching the Trio I waxed hysterical, jumbled the notes, missed the leap from the low D to high G, and ran out of the room without even pretending to finish.

This passed, and so did Miss Ellis, when I became too advanced for her. I got over my fear of dogs, too. I had been afraid precisely because I have never been bitten: the imagination being worse than the reality (for all I know). Thirty thousand New Yorkers are bitten every year, but up in West-chester—for which I don't have figures—I actually ended up living with a canine friend. Other problems, other fears.

A boy *is* supposed to have a dog, especially if he's been lucky enough to lose his sister. From ten till sixteen I had a Pekingese. Some would say, some did say, that that's not a dog. I've never been able to get to the bottom of the common prejudice against Pekingese dogs. Is it their small size? They are bigger than toy bulls. Consider the Chihuahuas, miserable hair-less creatures fit only to be inserted in the loving cup that some other dog has won. Is it the pug nose that mockery descends upon? Have you ever got close to an English bull? San Toy was just as stalwart as an English bull, and infinitely better looking. She had what in women are called delicate features—jet black nose, ears like the petals of a flower, nuggety cream-colored teeth that the triangle of her mouth would give tantalizing glimpses of, as if she wanted you to know that she could throw you a smile if she ever thought you worthy. Like some short people I have known, she was fearless, the Napoleon of street and home. She would go up to a dog of any size and stare him down. So what more can you want than bravery and beauty? Propping on my stomach the eight by ten studio portrait that I keep on my night table, I am seized sensuously with how exquisite her coat was, brushed or unbrushed, which is more than you can say of the hair of a multitude of women. She had this advantage over humans, also, that different strands had different shades, ranging from sand color to chestnut to autumnal red, all the spectra of brown. We know that a man's moustache may be a different color from his hair, and a woman's eyebrows from her hair, but this sort of variation is usually just embarrassing and suggests—and of course often is the consequence of—dyeing. (I seduced a housewife once because of simple curiosity as to whether she was a real blonde. She wouldn't tell me, but her pubic hair told me she wasn't. And they say vulvae don't speak! A really smart dame

38

would dye *that*. In all fairness—pun intended—though, I have just read that Rothe, "in his Berlin practice"—practice of what? —found extreme natural diversity among "977 North German women" he examined.) San Toy's silken coat that she kept pretty free of the ground was a joy to the eye and the hand.

Officially she was my mother's pet, a present for her birthday, and to ease the blow of Sis's elopement. Dad and I went to the pet shop, and I contributed $1.87 toward the purchase price and Dad the rest. The rest was a tidy sum—I don't remember how much because I didn't pay it, but my contribution must be seen in a proper historical light. In those days $1.87 could buy considerable (for instance, a Meccano set, which came with a perilous screwdriver), even if it couldn't buy a pedigreed dog. It was, moreover, all I had. I resist the cliché that I was giving what I wanted for myself, though superficially it looked like that. For San Toy soon began sleeping on my bed, and, when she was cold, even in it. Also I did raise my voice loud and clear in her favor while Dad was looking in another cage at a Siamese cat. If we're going to have something black-mugged, let's at least have something affectionate, I argued. A kitten might have had a chance, but the cat was months too old to be anything but cold and arrogant: it would scarcely look our way. It apparently didn't care whether it lived in Philipse Manor or not. Who but an adult would pick it over a puppy? Call me immature, but I still prefer a female that gives out signs of friendliness, that wags, as it were, her tail.

San Toy was so friendly that she wouldn't sleep in the guest room alone. Shut up there for the night, she incessantly moaned, yipped, and scratched at the door. Dad wouldn't have her in the master bedroom. So there was nothing for me to do but volunteer, although there was anxiety all round that I wouldn't get any sleep. And it is true that for some nights I ran short until we got used to each other, and she could loom suddenly as a living nightmare. She wouldn't lie still at the foot of the bed where an

39

old plaid blanket definitely marked out her area. I don't know who has ever shown greater interest in my face.

We had been bed-companions for several nights before I got her name straight. I assumed it was Sand Toy. I didn't know why she was named this, but I wanted to get to a beach to find out. My best guess was that she threw up sand dunes with those scratchy nails of hers. When the pedigree came in the mail I saw her name spelled out at last in purple ink that rivaled Dad's Bowdoin diploma: she was San Toy *by* Waikung II *out of* Ming Foy. Those prepositions, I backwardly failed to inquire all they meant. I was busy regretting the loss of a meaningful name; when we finally got San Toy to a beach, all she did was sink.

My growing years were perforated by anxieties over distemper, fleas, snarled hair (especially around the ears), and male dogs of all breeds. When someone tuned a ukulele with "My dog has fleas," I squirmed. San Toy, a clean dog, rarely had fleas, but when she did they hopped over to me. We poured on her, but not on me, a sickly-sweet powder that I should have thought would attract ants. As for those certain days when no dog that was a wolf could keep away from her, we put a girdle on her, but it was no chastity girdle. Walking in the suburban streets we'd draw within minutes four or five urgent prowlers. I would have expected yaps and whines from them, but their hunger was silent, deep, and of unbreakable persistence: a shameless fact of life. Whether aristocratic or just mongrels, they were all driven in the same direction. I kept them at a distance with stones, but they followed us around Philipse Manor, and when we returned home they befouled—I am not just speaking figuratively—our lawn. I know more about male lechery than any woman; my advice is, keep a stone in one hand and throw it at the strategic moment. San Toy never had puppies, and I went on to become expert at horseshoes. It takes little for me to imagine each ringer as a blow for chastity on some male dog's intrusive and sensitive nose.

I mustn't give the impression that I took over San Toy—or

she took over me—completely. Evidence was by no means lacking that she was my mother's pet. Mother took her walking almost as often, if not as far. She went everywhere in the car, and guarded it when it was parked, looking very snappish. She spent a myriad daytime hours on the double bed, especially after lunch when Mother lay down for a nap. Also it was Mother—more often than I—who fed her. It was definitely Mother who took to pouring the rest of her coffee into a saucer and letting her finish it. San Toy lapped it up with her little spade tongue (there had to be plenty of sugar and cream) the way cats are supposed to lap up milk (but often don't). In the long run, however, it seemed to be bad for her nerves. She got jumpy, and in her latter years her head shook, palsy-like. I must have been about fourteen when I came in at the end of one of the joint afternoon rest periods just in time to see San Toy wake with a start and nip Mother's lip. It didn't amount to anything—didn't draw blood—but never have I seen a creature so ashamed and embarrassed at her silly and involuntary mistake. She put her head between her paws and seemed to wait to be whipped, though she could scarcely know from experience what whipping was. Not only for that day but for the rest of their lives together San Toy and Mother were closer, the one forgiving, the other forgiven. There is nothing like a little incident of that sort to seal a companionship. One remembers that the reason that the Prodigal Son was welcomed so heartily was that he had gone away. No, busy with school and the piano (two hours' practice a day) and too young for a driver's license, I did not and could not preempt that birthday gift.

I only shared it. Sometimes, to be frank, as I got older (and, Dad said, lazier), walking San Toy was just a chore (like helping some small sister, if I had had one, in the bathroom) on a par with mowing the lawn. I would wait impatiently for her to do what we had come out for, and she, knowing that, perversely put me off. She would march up to a tree or a lamppost with every sign of purpose and sincerity, but it was only a sniffing act, an act of Pecksniffian hypocrisy. This could go on for ten or fifteen minutes. Sometimes I had to return her, she alone looking chipper, and try her again an hour later. What I learned—for future use—about feminine arts and whims and shilly-shallies!

Five weeks before my sixteenth birthday (I had been looking forward with a certain amount of paroxysmal tachycardia to my junior driver's license) Mother suddenly died. She was well for breakfast, offering me her cheek for the last time and San Toy a morsel of buttered toast. (It had to be taken from the soft middle—San Toy wouldn't cope with crust.) She passed away in the so-called "recovery room" of the Tarrytown Hospital in the late afternoon. When I was summoned from school just before noon she was on the operating table. Her appendix burst—and this was before there were the miracle drugs to clear up the infection. Dad and I were waiting in a little anteroom when the news—the final news—came. He looked at the big electric clock over the door and I involuntarily did the same. I had been keeping a diary. That night I printed in it in red crayon, "Mother died this afternoon at 4:23."

This was the last entry in the diary, which I am rather sorry now I put in the incinerator. One traumatic experience I was spared—seeing my mother's body. (I had not yet seen a body.) In accordance with her wishes, even Dad didn't see it. She had expressed herself with passion a year before, after having been to a funeral. "I don't want to be seen dead. That's not decent. I want to be remembered only as alive. Let's save on embalming and keep the lid shut." She was embalmed—I don't know for whom—but the lid was kept shut.

I have my doubts, after all, whether this is best for the survivors. You see a box lowered into the earth, but you can't be positive who's in it, or whether anybody—any body—is in it, because at no time have you seen with your own eyes. Your mother was alive the last time you saw her. The casket seems light enough to the ropes, and the pallbearers could have been pretending that they felt weight. So much pretending is done at funerals anyway. You come away with a weird feeling that she's not dead, just in hiding, for reasons that will eventually be explained. In her closet you see her dresses and her shoes—material evidence. A dog is lying on the double bed as usual. Everything is ready for her return, and you have no material evidence that she is dead, although you attended a funeral service. That could have been a deep trick played on you by your elders. An initiation, a rite of passage—to maturity. When the time comes they will break this solemnity and say, "You have passed. We were just testing you. You may take your place as a man now, and now that you have proved that you could get along without her, here she is." And a door would open and she would come in, maybe with a suitcase.

She was forty-two, a young mother (say I at forty-seven). If it would be partial of me to assert that she was beautiful (you know how everybody says his mother was beautiful—and then you see the picture, or, worse, the mother), I can at least report that she was widely regarded as good-looking in a rather athletic, very trim, blond way. She played a pretty good game of tennis. She applied but lightly to her own face the cosmetics that she hated to see on the faces of the dead. She was outstandingly sociable, received and accepted and gave numerous invitations, loved parties. (The pace she set herself necessitated the naps. She was at her best at night. I think if she could have lived till night she would have passed her crisis.) I could have taken her to dances. I wish I had.

Sis could not even be notified, having departed from her last known address.

How much San Toy missed Mother is not easy to say. San Toy was getting old. Pekingeses have a shorter life span than Pomeranians, for instance. The car, undriven now in the daytime, San Toy had become indifferent to anyway, had ceased to run for it, scramble spontaneously up the front seat; perhaps it was too drafty. She was habituated to her comforts; irregularities irritated her. The years had taught her to expect coffee and toast,

43

clean sheets, soft pillows, a walk whenever, at reasonable hours, she hovered by the hall closet where her harness and leash were hanging, and barked. I and a part-time maid had to replace Mother for her. I didn't drink coffee and Dad drank all of his, so extra coffee was brewed, and I gouged out my toast. At first San Toy padded all through the house, upstairs and down, in what we were reasonably sure was a quest. At first, too, she got on the double bed for a nap, but, the human warmth not being there, she changed to curling up *under* the bed.

Which leads to the question of how much Dad missed Mother. When a man marries again soon after having lost his first wife there are two lines of conjecture. One is that he couldn't have loved his first wife very much. The other is that, on the contrary, he missed his first wife so much that he was driven, in desperation, to do anything toward filling the gap, reach for anyone at all, swiftly and blindly, even the most miserable of substitutes. In short, Miss Warren.

Dad was not given to showing his feelings. He had been an officer in the First World War. He retained a military bearing. When I was six he started taking me walking with him, but it wasn't walking, it was striding, it was marching. He had me go at a pace too fast, and keep in step, left right, left right, hut, hut! No wonder he never took San Toy out. She would never have stood for that, the way I had to, my little legs working like pistons. Or rather she would have stood, digging in with her nails, mulish, the way she acted when you were trying to get her to ford a puddle: you could scoop her up in her harness, but when she said "No" she meant it.

Mother was the only one who could make Dad unbend. "Don't get excited," she would counsel, when I thought the whole trouble was that he never got excited. But she could measure his inner temperature, which showed only in a slight redness of the face. She did everything necessary to keep his inner and outer calm (and presumably contentment) equal. I offer no appraisal of the marriage. They didn't see a great deal of

44

each other. They went off in different directions, not really living together very much. He worked hard; she played hard.

I owe it to his memory as well as hers to report the possibly supernatural occurrence in our garden two months after her death. He and I were sitting in the rattan chairs on a Saturday just after lunch. It was June, her birthday month, a cloudy day, but you can smell the honeysuckle better when it's damp. I was hoping it would rain, giving me a postponement on pushing the lawn-mower. I didn't go so far as to scan the sky, for that would have reminded Dad that I had better "get to it." Suddenly a small white butterfly appeared on the scene, darting among the roses. Usually, of course, they come and they go, but this butterfly hovered, drew elliptically nearer. After visiting the flowerbed next to us it fluttered low over Dad's lap and then actually came to light on me, my left knee. It slowly closed and opened its wings, as if signaling. I knew that Dad was watching with the same fascination that held me, and he had the same thought, which he strangely whispered: "Maybe it's your mother's soul. The Greek word for butterfly and for soul are the same." The soul stayed there so long and so trustfully that I felt I could have touched it: it was looking directly at me, communicating, telling me, us, what it knew we needed to be told. It was all white, no spots. It did what church has never done. Never had I felt closer to both him and her.

Another three months, and he was married. I believe that Emily Post advises it is decent to wait a year. Still, five months— it is long enough, surely, for the funeral meats to cool. I don't wish to indulge in Hamlet's tragic exaggeration. I was even given some notice, but a thing like this is, naturally, carried out in a rather quiet way. I was told the week before, and I attended the civil ceremony, Miss Warren not choosing to wear the white wedding dress to which she was entitled as being beyond all doubt a virgin.

I don't blame Dad. I blame the matchmakers. Every community has them. Their idle chatter takes a turn in the direction

45

of this widower (poor Frank—he makes a good income, you know) and his poor unmothered boy (what's his name?), and they feel terribly, terribly sorry for all who are not married the way they are. Above all they feel sorry for some hatchet-face whom they've occasionally used as a fourth at bridge. She is in her forties and looks older, looks hopeless, and she runs a lonely millinery shop on the Old Post Road, standing woodenly near the window behind some sky-high price tags—like an old post, and I don't mean Emily.

She had not, to the best of my knowledge, seen the inside of our house till that September afternoon when she received her joyous new name, and the three of us disembarked from a taxi after the ceremony. Where she and Dad had had their clandestine encounters that shaped all this I don't know. It isn't easy for me to imagine him petting in a car, but now that my best years are behind me I must admit you never can tell what a middle-aged person will do. Anyway the three of us piled out, and I led the way up the path to the porch where, behind the screen door, stood San Toy. Miss Warren—let's forget her legal name, because that's what I was prone to do—didn't see her because she wasn't expecting her. As I opened the screen door San Toy padded out and sniffed at the stranger's ankles. She didn't snap and she didn't bark; she just ran her little nose around the edges of the black pumps. It was neither an unprecedented nor an unfriendly act; she kept her mind open, not her mouth: would there were more of this.

Miss Warren stopped in her tracks twenty inches before the welcome mat. "Why, what's that?"

"That," I replied, "is my mother's dog."

The hat full of purple bell-shaped flowers—dyed lilies of the valley—bobbed. "I don't like dogs. And if I did it would be a police dog. A watchdog."

"San Toy barks and bites," I said. "You don't know how lucky you are."

Dad reached down and took her up.

"Isn't she the ugly thing, though," came the distant comment. "What's wrong with her eyes?"

"Cataracts," I answered. "She has to get close before she can see anything any more. They have to get worse before we can do anything about it."

"It's disgusting. Like milk. She should be put away."

She passed into the hall. You can't make a retort to someone's back, even if you've thought of one. I've pondered more than once since what my answer should have been. What do the French call this futile practice, *l'esprit de l'escalier*? Should I have replied that I like milk, which is still a fact. Should I have conveyed the sharp point that those who obviously aren't ever going to have any milk naturally have a sour-grapes attitude toward it? But then I would have been thought to be revealing (by pretending not to have) anxieties about a future half-brother or half-sister, crude worries that I could not have entertained about a woman so clearly past her primipara.

The next week or two was a nightmare. I don't mean for San Toy only, who whimpered in her dreams in her favored position between my head and the wall. The new regime brought hardship to Dad too, though he stuck it out till the day he died: that is, for eleven years. One of his first discoveries was that his bride intended to go on playing bridge, with him as a partner. This was precisely and totally what marriage meant to her: giving up the millinery shop and having a partner for bridge. Marriage contract—contract bridge. Dearly beloved, we are gathered together for contract. My mother never played. She said so far as she could see it only led to quarrels. How right she was. Dad played badly, neither liking nor being used to the game, and Hatchet Face went on endlessly about his mistakes, for which she had a technicolor memory that could keep her going hours afterward. At odd times when they couldn't get opponents, she dealt out the cards anyway and under the guise of instruction she assailed his stupidity. "Now tell me, why did you lead the five of hearts? I was under the impression that I had given a full explanation of why you should not lead from weakness. But of course that was some minutes ago. Your memory, dear, is perhaps not what it was when you became Phi Beta Kappa. *I* never went to college. *I'm* not a clever businessman. But I've never thrown a rubber away through idiocy, blind mindless idiocy. We've got plenty of time. It's not late. It's early in the week—you can't be tired. Just give me your reasoning. You led the five of hearts. Your eyes weren't closed. You seemed to be looking. If I can know what's going on in your mind. Just a peek. I don't want to seem impatient. Maybe the tenth explanation will succeed where the ninth failed. Just give me *your* side. You haven't been drinking. You threw down that five in cold open-eyed soberness, although you had a choice of six other cards. *Six* other cards, not one of which wouldn't have been better than the five of hearts!"

But San Toy, who was entitled to a comfortable old age, bore the brunt those first days. Miss Warren was far from inclined to share her coffee with her. Dad made the mistake of giving San Toy some of his, which he had never done before. This was on the second morning of what would have been their honeymoon, if they had had one. It produced an explosion that subsided only when one of the component parts went off to work. But a firm decision was announced. San Toy was to have neither coffee nor toast. Miss Warren rushed out in the car and triumphantly returned with dog biscuits. "She's a dog, isn't she?" I examined one. It was shaped like a bone, but it should have been shaped like a stone. I tried it on my teeth: gritty granite, that's what it was.

"San Toy can't do anything with this," I said, rapping it on the kitchen table.

Miss Warren graciously proposed softening it with milk, perhaps.

"San Toy doesn't drink milk without coffee in it," I explained.

Miss Warren also said the blind filthy thing should be shut

48

up in the basement at night. "It's bad enough having her around in the daytime, infecting us. I feel germy already. But in a bed—a human bed! How could the sheets ever be made clean enough?"

I pointed to a moderately good health record, apart from colds and headaches and palpitations. That night, San Toy became almost literally the object of a tug-of-war between the bride and me at the door to the basement. I won.

A few days later I lost. We discovered that Miss Warren was not above taking a drink or two, a nip of bourbon as the afternoon wore on with no slams except door slams. The night I shall always remember, Dad came home late, and Miss Warren was in an uninhibited condition. *In vino veritas*. She and San Toy greeted him at the door, the one with a chip on her tipsy shoulder, the other with a gently wagging tail. He took the wrong one into his arms (in my opinion, the right one). "That bitch!" she shouted. "That blind stinking flea-bitten bitch. You have your wife before you and you take *her* up. I know why. I know why you keep her. She reminds you of—. You love that dog better than me. That pampered stinking bitch, good for nothing but bumping into the furniture and tripping me up. Your first wife's pet! Well, mister, you're going to have to choose. Either that milky-eyed bitch goes this very night—or I go. Take your choice, *darling*."

So she was exterminated. She really was bumping into the furniture, but I think she could have been operated on.

4

I have to say something about metaphysical fears. I was never led to see the comforting side of Christianity, came upon Thomas Paine and Voltaire at my own age of reason, and gave up Christianity as a superstition I had outgrown. Only now I'm old enough to know that I don't outgrow anything.

Dad, of Scotch origin, belonged to the Presbyterian church. Having got over stage fright I was roped in to play the piano for hymns during services at the local edifice, which was always *about* to get an organ. They didn't give me any money for this, but as I sat through hundreds of services there was dinned into me the gloomy likelihood that I was a goat, doomed from all eternity and to all eternity. There were very, very few blessed and predestined sheep. Gottschalk (the monk, not the composer) gave the number of saved as 13,768—or something like that. You were, as seen by yourself and others and in all mathematical probability a goat, personally singled out by Deity for damnation long before you were born, and there was absolutely nothing you could do about it. You couldn't even say, "Oh, well, what the hell!" and enjoy yourself (if possible) in *this* life, for you were told to behave *as if* you were a sheep, which *might* cause God (you never knew whether He was immovable or not) to put you in one of the better instead of one of the worst circles of Hell. Every little failure or sin or weakness you displayed added to the inner and outer conviction that you were going to the place of fire as surely as an unbaptized babe and the Jews and Mohammedans and Hindus.

And in your depravity you were always being watched by the All-Seeing Eye. Santa Claus had been bad enough. You had to behave yourself the week before Christmas. Santa Claus was watching to see what presents, if any, you deserved. But God was infinitely—and I choose my adverb with care—worse. He watched you fifty-two weeks a year. If you masturbated, He watched you. You had no privacy anywhere or any time. He even knew your thoughts. It was God-awful, and if you couldn't repress the thought that this was an awful God and you would like to be under a different dispensation, the Absolute Omniscient Monarch, who had been considering consigning you only to red flames, marked you ineluctably down for the hotter blue. At the same time, you were told to pray, God knows why.

When I came upon it years later I thought Pascal's bet contemptibly calculating. Maybe it appeals to bridge players and the lost souls at Las Vegas. "Let us weigh the gain and the loss in wagering that God is. Let us estimate these two chances. If you gain, you gain all; if you lose, you lose nothing. Wager, then, without hesitation that He is."

I have a lot of hesitation about this. In the first place, if God is, it may be eternally worse for you and me than if He isn't. But now that I'm forty-seven years close to the grave, and very sick, maybe God and Hell are, and I and Paine and Voltaire haven't exorcised them. The old ghosts come back, including the Holy Ghost, which I always envisioned as a white specter (taller than the others, of course). I am hound-of-heavened and hound-of-helled, losing my rationalistic nerve. *"Le silence éternel de ces espaces infinis m'effraie."* "I fled Him, down the arches of the years." Besides, they kept telling me I might see my mother again.

But, enough of theology or philosophy. I never was a thinker, just a feeler.

At the public school I was considered a freak because I played the piano—and long-haired stuff at that—instead of basketball. All the girls clustered around the athletes. Silly things, their mothers and grandmothers used to tinkle away, but the radio and records killed all that. Who wants to hear an amateur when he can put on Horowitz? But of course it wasn't

Horowitz that they put on. Well, if they didn't look at me, I wasn't going to look at them. I dimly knew already, and the boys passed on stories, that girls meant trouble.

At home my upright was moved to the basement, so Miss Warren would complain less about the practicing. I had British, Himmler-eyeglassed Mr. Claveridge as a teacher, a good theorist. He put up with no nonsense. "Don't be brilliant, and stop faking it." What he meant was that I could play faster than he could. I was a romantic; he was dry and academic. He had a nice trill, as in the Bach C Minor Fantasy, but I left him miles behind in Liszt's Sixth Hungarian Rhapsody. Which, when he perceived, he bade me drop. "It's just trash." I felt the terrible excitement of competition. There's that poem of Crashaw's, "Music's Duel," in which a nightingale, trying to out-do a lutanist, drops dead in his strings. It was my fate, as an adult, to be in the audience at Carnegie Hall when the phenomenal Russian virtuoso Simon Barere dropped dead while playing the Grieg Piano Concerto. He had just started it, and it was apparent he was going to take it at a dizzying pace—in the spirit of that miraculous 78 rpm of his of Schumann's Toccata in C (he breathtakingly got it on one side; Josef Lhevinne needed two)—when he keeled over. So don't tell me playing the piano isn't dangerous. I was also in the throng at Madison Square Garden waiting for a last chance to hear Paderewski, waiting for him to start, long-maned, his program, which he never did on account of a heart attack an hour before. Now it's my turn not to play—to nobody.

At least, that Paderewski had had a heart attack was the official story, and he sailed back to Poland, never to play in public again. The 20,000 who had been waiting in the Garden were given refunds, but I kept my ticket, sentimentally (not that the experts ever thought him very good). As it happened, I was memorializing an old Struldbrug. The inside story, even scarier than the official one, soon reached our shocked ears. Senile, when it was nearly time for him to go on, Paderewski said he had already played the concert, and they couldn't budge him from this insistence. I can see how it happened. Having practiced the program, he felt he had played it. I suppose if they had pushed him out he might have acted as crazily as de Pachmann, whom I've seen dance a jig upon his stool. Anyway, I'm getting the same way. The other day I broke off in the midst of the Chopin A Minor Mazurka, Op. 17, No. 4, when I realized that I was, obsessively, repeating the middle, which, goodness knows, is already repetitious, but there I was (no audience, of course), going on and on and on, dumty-dum, dumty-dum, like a broken record (which, you'll say—I give you this cliché free—is a good description of me).

A mean stepmother presents dangers, also, Grimm come true. I must not, in my corner at the bottom of the house, play too loud, or she would descend upon me, clattering down the steps with her wooden slippers and wooden face. Piano piano. Just what volume would bring her down? When would she go out and let an introvert be an introvert? I mustn't further jar an unhappy marriage with audible harmonies.

I was trapped, repressed, every way I turned. Only, the night brought something, after I awoke to the fact that the window opposite mine provided a view of the bedroom of my old flame, honey-haired, hay-sweet Agnes Rooney. It had been, last I looked, her divorced (or annulled—weren't they Catholic, with a name like that?) father's room, but apparently they changed, which was very good of them. Agnes had graduated and become, I regret to say, the gum-chewing waitress at Towne's Luncheonette, where she flirted with everybody but me. "No kiddin'?" she'd riposte to middle-aged truck drivers. "Bet you say that to all the girls. Now how about the chili con carne?" I wasted my allowance on banana splits, but I was not old enough for her to go swimming or anywhere else with, it seemed. Not that I asked her; I caught on wordlessly. Finally—and I had been leaving real show-off tips—I discovered I could see her for nothing.

I literally woke to it. That room, perhaps fifteen feet away, had long been dark, for months, and all I could have expected to

53

see, anyway, was her father, and I certainly wasn't interested in him. True, I had looked up the intimate life of Oscar Wilde, whose beautiful fairy tales I had gone around praising—"Far superior to Grimm and Andersen, you know!"—until my English teacher stopped me short. "Wilde?" he said, lifting his bushy brows. "*Fairy tales? Fairy* tales indeed!" So I read about his imprisonment, without being able to figure out, even with the aid of a dictionary, exactly what it was that he did. Some of my jolly classmates and one or two upperclassmen had endeavored to cast doubts on my masculinity, because of what I did (did Oscar Wilde play the piano?) and didn't do, such as not running around on the basketball court or with girls. The nearest to being disturbing was a budding scientist—he ultimately became our valedictorian—who prided himself on his powers of observation. "Look at your fingernails!" he said to me suddenly, outside the assembly room. In consternation, fearing that something awful had happened to me that he saw but that I couldn't even feel, I held my left hand up. "Ha, ha, you do just like a woman. That's what I thought you'd do. A *man* will *make a fist* to look at his nails." He brimmed with self-satisfaction. "I'll bet you stir liquids clockwise, too," he added. "A *man* will stir counterclockwise. I've been observing the girls in home ec." I didn't stir at all, as he turned away that conceited smile that I had had to put up with year after year, getting small satisfaction out of beating him at ping-pong. "It's just a sissy game, anyway," was his repeated comment. I've never been able to talk to scientists. He was plump, even plumper than my sister had been—there was so much fat around his eyes I don't see how he could see out of them—and of course he had no girls either.

But I possessed with my eyes Agnes Rooney, I at sixteen, she at eighteen. She had the same effect upon me as she had had nine years before. What does the old song say, "It's a long time between—"? I had gone to bed early—I worried so much about not getting enough sleep that I got quite a little, at least compared to now. My brain was crisscrossed with Euclidean

54

theorems, the ones I couldn't do in the daytime. Very possibly, the light newly at the window touched my eyelids like a magic wand, to summon me to life, after death. Something caused me to open them, and I crept forward in time to see a naked girl, moving before a bureau. She was searching for something in a drawer—maybe, oh, blessed lack! a nightgown. She stooped down, her breasts in profile, an exquisite curve of gleaming back. She was the archetype for unclothed female beauty, such as I had never seen before, the model for all I have seen since. I was so taken, and my blood was racing so, that I didn't identify her: her name was Woman, her name was Beauty. For the moment I was a Platonist, though in bursting tension a carnal one. Then she turned to the window and I saw with breathtaking clarity more of the honey hair than I had ever seen before—all beautifully in tone above and below—and it gloamed upon me that this was my neighbor Agnes Rooney, without her gum and very much without her apron, unfallen Eve. But now, having favored me more than any boy deserved, she was pulling down the pale shade and leaving me to shadows.

I didn't sleep well that night, and night after night I stayed awake or forced myself to wake up, at her late hours, and waited for a sight, but never again did she neglect to draw the shade before undressing. The light would go on, I would rush to the window, she would move around in her dress (I deduced that her bed was on the left, out of sight), maybe even comb her hair in her slip, but beyond that down would come the hateful yellow shade, extinguishing me.

Except for once. Once—it must have been in the middle of the dog days—I heard her speaking, she stood facing somebody (I couldn't see her door either), and then she went toward the shade but a man's voice said something about its being "too hot." All she did at the window was push the French panes farther apart. Then I heard, or thought I heard, the creaking of a bed, and no one came within sight anymore. I was staring at the blank farther wall, where a tasseled floor lamp mocked me with its grotesque resemblance to a lean, poky, overdressed female form. Suddenly I became ingenious. I moved to my other window, on the left, and looked diagonally out. Reflected in her right French pane (like a truck mirror) was a couple in naked-shouldered, loosely sheeted embrace, as in some French film. Unlike Mother, she made no sound. It was a wrestling and a rustling, in summer heat, and believe it or not, I didn't keep my post but went back to my own sheets and put my head under. Couldn't they, wouldn't they at least have the decency to turn out the light? I wanted her alone, and to look upon her alone. I was miserable, and what would she tell the priest on Saturday? It was probably a middle-aged truck driver, with eight kids, and if she had only turned to me, and given me one night (me with my trained hands and short, in fact bitten, nails) I'd have been her husband-slave for life.

I instinctively knew the facts of life. That Greek romance in which Daphnis and Chloe hug each other but don't know what further to do (until Daphnis receives instruction from an older woman) is one of the stupidest things to come down from antiquity.

Crazed with lust, I went to the beach next day. I felt like raping somebody. (This is Fear No. 33, fear of being a sex criminal; No. 32 is fear of being a sex deviant.) I scrutinized the girls in their summer suits, which in those days were never bikinis. Whom might I bear off, on my thin shoulders, behind that promontory? I wanted to strip every female under thirty, even the ugly ones. Indeed, the ugly ones might be more complaisant, in gratitude for my display of interest.

But it turned out that I was afraid to approach anyone even as old as I was. I understand the little-girl-fondler: he has no confidence in the presence of knowing maturity. Although there were other acquaintances there, I singled out Helen Trudeau, who was assisting her little brother with a sand castle and who had a reputation for not being very bright. Her older brother, who was also dumb, was a classmate of mine, and she and I had often tipped our foreheads to each other in the school yard.

Getting close enough to sniff her, as she bent over in her suit of green sheen, puffed or purfled around the breasts, I felt no prejudice—since she filled her suit well—against her for the word that had got around that she was going to have to repeat the eighth grade.

"Helen," I said, wasting no time. "Let's play Helen of Troy."

"What's that?"

"Come over there with me, and I'll show you. It's a game. We can't play it here. We have to play it over there."

"I can't leave *him*."

"Of course you can. How old is he—five? He's old enough to make his own sand dunes. Johnny—what's your name?— we're *both* going to help you in a few minutes. Just stay right there. Here's a full pail for you."

Little brother was being lapped at by the sea, which he needed to wet his cement. Would he be idiotic enough to drown? I didn't see that one sibling more or less would have made much difference, but I had to placate his sister.

I picked him up and deposited him fifteen yards farther from the waves. Then he bawled because his castle had been left behind. So I picked that up, but it crumbled. With trembling hands and Sister's help we did an elaborate construction job, with four towers and a moat and arched gateway.

I started running, like a criminal. I didn't want to be seen paired with her. I scrambled over rocks in the cove that no one went to because it was all rocks. Out of breath, I faced her, as she stood above me on a higher rock, already pedestaled.

"Now this Helen of Troy, she was the most beautiful woman in the world. And anyone with the name of Helen has to be beautiful. And I want you to prove to me that you are. But it's not just the face, you know. It's the whole body. So—so take off your suit, and I'll tell you whether the Greeks would have called you Helen."

"I have a cousin up in Troy. So what's the game?"

"That's the game—Helen of Troy."

She giggled. "You're foolin'. That's Show Me."

"All right. Show me."

"That's for two. You have to do it too."

"'Look. I'm bare to the waist. Tit for tat—" and I actually put my hands over my tits. "Now you be."

She wriggled out of her straps and rolled down to her belly-button, my eye following to that entrancing dimple and then up. My breathing stopped like a clock. This was not through screens and darkness and fifteen or twenty feet away. This was real, two pliant scoops of raspberry and vanilla that, inches near, I almost fell upon with my mouth.

One hand on her belly, she flipped with the other toward my trunks. "Now you."

"No, you first. Ladies first."

She looked around, then pushed her suit down her thighs until it was down to her knees and would have dropped to her ankles if she had not held her legs apart.

I stared for eleven seconds. Then I picked my way toward the sea, the nearest exit. I would take it, rocks or not.

"Hey!"

"You're Helen, you're really Helen," I flung over my shoulder. I had a head start, and she couldn't run with her suit like that.

I was on my half-covered belly in shallow water, easing my way over the slimy rocks.

"Beautiful," I said, as she stood watching with an expression that I didn't look up to see.

"Welsher! Sissy! Snake!"

The water was deepening. I could almost take some strokes now. I would drown, be battered on the rocks like Leander, so long as my corpse was found with my trunks still on. Coward, liar, cheat, I just couldn't take them off. I just couldn't. What did I have that had to be kept private? My privity, a sight for me alone (not counting God) and not one that I myself was invariably satisfied with. *Mein Scham,* as the Germans say. I just couldn't expose myself. I didn't even take showers in the gym. I always made some excuse—didn't need one, had a cold, an appointment. And to show a girl—just like that? Cold, like that? Or worse, hot? To be naked, stark naked, in front of a girl. Boy, if I ever did it, you know what, I'd use my fly! And to think that there were said to be nudist camps, even one only two miles away! My blushes would burn me alive. Even Sis—I caught her a couple of times without wanting to—used to put on her nightgown like a tent, withdrawing her underwear from under its folds. I'll bet there are married couples that have never seen each other naked. Babies right through the fly or under slightly raised gown in darkness. Kinsey reports it's the lower, uneducated classes that insist on darkness. OK, forget about college. Swim, boy, swim.

These titillations all came to an end. The second autumn after my mother's death, one afternoon a week before school opened, I was summoned up from the basement by the shrill voice—a discord in the BC range—of Miss Warren. What had I done now, *poil de carotte?* I hadn't even been playing the piano but musing in a chair. Maybe that was what was wrong. She was also capable of complaining that I *wasn't* practicing.

I glumly entered the shaded living room and made out a tall figure in black and white that was introduced to me as "Miss Ryder, our new neighbor next door."

"Next door?" There was only a vacant lot on the other side.

"Yes, the Rooneys have gone, and while I wouldn't want to say anything, Miss Ryder, against people who were emphatically no friends of ours, let me say that it is just as well, and you are doubly, doubly welcome."

59

She hadn't even said good-bye. It had been dark for two nights.

There was no one for me to rest my eyes on but Miss Ryder, the most spinsterish-looking spinster ever to step out of a history book. With the arrogance of youth, I assumed her to be about fifty-five, although she was in fact thirty-eight. She was dressed like the nineteenth century, with a frilled shirt covering her throat to her chin, and pearly buttons at the ends of her long, billowing sleeves. It seemed as if September were going to break August's heat record, and I couldn't comprehend how the visitor, whatever her devotion to Queen Victoria, could physically endure to throttle herself with that high collar, constrict her delicate wrists, and let a black woolen skirt drape not only her unmentionable ankles but her feet, which might just as well have been bare (though I knew they by far were not), for all you could see of them as she sat balancing her teacup. She bent, in greeting, her fine profile; the feathered toque topping her high-piled hair darted like a quill being dipped in ink. I saw hatpins that could have stabbed a man through and through.

But what I really stared at was the teacup, which was steaming. I turned to my stepmother; she was having the normal glass of iced tea.

"You're having hot tea on a day like this!" I blurted.

"Try to restrain your rudeness," intervened Miss Warren. "Miss Ryder has just told me that hot tea is actually more refreshing than iced tea when you're hot, and next time I must try it myself."

"Yes, young man, such is the fact. You can believe me—I'm the new biology teacher at your school. I've had many boys like you, and at first they don't believe me either. It's the homeopathic principle. Treat like with like. Do you know what you apply to frostbite? Not hot water, but ice bags. And if you ply a starving man with food, you'll kill him."

"Live and learn," I said, pouring myself a glass of iced tea.

"He's not at his best today," came the sarcastic explanation. "He doesn't know what to do with himself. When he's not banging on the piano, he bats ping-pong balls, looking for a partner. Boys would be better off working in the summer."

"Ping-pong? I will play with you."

I looked toward her feet, still invisible. Wouldn't she trip if she tried to cross the room? It was really baking in that living room, and no fans. I had had enough by that time of adults saying things they didn't mean, and I wasn't going to let this pass as a gesture. Always politeness that crumbled when you tested it. I had liefer be honest and rude, if they wanted to call it rudeness. This was my adolescent—not rebellion—but ripple.

"All right. Right now?"

The hostess raised a hand in protest, but Miss Ryder stood up immediately, revealing the mono-bosomed, carefully S-shaped figure that I wasn't yet in a position to label as the Gibson Girl. But I sensed, to my surprise, athleticism—provided her skirt let her walk.

It did, briskly, and Miss Warren, bored and outmaneuvered, called after us that she would go shopping, as we descended to my den and started to size each other up from opposite ends of the cool green white-lined table, which has always been an oasis for me, wherever I have seen it. (Green is supposed to be the introvert's favorite color. It sure is mine. Emerald is my birthstone, and I read about fifteen Oz books.)

She had quite a forehand drive. The game was speedier in those days, with the sandpaper paddles. Miss Ryder would take one side-step and really lay it on. I felt like a "partner"—Miss Warren's bridge word—in a minuet. It would be ungallant to beat her.

Soon I learned that there was nothing, absolutely nothing, for me to hold back, for she was the better player. When we started keeping score, I was behind from the beginning and stayed there. I rued, as I have so often since, that I had learned the game with—and was irremediably committed to—the penholder grip (it's rather sissyish too), whereas her racquet fore-hand, swung in the long arc of her billowy arm, scored winner after winner. It was ridiculous—I even started jumping up and down (which distracts some opponents)—but this thin Victorian wraith just had too much power. I'll never forget the scores—21–16, 21–14. I can't forget either that I lost my temper with the last point of the second game and cast my paddle on the table, in a true but overemphatic (all right—"rude") expression of disgust.

"I have had a good head start on you," she consoled. "In 1910 ping-pong was all the rage."

We were resting side by side in two wicker chairs. She took up and asked me about a color photo of my mother. After the second marriage I quietly removed it from the master bedroom, no one commenting or dissenting.

She turned and moved her elegant head startlingly near. Goodness gracious, was I irresistible to spinsters?

"You have beautiful brown eyes," she said.

Some change of subject, that was!

"Shall I tell you something about your father, whom I haven't seen?" she went on, touching my arm. "He does *not* have blue eyes."

"Oh, doesn't he?" I parried. "And why not?"

"Because your dear mother had blue eyes. And two blue-eyed parents can't have a brown-eyed child."

"No?"

"You haven't had biology, have you?" She mentioned Mendel, and launched into an explanation I didn't follow about dominant and recessive traits.

"Are you sure that two blue-eyed parents can't have a brown-eyed child?"

"Biology doesn't lie," she frowned. "People may. But this is an incontrovertible fact, and has been used in paternity cases."

"Live and learn," I said, getting up. There I didn't want to stay, nor with her. "Look, I'm supposed to go swimming now.

Thanks for the games. Do you want me to show you back to the living room? Someone should come home soon."

In fact, my father was due soon. Or rather, the man that in this narrative I have been careful to call "Dad," never "my father." We don't want any scientific inaccuracies. What would Miss Ryder say when she saw this blue-eyed man? I was entangled in a spider's web of thoughts, as I went down the breezeless street. Who was—and where was—my father? If I encountered my blue-eyed mother in Heaven, would I be saintly enough to avoid a forbidden subject? And what about my brown-eyed sister, if I ever had to face her again? There were angles on angles. I had always thought Sis was more different than a sister should be. I don't mean just her character, but her Roman nose. Whoever my father was, was my sister's father the same? God, the Ivory that it would take to clean all this out!

As you see, and as it usually does, life went on, right to the end of that week, and that month, and year, though I nearly flunked trigonometry. And there are always explanations and retractions. Miss Ryder, visibly shaken, made hers Saturday afternoon, when I turned the corner of her hedge, on purpose, as she was clipping it. She rushed out and grabbed me and said, "I was so stupid, so stupid. Your eyes are hazel, they aren't brown —they've got blue in them. I must be getting color-blind in my old age. Understand?" She clenched my arm.

Sure, I understood. It's great to be slim and blonde and blue-eyed and beautiful. What does having an attractive mother mean if it doesn't mean that she attracts more than one man? Sometimes I work at being glad, and proud.

Having been afraid, like a shy virgin, of letting others see me naked, I became afraid to see myself naked. I thoroughly hated myself, all pimples and blackheads, with the stiff carroty top (I'm talking now about my head), and there was no one I loved. At school my grades sank.

I also became accident-prone. I backed the family car against a tree, denting the trunk, and was forbidden to drive it any more. I ripped my already scarred pinky working at the glissando octaves of the Brahms Paganini Variations. They aren't easy, but managing to injure yourself on the ivories isn't easy either. Psychoanalyze it as penis-rejection. Worst of all, I literally stumbled out of high school.

It was Commencement, and I fell down the steps before the crowd, after receiving my diploma. It was a terrible bang. I howled and couldn't get up. When they got me up I couldn't stand. Something had gone wrong with my left knee (the same one the butterfly had alighted on). Was this the Fall of Man? Was it fear of entering the world, growing up, commencing?

If I dared to be a critic of the Creator, I would say that knees, though built with some cleverness, might be better crafted. We're always hearing—are we not?—about trick knees, arthritic knees, knees that spontaneously swell with pain or abruptly give in or go awry and puzzle orthopedists. I was told that I might be lame for life. They just couldn't say. Time would tell.

Meanwhile I limped, with an ugly lurch to one side, which of course put the crowning touch on the self-hatred. Of course, too, this was the summer that I went looking for a job, now that I was scarcely fit for any. Dad said he would see me through college—I had applied to six colleges, and only Dartmouth offered to take me—but I would have to work in the summers.

This was fair enough treatment from the blue-eyed widower of a blue-eyed wife who had had brown-eyed offspring. Off I would spring, with my stepmother giving me an extra kick: I complain only about the irony (iron knee?) of a very unspringy knee.

This was a memorable summer that I shall have to deal with in some detail. It was the year 1939.

Part
II

Part II

5

As I descended the steep steps of the train and the conductor handed down to me my suitcase, I remember trying to remember whether conductors usually did this for male passengers. Probably I was being singled out. I had started down the aisle with the suitcase and the conductor had sneaked up behind me and taken it out of my grasp so quickly and so silently that I had been too surprised to offer any resistance. I had just hurried out, hurried, in fact, a little too much, under the dead weight of the confusion that now came over me whenever I knew I was being watched as I walked. The conductor was saying, in effect, "Let us see what you can do *without* the suitcase." Let us *see*. I should have refused his help, as I had coldly rebuffed the woman on the trip to New York who had loomed up to me when I was struggling with more luggage than this, but she had only spoken, while the conductor acted, and even so the conductor would still be behind me, and it *was* easier without the suitcase, or it would have been if I had not felt hurried. But maybe the conductor was only doing what was customary. I should have stared out of the window less and noticed. I'm always wishing that I had noticed something that I hadn't.

Anyway, I thought, as I turned half around in the shed that was all the station there was, a shed barely wide enough to contain the faded letters of the sign with the long Indian name on it, anyway it was good that MacSwain was not there to see his new employee being helped, that is to say, as he would certainly have interpreted it, being helpless, right at the start. That would only have strengthened the doubt he had catapulted at me in the interview. "By the way, Holm, is your health good?" The beady eyes had bored into me, goading me not only to say yes, but yes

67

I would take the job. It was just as well no one was there to meet me.

Out in the full sunlight a freshly painted sign pointed the way along a road that was overgrown with high weeds. The neat red letters of the sign, curved against a black background that was still sticky, somehow struck a friendly note in the uncouth, very un-Westchester wilderness. A human being had lately been there and had planted or renewed this mark of encouragement, telling the wayfarer not to despair, that Silver Lake Camp lay ahead and would be infallibly found by anyone who went in the direction indicated. Here stood one brave, even gay certainty in an uncertain world. It was an outpost of promise that did not, like the tall grass, waver in the breeze.

It was late in the afternoon but still hot. The gusts of air that fitfully touched my neck and ears added nothing to my comfort. I felt as if I were being breathed on from behind. Perspiration ran down the nether side of the arm that held the suitcase. As I limped along, insects jumped on and off the legs of my trousers. I don't take to insects; if ever I discover my real father I wouldn't be surprised if his name turns out to be Muffet. On my shoulder I observed what looked like a piece of yellow weed that suddenly came to life and flew away. Was this the motion that rolled through all things, perhaps? If Wordsworth was right, I wished I had a little more of that propulsion.

The road wound up and down for about half a toiling mile, and then, after one last upward slant, revealed the camp. As the circular had said, the camp "nestled" in a valley among the Berkshire hills. From the crest of the hill that I had just climbed I looked down on my right upon two rows of small uniform log cabins, in front of which was a somewhat larger cabin that seemed less crude and had wires running from it. On the left, and completing the family, stood a structure of the same shape as the others but four times as big. The cabins faced and with the main lodge formed a right angle to a lake that glimmered pleasantly between hickory trees.

The wayfarer as he advanced saw no sign that anyone was there. I did not know whom to expect beyond the chef, Mac-Swain's pride. ("The salary is sixty dollars for the season and the food is excellent. We buy only the best. The chef is French.") The season had not begun yet. It was two days before the boys were due to give the place life. In my need to get out from under Philipse Manor I had accepted MacSwain's invitation to go up in advance and pick out a bed for myself and begin eating. Business would keep MacSwain himself in New York until the opening day.

The garbage cans behind the main lodge were covered and I resisted a passing temptation to peer into them. I could not see into what must have been the kitchen because both the screen door and wooden door were shut and the windows on the side were above my head and screened. The cabins on the right looked wholly deserted. They gaped at me, open-doored. Was I being observed from somewhere unseen—that most unfair of situations?

I headed for the building with the electric wires on its gable. When within a few feet of it I heard the whine of a screen door and a woman came out carrying a bucket. She paused on the steps.

It was a second before she saw me. For a second I had the view of her in profile as she looked off into the sky like a bird on the edge of flight. It was something to sculpture, or, motionless, *was* a sculpture, the upward tilt of her chin at that moment, a summary of grace and aspiration. Her hair was pinned up and the curve of the jaw to the ear was long and exquisitely clear. So much I caught before she saw me, before at the clumsy sound of my foot on the gravel she turned from the horizon and noticed me.

I was startled by the blue of her eyes, for her hair was raven black. She had got it out of her way by mounting it into an impromptu knot that made her look a little impish and was at odds with the gravity with which she greeted me.

"Oh, hello," she said without smiling. "Welcome to Silver Lake Camp." Then, in answer to my unspoken question, she added, "I am Mrs. MacSwain."

As a musician I am particularly sensitive to voices. Hers hovered uncertainly in the upper register, it had none of the depth and assurance of a grown woman's, and I wanted to protest that she was too young to be MacSwain's wife, that she was too young to be a wife at all. It was an incongruity for which life hadn't prepared me. She was wearing over her short gingham dress what looked like a child's pinafore. It had as design innumerable pink teapots. Her legs were bare except for a girl's socks fringing the crisp new sneakers.

Instead of protesting, I only said, "I'm here as the music counsellor. My name is Holm, Kenneth Holm. I thought it would do no harm to come up a couple of days in advance."

"And what harm could it do?" She was smiling now. "Come, let me show you your way around. Let's first find a cabin for you."

She set down the bucket and began to stride briskly toward the rows of cabins. It was uphill, and there was hardly any path. You had to be sure of your footing. I started lurching with my suitcase, feeling like the Hunchback of Notre Dame. After a glance in my direction she was back beside me, restraining her pace to suit mine.

"I've never been a counsellor before," I confided.

"Well, this is my first summer here too." She seemed to be studying the grass. "I'll be on a kind of honeymoon, for when Harry and I got married in February he couldn't get away from his teaching except for a weekend, and I've been looking forward to the country ever since. We both have. The cabin I came out of is ours. I've been fixing it up. You must come and admire."

We went into the nearest cabin of the front row of seven. Three cots, painted silver, their striped mattresses bare of sheets, had been placed head to foot on either side, leaving a three-foot aisle in between. Light came through two screened openings on each side, which could be closed by shutters from the outside. Mrs. MacSwain walked to the end and turned around.

"They're all alike, these cabins, but this one is probably the most conveniently located and you may as well take it as yours. Have you sheets? No? I'll give you some. And the nights are apt to be cool. You'll want a blanket. I used one last night. Let me see, I think there are some extra ones in the storeroom."

Sitting on the bed by the door, suitcase beside me, I tried to imagine what she looked like sleeping under her blanket. I kept it decent, for buried reasons. Did she lie still, the small lithe body a single wave, or was she restless in sleep too? Whatever postures she took, I knew she had to cease pretending to be grown up. Sleep would return her, as it returned everybody else, but especially her, to childhood. How was her hair on the pillow, and did the mouth, now pursed in the make-believe of thought, pout then?

"Well, we can go down to the lodge right now," she was saying, "now that you've found a place for your suitcase, and I can see about the blankets." She had entered with spirit into her role of guide.

Following her I found myself in a room that was impressively spacious after the cramped cabins. There was a fireplace of massive gray stone, around which some wicker chairs were arrayed in a perfect semicircle, as if invisible people were sitting in silent contemplation before an invisible fire. In the back were the long dining tables, unvarnished boards on horses. The sun streaming over the yellowish wood through the windows on the west seemed to be performing the last burnishing. It was also polishing, incidentally, the mahogany legs of a grand piano in the foreground.

"Your husband didn't tell me the piano was a grand."

"Oh, yes. A rich parent, a doctor whose son comes here every year, gave it to the camp last year. The son had refused to take any more piano lessons, and the father decided the camp might as well have the piano. It's beautiful, isn't it?"

"Has it been tuned?"

"I took care of that," she said proudly, waiting for me to question her.

"You mean you tuned it yourself?"

"No, of course not." Her laugh was frankly impish. "I must tell you. Harry never thought of the tuning. When I got here I played some chords on it—you know, I took lessons years ago when I was a child, everybody does. It was terrible—the piano, I mean. I immediately sent for the tuner. He came yesterday. But now the blankets."

She dashed off to the back where a padlocked door had been carved in the wall. I went over to the piano, which had no seat in front of it. I lifted the lid. Maybe I had exulted too soon. Grands were not necessarily better than uprights. It depended. I had been deluded by a fair exterior more than once before and then sat down to sour notes or even broken strings. But she said it had been tuned. The name of the maker was inscribed in fancy gold inside the lid, but it was unencouraging that I had never heard of it. However, the keys looked to be in good shape, and I wondered whether their cleanliness owed something to Mrs. MacSwain.

Pulling over one of the wicker chairs, I propped myself on the arm of it, for the seat was too low, and struck out some arpeggios. The big, barely furnished room awoke. The sound rolled out in waves to all the corners and up to the rafters, and more kept coming. The instrument was not a bad one, I decided, though it was not equal to my own upright, for instance. The keys were firm, the action not too loose; the lower notes had excellent deep tone, but there was some shrillness, a certain hysteria, in the treble. Probably too much jazz had been played on it.

There was a flash of color near my shoulder that steadied into the red and turquoise of her dress and pinafore and the flocculent yellow of the blankets she held pressed in her arms.

"You're good," she commented. "Can you play the 'Rustle of Spring' by Sinding? I mean, do you know it by heart?"

"I could play it, maybe, if I could sit down right," I answered, looking around. Together we piled cushions onto the wicker chair until it was high enough. As I swayed tentatively for a moment on the soft seat we had built, we both laughed. Then, hands close together, I began the piece she had asked for.

It was no favorite of mine. My taste for sweets was not what it had been—how many years before?—when I had come under the spell of its popularity and learned it. Mr. Claveridge had bit his lip when I played it for him for a surprise one day. I had been put on the defensive, as usual, had asserted it was at least as good as the A-flat "Liebestraum," but my teacher, without arguing that point, would grant only that it was a useful exercise, if one held back on the loud pedal. How young I had been, and this was not my earliest memory of it, at that. It carried me back to the days when great-aunt Francine (the one who's now in an institution), who thought the talkies were not good for small children, took me to a place where silent movies were revived, and learning to read was encouraged. There it was always brought into the piano score for scenes of spring and love. The hero and the heroine would be walking happily along a lane full of cherry trees, and there would be a close-up of cherry blossoms—or maybe they were apple blossoms—shaking in the wind, and the pianist down front would break into "Rustle of Spring." He never finished the piece, he just gave the flavor of it, and went on untiringly to something else when the scene changed. My earliest remembered ambition had been to take the place of that anachronistic musician down front, alone under his little light, who played with careless skill so many different kinds of music for hours at a time.

I think that what appealed to me was his indispensability, and yet obscurity. No one was staring at him.

And now it was spring or summer again and I was playing

73

"Rustle of Spring" for Mrs. MacSwain, who had not outgrown it. It began very softly, the melody a faint sigh. The agitation increased. The winds were blowing harder, and they were getting nearer. Now they swept onto the scene, forces joined. What had been single notes became chords struck out grandly against a swirling accompaniment originating in the left hand. The crescendo mounted, and with it in me (I must admit) an exhilarating, even athletic sense of power that was compensatory. I was doing the thing I did best. My fingers on the keys were strong and sure and there was no feat they were not capable of. Whatever failures lay beyond the breached walls of my music, I was master here. I was the god of a storm that would now subside, only to rise again at the end, at my command. Let the winds divide and become faint. Reduce them to the first whisper. Fickle, their adieus were false adieus. Mark the crescendo with the left hand stalking down the scale. Sweep on to a finale. Crash out the last tonic chords loudest of all.

From where she had been leaning with cupped hands she looked at me, her face full of appropriate appreciation. "That was wonderful," she said. "I love it. It is so sad." And her eyes did express sadness, though the rest of her was smiling.

I was about to reply when I observed beyond her a sardonic Gallic face. Leaning out of the serving window of the kitchen, arms folded, the chef was gazing at us like a Cheshire cat, in a kind of parody of the attitude of an earnest listener. Do anything romantic and you face the prospect of fun being made of it. I could not help speculating how long he had been there unnoticed. We hadn't been doing anything improper, and yet I was annoyed. Doubtless the first chords had brought him to the window.

We went up to him, there at the window, and I learned that the chef's name was René. René stared at me. Oracularly he delivered himself of an observation: "You play the piano." Getting no denial, he went on, "You play the piano at night." It was impossible to tell from the level intonation whether this was a

74

statement or a question. But René had already resumed, with a nod in the direction of what must have been his *chambre à coucher,* "I have to sleep at night."

"So do I," I replied, anxious to conciliate this important person right from the start. While fearing that he might be my stepmother all over again, I hoped I had sized him up correctly as a character whose saving virtue was that he knew perfectly well he was a character and smiled at himself under his leering mask. This impression Mrs. MacSwain confirmed as we walked away.

"René may not be musical, but he is at bottom good-natured. Harry says he gets along splendidly with the boys. I must say I've liked his cooking the two days I've been up here. It's simple and wholesome, just what we need. Unlike the conventional French chef he has no goatee for the boys to make fun of and no fancy sauces to make them sick. Of course I direct the menus now. Tonight you're getting lamb chops and peas and mashed potatoes, and I guarantee you'll recognize all of them. Or maybe you'd rather not? Maybe you're a gourmet."

She gave the word its French value, exaggerating the "r" and snapping off the last syllable with a grimace. We were standing now on the porch outside the lodge. As we leaned over the railing the sun slanted on our faces and we dodged it by standing straight and turning our backs. At my full height I was almost a head taller than she.

Something—this loftiness?—had put me and perhaps her in a bantering mood.

"Ah, we are being satirical," I said, announcing it. "And in what grammar school, pretty miss," I queried, with a glance at the pinafore, "are you studying French?"

"My French!" she laughed. "That reminds me. I tried my *high school* French out on René the first day, and he listened patiently, even making replies in French which I didn't bargain for and didn't understand. Finally he said in plain English that he bet that in five years I could learn to speak so well that any

Frenchman would understand me, provided he had spent an equal length of time in New York! That was all the gallantry I got out of René."

"And when do you go back to high school?" I pursued.

"I graduated, one full year ago." Her face grew serious, the eyes under the dark brows seeking out the horizon again. At last she came back to me. "And you?"

"Either you're older—which I can't believe—or I'm backward. I just graduated, at which time I fell off the platform. I'm headed for Dartmouth."

At least I could boast of that, to this child.

She moved to the steps, and I followed her down.

"You can't see our cottage yet. I still have one or two things to do in the way of fixing it up," she said.

"What a tease you are," I called after her as she disappeared inside, "—what a tease you are not to let me see it!" And I added musingly to myself, "Not to let me see Honeymoon Cottage!"

6

It was ridiculous and yet rather beguiling of her to call a rough log cabin which looked hardly different from the others a cottage. This threw light on the question, which I had pondered over in the past, of whether women were more sentimental than men. Directly I had had too little experience. In literature, to which I regularly resorted for knowledge of human nature—a painless short cut—the issue was divided, so far as I could tell. The older novelists were lachrymose in their assertion that women had the corner on sentimentality, but living moderns like Sinclair Lewis and Bernard Shaw denied this, giving all the impractical tenderness to the men. It was a fascinating question, and now I had a chance to study it, along with other sexual questions, outside of books, with Mrs. MacSwain, whose voice and manner swung uncertainly between girlhood and womanhood, as my guide. I felt as if I had shut a dusty door behind me and was facing life for the first—palpitating—time.

Life was—baffling. Her alliance with MacSwain was even odder than my own. And that certainly was odd enough, though it had its reasons. Meeting her had set me to wondering about it all over again. Earning even sixty dollars was going to be harder than I had suspected. How would I perform my duties? I had disturbed on my walk to camp a bird with a clownish overlapping black crest and a long pointed tail. What species was it? A counsellor should know. The boys would ask me. Did they dress themselves? How old were they, anyway? Would I be able to practice?

I had taken the train to New York with the aim of getting a foothold on fame and fortune with four short piano compositions. Mr. Claveridge had given me a letter of introduction to a music publisher. My guardians had expected me to work all summer, but I would just sit back with this money, the substantial advance on royalties. I had heeded my teacher's advice to take out copyright on the manuscripts, to foil any thief who had designs on this pot of gold himself. This firm had once published a Lullaby by Mr. Claveridge, in G-Flat.

Well, it wasn't the humidity that did the final wilting. I was listened to by two Mutt-and-Jeff characters, who eyed each other like bridge partners. They said they liked the pieces but were afraid they would not be a good risk. Not just now. There were waves of taste and the public wanted clever, somewhat cacophonous novelties. When I finished playing, Mr. Cox (short) of Cox and Basch rubbed his hands together and said, "Charming, charming! . . . But a little like Schumann, don't you think?" I asked what was wrong with being a little like Schumann. Mr. Cox shrugged his shoulders. His hands went out in a gesture of dismissal. "Your pieces are old-fashioned, Mr. Holm. German romanticism, you know. It is not *the* thing. Next year it may be *the* thing. I can make no promises. But keep in touch with us."

Could I go back home empty-handed? I searched *The New York Times*. In the want ad columns I could not help but notice how full the C's were with the advertising of camps for counsellors. They wanted counsellors in woodcraft, counsellors in archery, in swimming, in canoeing and sculling. I did not even know what sculling was. But one ad I carefully tore out, and a half hour afterwards I had been myself not a little surprised to find myself waiting, in an outer room in an office building high above Madison Avenue, to see the director of Silver Lake Camp for Boys.

The two-room office, bare of rugs and short of chairs and with only one desk, seemed anxious to repudiate any connection with city life. Odds and ends of camping equipment were stranded there. An anchor and some rigging sprawled on the floor beside the desk where the director, in a tan open-collared shirt, sat talking with a fat mother and child. A huge glossy red canoe stretched out along the back wall, ridiculously far from a lake. In the outer room I stepped from one photograph to another that made up a framed series illustrating life at Silver Lake Camp in its various phases. Here boys were earnestly playing what was labeled "Tennis," while in the next picture, "Swimming," heads bobbed out of a lake, faces frowning in the sun. Nobody smiled in any of the pictures.

I had surveyed the pictures twice and was hesitating whether to pretend to study them again when I became aware that the eyes of Mr. MacSwain were on me, were ready for me. They were small black eyes, the shape of watermelon seeds, too small for the face, and they took in my lameness even before I had pushed aside the swing gate and begun to move toward the director's desk. This man I would have recognized as an instructor in physical education (my *bête noire*) wherever I saw him. With his broad, square build and rough-hewn face, he belonged to a type, the athletic man, now about forty, with a paid pride and joy in agile human bodies, especially his own. Limber-shouldered, he managed to sit at the desk like a man riding a horse, and he was in fact wearing riding breeches. He looked capable of brutality. A crop lay on some papers near his hand. I thought I had read in his first glance the easy contempt of the strong for the weak, and felt that there was already between us the antagonism natural between the halt and those who flaunt their sinews and their fleetness. This was war, and it had started with me, not MacSwain, on the defensive. I sat down angrily, though not a word had been spoken.

The words that were spoken were all in the line of business, and my nerves found nothing tangible to quarrel with until the end. MacSwain summed up the situation quickly. A counsellor was wanted who could play the piano for singing, which was a regular activity at the camp. On rainy days and often at night before going to bed the boys gathered in the main lodge and sang. They sang standard songs and popular songs. Could the

79

applicant play these? MacSwain mentioned examples, half humming. He sang baritone solos himself now and then, he confided. His laugh ended in a snort. He added that two or three of the boys might want piano lessons too.

"Larry Walker, our music counsellor last year, did all right on hymns (which we have every Sunday when the parents come, you know), but he played everything else the same way. Dead. No damn pep. Slow figuring out the notes. He'll be back this year, but I've shifted him to track."

I answered, without mentioning my church experience, that I was up to these musical requirements. I stated this merely as a truth without thinking about whether I wanted the job or not. I had been lulled into impersonality by the extreme casualness of MacSwain's manner. I listened like a visitor from another planet while MacSwain explained to me that each counsellor, besides his special activity, was in sole charge of a cabin of five boys.

As I still sat silent, MacSwain had let out the question about my health which roused defiance in me. The primitive opposition between man and man that had been signaled in the first glance came back. "By the way, Holm, is your health good?" What a nerve, and I wasn't even sure that he wasn't taking in *mental* health, my emotional stability. And I wasn't even sure he shouldn't have been. I would take the job, even—as the expression went—if it killed me. And if I were dying, this healthy animal opposite me would be the last person I would permit to know.

Then he was shaking my hand and telling me something about trains. The job was mine. I would never know why the director took me so readily. In after months, looking back from a dramatic height to a small beginning, I called it fate. It was at least something I could not explain, or rather something for which I had so many possible explanations that none would stick. I had been bought for seven weeks for a salary I was evasive about back home. But I was to find out it was a normal salary at the camp. Others presumably would have been interested in the job. Why had not MacSwain waited to see what other applicants turned up? Maybe there had been others already that morning. Maybe MacSwain, as casual as his word, was inclined beyond all reason to engage the first person who came: regardless that there were others who were worse pianists but better suited to his purposes, even so far as the "music" went. No character references either. As for experience with the outdoors and with boys, well, I had gone to school for twelve years, and that was it.

And the fact was not less sure for being unvoiced that I and MacSwain had instinctively disliked each other. We had squared off at sight as if for an encounter, and now we were shaking hands and arranging to meet again, under conditions of intimacy. It made no sense. Do you need your opposite to assert yourself? I could not comprehend by what law governing antipathies I was rushing into a job for which I was not fit, under a boss whose brutal swagger and overhearty laugh I despised.

Of course I was not really a free agent, because of my home situation. Who is?

But what accounted for *her* alliance with this man, an alliance that also could not be expected to last? (I had already made up my mind about that.) What kind of desperation had driven *her*?

She had aroused my curiosity, in more ways than one, and now I was waiting for her to satisfy it. Dinner had come and gone, a dinner eaten placidly and without much conversation by three seated at the benches of one of the long tables that ordinarily served—and would soon serve again—fourteen at a time. René put the plates at the serving window, and I or Bob Coutts picked them up from there and set them on the table. Coutts, a "junior counsellor" who had been at the camp for several days, turned up just at mealtime and spoke hardly a word. A scout by instinct, he was always busy at the outskirts of the camp, either on hike or down the road where the workshop was or in a canoe at the far end of the lake. Big but not gawky, at fifteen he was as sandy-haired and friendly and inarticulate as an overgrown collie, and I, for whom first impressions were apt to be decisive, liked him at sight. Sitting opposite us, she called him "Bob" and me "Mr. Holm," but probably that was a distinction of age rather than of intimacy. I found that this occasional reminder of my maturity pleased me. At the same time I caught myself wondering what her first name might be, surprised that I did not know it.

However, it was not her Christian name but her living quarters about which she had been coquettishly mysterious. We had been playing a game in which showing the cottage was evidently the next step. The game had been broken off. I fervently hoped it would be resumed. Meanwhile suspense would give me no rest; my inner excitement would not die. The suspense was general and hovered over the whole immediate future, but it had a specific edge in her allusions to the unseen cabin. She had thereby—with or without design—created a void which she had not filled. She had planted in me an interest in the interior of the cottage which was not normal and which I would never have had by myself, not being the interior decorator type. And now she was letting it lie fallow. After dinner she had glanced at her watch and hurried from the lodge as if she were late for an appointment. That was the last I had seen of her. Two hours went by while I aimlessly passed my hands over the keys of the piano, modulating and playing snatches. When René had looked out admonishingly, I dropped into a chair with the thick novel I had—with some bravado—bought to tide me over my leisure time at the camp. But the reminiscential subtleties of Proust over a mother's kiss were more than I could bear. The sentences on the crowded page twisted and turned out of my reach, their convolutions beyond my shattered powers of concentration. I got up at last and lifted a curtain at the east front window, still restless with expectancy, or more accurately, an urgent sense of incompleteness. The evening was apparently over, but I could not bring myself to admit it, like Bob Coutts, by going to bed.

Her cabin, a few feet away, gleamed comfortably in the night. It perfectly resembled a cottage now. It had not only an electric light, of which none of the other cabins could boast, but a glass window and yellow shade (always those yellow shades!) through which the light might shine. This triple refinement set it apart, even without the further consideration that she was inside. Married women, I guess, at least those who have not been married long, are particularly careful about shades. When, as I stood looking out, I thought I saw a shadow pass across it, I guiltily drew back from the curtain. I could not see her, but she must not see me. I had been wanting to look out for hours.

Extinguishing the last light in the lodge, I went onto the porch and stood there idly. Once I was outside, the wilderness stretched out gigantic arms toward me. It was only ten o'clock, but it felt much later. From the lake came the uncanny croaking of frogs, puncturing the curtain of crickets' voices and other hummings all around me. The hills back of the cabins, wan in the slit light of the moon, seemed to be beckoning to me to go out and explore them and penetrate the secret of the voices, but the invitation was of a clammy kind which I would not have dreamed, except maybe in a nightmare, of accepting. And I somehow divined that no matter how far I went the voices would recede before me and lie just ahead, or to either side, tricking me on. My own cabin looked sufficiently distant, up the steep incline, brooding beside the others, with no electricity to cut away the darkness. As I shivered in my polo shirt in the dank air, hands thrust in the pockets of my gray slacks, I wondered whether I was meant for life in the country, after all. To sleep up there alone? What animals would pad out of the darkness?

But her light still made a wide swath over the path in front of me. There was my beacon. Outside it was chilly, as she had warned me, but inside, where the light was, it would be warm, and surely—for me—friendly. I was so near now that I could hear the slightest movement of the shade when it nudged against the half-open window. But of her there was no sound, no trace. Perhaps she was reading. I ought to make some sign to her that I was there. She would come out gratefully, even if she had undressed for bed, and ask me inside, where she would warm me with coffee and with her flow of talk, showing me all she had done to make the cabin a perfect home. I had only to knock. We had got along so well. She must have noticed the harmony between us. She might be dressed only in a flimsy nightgown, with a red robe thrown hastily over it, but she would welcome me in, saying, "Oh, I had no idea you were still up! Why didn't you tell me? I've been wanting to show you the cottage." Her hair would be piled mischievously high again (she had tamed it for dinner), and her naked throat would be, as the Song of Songs said, a tower of ivory. At any moment now she would open the door and I would hear her voice.

The light went out. My disappointment was not immediate. I was waiting for her to come to the window to adjust it or raise the shade. Anything might yet happen. It was normal for this much to happen anyway.

But the seconds passed, and each one, that might have been so full, turned out to be empty. Nothing happened. The house stood there stolidly and would give no sign. Only the frogs and the insects and the listening night were alive. Hope had died. I could no longer keep my disappointment back. It rushed coldly upon me.

The rustling of the shade, when it again reached my ears, seemed a mockery. Quickly, for no one could see me, I clambered up the slope to my cabin. On my way I stumbled and my hands came in contact with the wet grass. The dampness I had sensed before, but this tangible proof of it startled me, for I had forgotten the feel of dew. It set loose most unpleasant associations. A worry crept into my mind that had not been there before, a fear of dampness, especially at night. I had had bouts of rheumatism lately in my bad knee. Of course I had not men-

84

tioned it to MacSwain, but now the memory, the mere memory, pierced me, at a time when there was no part of me left, inside or outside, that was warm. Presbyterian-wise, wise Presbyterian, I could not but look upon my latest fall and the resultant association of ideas as a premonition. I wryly recalled that someone had said, in a moment of great personal disaster, that it is what we fear that happens to us. In fact it was my friend Oscar Wilde who had said it. I was a coward before the pain in my knee that doubled me up and, defying all nurses and physicians, left me only in its own good time.

Stiff and uncomfortable, I groped about my bed and got into pajamas. The bed was already made. I had made it while it was still light, going up before dinner. It was then too that I had changed my suit for clothes that seemed more appropriate to the place and the temperature, as it then was. "Undressing for dinner" I had called it at the table. Now I was shivering between the clammy sheets. However, the shivering stopped while I was still considering whether it would not be better to get up and strip the bed of sheets and lie directly between the blankets. Turning on my side I attempted to concentrate on Mrs. Mac-Swain, but other things, various anxieties, particularly the new anxiety over rheumatism (how old it sounds, to have rheumatism!), got in my way. I found I could not bring her to life before me. She kept slipping. The parts—blue eyes, checkered gingham dress, a wisp of hair—did not make a whole. At best she was outside looking in, whereas before (to remember the feeling was not the same as having it) she had somehow been inside with me, and we were looking out together. The sense of her nearness, and with it all sense of pleasure, was lost. I was alone with my discomfort and my fears.

Yet these and the night sounds must have passed, by an undefinable transition, out of consciousness, and I knew nothing until the bell woke me at 7:25 A.M. My acquaintance with this bell as a sound had begun at dinnertime, when Bob Coutts had leaned out and rung it at the chef's bidding. A large and brassy

85

fixture at the entrance to the lodge, it was the strident herald of the camp's routine. It announced all the periods of the day. It was clanging out the first period now—Reveille. At ten minutes to eight it would call all to the lodge, warning that breakfast was impending. At eight sharp it would say that breakfast was being served. Its tongue was inexorable. I jumped up, nervously submissive.

I had become acquainted with other aspects of the camp's routine. The cabin adjacent to mine, the middle one in the row of seven, was the lavatory building, for instance. It looked like the others from the outside, except that it was more transparent, having glass windows in front. The stalls had no doors. I saw this was going to be a problem, but the only one I had to watch out for at present was Coutts.

The modern plumbing therein did not include any faucets. Life in the rough and no doubt MacSwain's economy demanded that the boys go down to the lake with buckets and carry back their own water for their washing. I discovered that two-thirds of a bucket was a very full load. When I had dragged it to the rear of my cabin, and dipped a finger into the cold of it, it was filthy—I suppose I had gathered in some of the lake bottom— and contained an ugly little tan frog. I dumped it all out.

It was a drab lowering morning, with the sun skulking behind mists. I wore an old windbreaker from school to breakfast. I borrowed a glass of water from René on the pretense that I was thirsty; went around the corner with it and sprinkled myself and rinsed my teeth. It was like going to the dentist. The water probed with merciless metallic fingers every crevice in the mouth.

"Cold, monsieur?" said René from behind his window (was he referring to the windbreaker, or his precious water?). He nodded the next moment, without relaxing his grin, to Coutts, whose face had a cat-licked look, to ring the final bell.

Like an actress who has been awaiting her cue she straightway swept in upon our little group, her hair parted in the middle and plaited in a chignon, her green dress longer than yesterday's, which had left her knees bare. Her eyes stirred in me dim recollections of the sea, which seemed far, regrettably far, behind me. The lake and the sky that morning were muddy by comparison.

As if taking cognizance of the fact, she remarked, "Not the best of mornings, is it? But the sun may yet break out." At any rate, her cheerfulness kept breaking out.

When our breakfast had come around to the toast-and-coffee stage, she flung out a question. "What are we going to do on this the last day before the boys come?"

"Have you finished your interior decorating?" I could not resist saying.

"Yes. Any interested persons may come and see," she smiled. "But it will not take all day."

Bob Coutts told of having discovered nearby a field where blackberries grew. She took him up enthusiastically.

"That's it! We'll have blackberries for lunch. We'll all go picking blackberries. René," she called, "how would you like me to bring you back a bucket of blackberries?" The *b*'s tumbled gleefully from her lips. She might have been reciting a nursery rhyme, a relatively wholesome one. There was one I never could say, but it began, did it not, "Peter Piper picked a peck. . . ." Of course that was far behind me, like the sea.

On our leaving the lodge Bob Coutts moved off toward the cabins, murmuring that he would be back in a few minutes.

"And I have to change," she said, as I lingered with her at her door. "But you may as well come in and see the interior decorating, such as it is."

"Said the spider to the fly," I answered, following her up the steps.

The interior was as neat and cozy as I had imagined, and everywhere, more than I had imagined, was the prettifying woman's touch. The biggest thing in the room was the double bed, the foot of which extended halfway past the window. It had a pink coverlet, with cottony white strips as design and borders.

Pink also was her color for the curtains, trimly tied back, and for the tiny dressing table next to the bathroom. For the rest there was room only for an oaken flat-top desk to the right of the entrance. This was virile, this was MacSwain, but at least she had been able to find a pink blotter for it. Gazing around I added up appreciatively all the comforts—the telephone on the desk, the lamp over the bed, the bath with enamel basin, the two soft scatter rugs that resembled decapitated and flattened polar bears.

"You have everything here," I said. "The curtains are splendid." I wondered why I had not noticed them from the outside. Of course at night they had been invisible behind the shade, but I should have seen them in the daytime if they were there.

"Tulle," she explained. "Normally white. I did the dyeing myself. Even the dressing table is homemade." She went over and lifted its satin skirt. "See? Two egg crates, with the space inside for clothes. Bob gave me the idea."

She searched my eyes for admiration. "Of course," she went on, "if you were a woman you would ask immediately whether there are any closets." She opened a door next to the bathroom. "Here is one."

It was crammed with dresses, and underneath were more pairs of her shoes than I could count at a glance.

"And where is your husband's closet?" I joked.

"Oh, there'll be space for both of us. Now that you mention it, Harry's things are coming this afternoon. I remember now, we *will* have *something* to do. All the luggage is coming. The boys' belongings will have to go in the proper cabins. We'll need to work out assignments. Harry hasn't made any. We'd better not take too long on our berry picking."

"I'm glad you put pleasure first, at any rate."

"Well, I don't really expect the truck until fairly late in the day. And food *is* important," she smiled. "Now if you will excuse me while I change."

When I had passed outside I looked back over my shoulder

88

at the window, the interesting window. The curtains formed a pink bulge on either side. The cottage was perfectly set for a honeymoon, I had to grant, except that it was still empty of signs of the approaching groom. Come to think of it, there had not even been his picture. That was a strange omission in one only four months married. I knew now I had been set to see her in the customary white dress and veil, clasping her bouquet, posed beside her groom, but there was neither this picture out, nor any other. To declare MacSwain, there had been only the double bed and, over in the corner, the oaken desk and chair. Her personality reigned. The cottage was yet daintily unconscious of its master.

7

I'm not an outdoor man. I really belong in the bedroom, except for a little swimming.

Picking blackberries on a sullen day that would neither rain nor shine turned out to be more like business than pleasure. The three of us talked very little. While the field was not far away, we had to get over or through several barbed wire fences to reach it. Mrs. MacSwain, who had protected her legs with slacks, approached these barriers very gingerly, exclaiming that she would be hurt. She got through them unscathed. It was the men who were hurt. Bob, who had been scaling fences with nimble bravado, tore his hand on the way back, and I, increasingly impatient of my own clumsiness, ripped my trousers and the skin of my right calf when I misjudged the height and resiliency of one of the wires. (She brought us both into the cottage afterward for iodine.)

The brambles added their quota of scratches too. What hurt most, however, was the fact that the party soon separated on arriving at the field. It was not practical for us to keep together, because there were not enough ripe berries in any one patch. Each picker had to seek out individually and a little laboriously the fruit whose black blotted out the red. I, who had expected nature to be a pliable backdrop for conversation, was reduced to giving or receiving, at best, a shouted word now and then. The full pail that our joint efforts resulted in failed to stir in me enthusiasm, either when we carried it home or later when I met its contents, rather sour, at the lunch table. I considered that my education had not advanced the way it might have under different auspices. I had known that blackberries bled red without staining my hand on their juice. This particular rose was not worth its thorn, even with sugar and cream. And how good was the cleaning—might there not be bugs still?

The time between berry picking and lunch I spent at the piano, going through some of the preludes and fugues in "The Well-Tempered Clavichord," and I was moving toward the instrument again after lunch when she recalled me to a sense of my new duties by asking me to help out now with cabin assignments. I obediently followed her and Bob into the cottage, where she sat at the desk with a counsellor at either shoulder and a sheet of names and ages in front of her. The rule was to put boys of like ages in a cabin together. There were thirty-seven names, and the age range was from 6 to 14.

"Of course there may be a number of last-minute additions, but this is the list as of last night when Harry called. So let's make the best distribution we can, leaving any changes to the director. Now Bob, you like to have the oldest boys, don't you? That's cabin 10 for these five." Picking up a pencil she enclosed with a rectangle the top five names and ages, and wrote within it the assignment. "This bottom group, the smallest and the most difficult, always fall to our senior counsellor, George Gorman." Another rectangle shut off the boys of six and seven and one boy who was eight. "There now, the youngest counsellor has got the oldest, and the oldest gets the youngest. Mr. Holm, have you any preferences?"

I could not think of any, but said, pointing, "Suppose I take these five who are eleven. That's a benign age, isn't it?"

She solemnly inserted my name and the number of my cabin, number 3. In a short time all of the names had been distributed among eight of the ten cabins.

Destiny had about made up the cast. It remained only for the actors to take their places and the seven-week play to begin. I was tempted to make use of these dramatic terms when the truck had come and gone and I was surveying the luggage that had been tossed on the cots in my cabin. On Mrs. MacSwain's sheet I had looked at ages rather than names, but now I was moving about noticing names. It was indeed like being in a theatre before the curtain went up. Only, I bore the uncomfortable awareness that I myself was on the stage; that, far from being a passive spectator flipping idly through a program, I would have to act too, regardless of whether I knew my part or not.

I wished I could have built up some sort of picture of my charges from the superscriptions on the tags and labels of their duffel bags and suitcases. Was Frank Case fat or thin, and what relation did his appearance bear to his personality? Did John T. Livingston, little Johnny, bite his cuticles or go into tantrums, and if he did, what countermeasures, if any, was his counsellor supposed to take? I was supposed to correct everything, including faults or immaturities I myself had. Parentless, I was being rushed into parenthood. What manner of creatures, posing what responsibilities, were B. L. Combs and Ernest Vandevanter? My imagination found nothing to feed on in any of these names. Claude Bryant, the legend printed in yellow on a hand trunk on the cot opposite mine, did give me pause when I returned to the front of the cabin, because it struck me as a euphonious combination and at the same time not an ordinary one. The unusual first name I took to be French. On the other hand, there was nothing foreign about the surname, and I could no more dress up with satisfaction Claude Bryant in a beret and a French accent than I could expect Ernest Vandevanter to know Dutch and wear wooden shoes. No, there was no promise of unusualness in the names as names.

But as I sat brooding on my cot the yellow letters above the handle of the blue hand trunk stubbornly drew my attention, as if insisting that here was an exception. Maybe Claude Bryant was a combination no more euphonious really than Frank Case or Ernest Vandevanter, but it became more and more poetical the longer I stared at it. The power of the Word. Later, when, repressing superstition, I tried to analyze the aura surrounding this early contact with the name, I could only attribute it to the physical accident that the lettered hand trunk had been left right side up on the cot across the way from mine, squarely in the line of my vision when I sat down. Any name—even or especially one's own—becomes strange if it is repeated often enough without interruption. Claude Bryant, yellow against a blue background, became hypnotically beautiful.

Suddenly she was standing at the open door. Without getting up I questioned her. "What is your first name?"

"Marjory. And you may as well call me that, *Kenneth.* I looked in to see if you would like to go canoeing on the lake." Then she added, as if it were an explanation for all the kindness she had just heaped on me, "Bob has gone off to the woods somewhere."

As we went down to the lake I asked her if she knew Claude Bryant.

"No, I've met hardly any of the boys. I'm new at this business, you know. He may be a new boy this year, but if he was here last year Bob will be able to tell you about him. Ask Bob."

I took in again the fine lines of her profile, which abounded in a tenuous strength. Her small straight nose flung a clear-cut challenge at the world, a defiance that her chin and mouth and throat caught up and cradled in curves. The uncertain lights and shadows of a premature dusk played tricks with the whiteness of her childlike skin as she moved.

Beside her, walking was almost a pleasure. She adapted herself perfectly to my pace, and I was less conscious of my own heavy rise and fall. In fact, she acted as if it would never occur to her, even if she were by herself or with someone else, to walk any faster than she was walking now. From sheer exhilaration I kicked aside with my good foot a pebble that lay in the path. I still see it after all these years, round, tending toward orange, with a dent in the middle.

At the landing beach, where a canoe, red like the one I had seen at the office, lay upturned, its bottom slanted at the mottled sky, I felt no hesitation such as might come to one who had never been canoeing before. I fairly pounced on the canoe to lift it, like a young Hercules, into the water. It proved to be heavier than it looked. She recommended that we both take hold of the sides and ease it in gradually. When we had thus got all but a sliver of the canoe afloat, she looked at me and hesitated.

"Shall I get in first?" she inquired.

"Yes, of course."

She made her way to the bow, paddle in hand, and sat facing forward. "Shove off when you're ready," she called back. That was easier said than done. I could not trust my left foot to hold my weight while I pushed off with the other; still less could I use my weak foot for shoving. I solved the problem by standing in the canoe and prodding the graveled beach with the blade of my paddle. This manner of launching was violently successful when I least expected it to be. For an awkward moment as I crouched and the canoe swayed drunkenly, I thought it would overturn, but I gained my seat without mishap and began to make deep swaths with my paddle. She, after a backward glance, paddled on the opposite side, and we made good progress. I felt like the last of the Mohicans. Canoeing, I gathered, was really a simple matter, unlike rowing, which I had tried once on a municipal lake only to discover that the oars would not stay in the locks, which, for some unfathomable reason, were wide open.

In the light of later experience, however, I am surprised at the luck that, faithful to fools and little children, kept the canoe right side up during that first, rather wordless excursion of ours. More than once we disturbed the delicate balance of our craft. While gliding near the rushes at the far side of the lake I discerned a frog staring bloatedly and I reached out to pat it with the paddle. The canoe shook; the frog vanished like a practical jokester. Or like a prince that had been considering absconding with my girl.

Another time, when we were resting our paddles at about the center of the lake, I was daring in a different way. Masking in mock gallantry my sincerity, I said, "Your back is lovely, Marjory. But I should like very much to see your face."

94

"Do you know how easily these things turn over?" she protested. "It is no day for swimming. Besides I have my watch on."

"Please turn around," I persisted.

"All right." She arose cautiously, hands reluctantly leaving the sides of the canoe. Stooping, she turned around and faced my way, her eyes serious with the delicacy of the maneuver, her mouth amused. The canoe shuddered as she got one bare leg over the straw seat, and its paroxysms increased as she followed with the other leg. But she managed to sit down without the final infinitesimal tilt that would have meant an upset.

"I suppose it would be dangerous for me to applaud," I greeted her. "But thank you very much."

I was more grateful than I could say. Yet, face to face with such beauty, I did not know what to do with it. It was impossible even to stare at it. True, in the morning, when we had been picking blackberries, I had been chagrined that there had been no opportunity for conversation. Now I was alone with her under conditions ideal for intimate talk and I was speechless. Perhaps I had nothing intimate to communicate, for she must have known her effect on me. I was conscious only of wanting to look at her at leisure, which meant to look at her without being seen myself: the Peeping Tom complex. It had not struck me with full force before what a precious gift invisibility might be (whatever, as Plato said, it might do to morals). Had she been a statue or some other immobile work of art I could have gazed and gazed (or had she only pretended to be, like Hermione), but being disturbingly alive and opposite me, so near that I could not escape the rise and fall of her shirred bosom, she caused me to look away and to take action against the spell that embarrassed me. I began to paddle toward shore.

The wristwatch she had not thought to look at before, she now regarded with mute surprise and resumed her paddling. Still alert to etiquette between the sexes, I said, "Let me go backward, and we'll land that way." I paddled in reverse, we swung completely around, and within a couple of minutes my end of the canoe struck the beach. But we had made a bad landing. The canoe was stuck without being high and dry. Turning, I saw about two feet of shallow water between me and dry land.

With me, lately, it was an ironclad necessity to put the best foot forward. My right foot stretched safely onto hard dry ground. With an effort I got my other leg free from the canoe but I could not bring it the same distance. For a moment it seemed clear of the water, but as I put more weight on my left foot it sank in mud, and the water sloshed over my sneaker. However, I was able to drag the canoe farther up on shore, and she got out without taking any notice of a clumsiness that had brought the blood to my cheeks.

What, if anything, we said between the landing beach and the lodge I fail to recall. My attention was focused on my sodden foot. It dragged along like something that was not mine but was unpleasantly next to me. My sneaker, darkened with mud and water, might have been a piece of oozing garbage. Worse, because more intimate, was the slobbery embrace of my sock. Disgust, backed by common sense, bade me go to my cabin and change, but while I was making the decision Bob Coutts rang the dinner bell. I looked at my companion to see if she was going to stop at the cottage, to wash her hands, for instance. I even looked at my own hands to give her the idea. But she was insensitive to me. She went straight ahead, instinctively quickening her steps at the iron summons so that she was a little in front of me. I felt alone, and yet bound to her. Had she turned aside I could have done likewise. As it was, all three of us sat down to dinner together.

In my mind I reproached her like a jilted lover. She ought to have noticed my situation and insisted that I go and get dry. I would then have done so, or at least have got credit for not doing so. But I could not mention my plight to her or to anyone. I could not face the embarrassment of making a detour and being

96

noticeably late for reasons that I would have been under a compulsion to blurt out, drawing attention thereby to my physical defect. The accident, I knew, could have happened to anyone, but everyone, the moment I began to tell of it, would apply it peculiarly to me. Besides, I had got used to the sogginess, which felt warmer now, like perspiration. I had had rheumatism when my feet were dry, and if it was coming it was inevitable, and I could not expect to fence it off with one thin dry sock. That would be comparable to tweaking the nose of fate.

The premonition would not down. As I mechanically shoved meat and vegetables into my mouth and bandied casual words, underneath I was waiting, listening for the pain. I well knew how subtly it insinuated itself, and I was morbidly fearful of not being alert to it. There would be faint twinges at first, raps, like the swinging of a cane against the bone. Then the pain would enter in earnest and go to work, and God knows when it would stop. Strangely enough, it was the warning twinges that I best remembered; my recollection of the main affair was mercifully inadequate.

But the mind had its own anguishes, including this of waiting for pain that did not come. If I had been by myself "at home," it would not have been so bad. But here I was exposed, it was like having to undress before all the world, there was no place I could withdraw to without somebody's noticing me. In a few hours the whole camp would be there, ready to stare at whatever there was to stare at, argus-eyed. When would the pain come, and how often would it run foul of me this summer? I had given assurances to MacSwain, and now I faced not only pain but public humiliation. There was no place to hide from the ghastly nakedness of camp life: you could not even go into the bathroom and close the door. There would be whispering and giggling about me among the children: sick or well, I would limp and they would notice with the cruel frankness of their years and their animal health.

So far my mind had made a hell out of nothing. Dinner

came to an end, and nothing happened. I was now free to go to my cabin and unswathe my damp foot. I left the lodge with inner if not with outer haste, glad of motion, shaking off the paralysis of thought, not stopping to imagine the reaction of a personified fate to this belated gesture of defense.

It was while I was sitting on my cot, a bath towel around my foot, that what I had so acutely anticipated happened. The first signal went out from my twisted knee, a slight twinge, the lightest tapping on a minutest particle of nerve. Then dead silence: if I had been asleep I would not yet have awaked. But the next twinge was more insistent, as if the outsider were not to be kept waiting. Those that followed shortly after were imperious.

I started biting my lower lip and going through little helpless motions on the bed. Once when I had had a toothache I had found some relief from the torment in pacing up and down. This diversion was denied at a time like the present, when walking only made matters worse. Yet it was impossible to keep still while the nerves of the knee were being plucked, one by one, in quick relentless succession: some fiendish cellist.

Someone knocked at the closed door. This was exactly what I thought would happen, and there was no bolt. I half rose to open. It was Marjory, standing there as she had stood a few hours before, but with a look of anxious inquiry on her face.

"I saw you go to your cabin, and you did not come out, and I thought maybe you were sick."

"I am having—some trouble—with" [ridiculous word!] "—rheumatism," I eked out, sinking back.

"What an awful thing!" Her voice was deep with sympathy, deeper than I had ever heard it. "You were in pain at the table. I knew it. There must be something that we can do."

"No, nothing." I bent forward, both hands gripping my leg below the knee.

"What about liniment? Or hot compresses?"

"No good, no good at all. It has to go of itself. Electric pad sometimes helps. But I don't have one."

"I have one." She turned and called for Bob. "I think he's still in the lodge. We'll get you down to the cabin and attach the electric pad. The pain must be awful."

I had a little corner of consciousness with which to appreciate her concern.

Bob came briskly and, on being informed of the situation, asked me if I could walk. Not fancying the tragicomical alternative of being carried, I said I could. I slipped a shoe over my bare foot. Leaning heavily on Bob's shoulder, I hobbled down to her cabin. It was hard progress, excruciating. She went alongside at first, then hurried ahead to make preparations.

When at last I had got inside I found the coverlet had been removed from the bed, baring a yellow blanket on which lay the electric pad already plugged in. I sat on the bed, was helped off with my shoes and required to lie with my head on the pillow, on two pillows in fact. She laid a blanket over my feet. This I drew further up and underneath it hoisted my trouser leg and applied the pad to my tortured knee. In the warmth that came to me I had immediate faith. The pad had itself a woolly exterior like a blanket, but the heat it gave could be nicely regulated according to the degree the red button was pressed. I had a feeling—which, however, I did not seek to corroborate—that I had seen this pad when I was in the cabin before. Had it been out somewhere in the bathroom, or had I glimpsed it when she lifted the skirt of the dressing table, or was I merely confusing this particular pad with memories of others that were also tan and woolly? I could have asked her where she kept it, but it was much easier to lie back and say nothing, while the pain came and went in jagged waves, and the heat flowed steadily on, promising comfort even if it did not bring it. Nevertheless, I could not quite clear from my mind a word that was still fairly new to me and very disconcerting—the word, the accusation, *psychogenic*.

8

She came in from outside. I looked at the luminous traveling clock on the homemade dressing table. It said ten minutes to nine. I had been lying there in growing darkness for close to two hours, which is a long time, clocked by pain (of which let us not forget my low threshold). My variations from the flat recumbent position, my flinchings, my movements of hands and legs and trunk—would have tortured even someone else to count. It was a part of my life I would gladly have sliced off in advance, being willing to die two hours sooner later on as the price of such a dispensation. Yet, no such supernatural bargain having been offered me, I had apparently got through the worst of the siege, fortified by the electric pad whose heat became synonymous with hope. The pain was lessening, and some pleasure in being alive was returning. I began to take interest in my surroundings again. And I spoke to my nurse, to whose goings and comings I had been indifferent, almost oblivious.

"Hello. Are you here again?"

Her dark form moved toward me.

"I feel better now," I said. "I think the main bout is over. Your pad has been a blessing. But I'm afraid I haven't been a very sociable visitor."

She was alongside now. Her arm reached over my head to the bed lamp and switched it on. Her eyes studied my face diagnostically.

"You were in very great pain, and I didn't know whether to go or stay, or what to do. I offered you aspirin but you shook your head. This is the first time you've spoken since you came in."

"Well, it's a matter of wrenching out words at such times. Quite spoils my usual garrulity."

Of course I was being defensive, or hoping to be praised for what I did *not* do. And that was what she came through with.

"You're not serious. You talk very little, in fact. But I like your silences. They are not uncomfortable—except for this last one, of course. Some people seem to be silent out of meanness or emptiness, and I hate that. I talk hard at them but it's like throwing stones at a watchdog. They're guarding something, or nothing, and won't let you in. But you're different. And Bob is different."

I did not like sharing the cup of compliment with Bob. Was she herself being on guard in these last-second references to a lad of fifteen? It looked almost like teasing, but teasing seemed to be as alien to her nature as it was congenial (I was beginning to think) to mine. Whatever the sex's reputation for disguise, I could not believe that words spoken so earnestly were the instrument of a jest. Her very youth seemed to be a guarantee of sincerity, for my general impression of children was that one either got the naked truth from them—witness "The Emperor's New Clothes"—or else a very big penetrable lie.

At any rate ours was an alluring game, and I felt well enough to play it again. The shoots of pain that still went through me occasionally kept me sensitive and alert. I compared my situation to that of the celebrated author who always wrote best when he had a headache. I had been right in refusing aspirin. In such cases aspirin only deprived the organism of the natural aesthetic benefits of overcompensation.

"I suppose I ought to be going," I said, trying to sound casual. "Everybody goes to bed early at a camp—and well they might, considering the hour at which they get up. I suppose it's your bedtime. . . . The worst is over, as I say."

"You may as well stay and go on using the pad. It's not at all late."

This was my dream girl. I could have been writing her speeches.

"Are you sure you don't mind?" I queried, with very faint persistence. "I could sit in the lodge and plug the pad in there. It has done me good, I think."

"Stay. It's no trouble at all. I would tell you if it were. It's begun to drizzle anyway, and I don't know what effect that might have on your rheumatism if you went out."

I rather thought it would have no effect at all, but I was silent as I watched her go over to the window and draw down the shade. I was reflecting on the circumstances whereby I was inside the cottage that I had surveyed with longing and infinite regret from the outside the night before. To complete my satisfaction and give the wheel of fortune its final twist, it was necessary to imagine that someone else might now be standing outside in the rain, might have turned to the window just in time to see the yellow shade go down. For the sake of contrast there ought to have been such a person, even if it were only René with his antic leer. Insiders required, in order to savor to the full their good fortune, inclemency and envy and deprivation outside, to close the door on and tantalize with shades that are translucent without being transparent.

Yet the change from have-not to have was so new that, although ready, I supposed, for anything and sure there had been a change, I still did not know what it was that I possessed beyond a vague euphoria, a sense of warmth and light and blankets and companionship. The companionship included the whole interior of the cabin. The four walls, log on log, enclosed me in stalwart and hairy arms. Yes, at the moment they seemed friendly and strong, but how reliable was a wall? A part of me kept insisting that the wall between pleasure and pain, between elysium and torment, was at best thin. A false move would crack the flimsy structure of paradise. I had the nouveau riche's fear of losing all I possessed in an instant of rashness. It could all go at a word. I had to explore, to feel my way carefully.

"Out of pleasure pain," I said out loud.

"What?" The bed gave under a new weight and the blankets tightened over my legs. She had seated herself at the foot on my left, one leg drawn up under her. If she had been disconcertingly near when she faced me in the canoe, she seemed even nearer now. As the bed offered no support for her back, she leaned forward, and at the base of her throat her clothes tilted away from her in a perceptible cleavage. By sitting up a little I could have touched with my hand her purplish skirt where it bordered her knee.

"I was remarking that pain seems to be the ordinary sequel of pleasure. This afternoon I had the pleasure of going canoeing with you, but I got wet, and this is the consequence."

"How moody you are. But you look better."

It was like a woman to be personal where a man was trying to be impersonal and draw general rules. If this was her way I would take deliberate advantage of it.

"And you look very good yourself. I don't think I've ever before met a woman with black hair and blue eyes. I can't get over being startled."

Contrary to my nervous expectation she neither blushed nor frowned, but only smiled in amusement. "I was of course referring to your health when I said you look better."

"But why should beauty be any less legitimate a subject than health? We ask each other how we are as soon as we are introduced, not that we expect anyone to tell us, and in fact the clinical details would bore us. Yet if we openly admire a good face when we come upon one, it is considered rude. Why? A simple admirer may praise the beauty of a tree. Why may he not without umbrage tell a woman face to face that she is beautiful?"

"I dare say because, in the woman's case, he is open to the suspicion of making love."

"Well, it doesn't hurt a tree to be loved."

"Oh, but women are different," she responded. "And even

with a tree, if I had a tree that someone praised too highly, I'd immediately raise a fence around it, or buy a watchdog."

At the time I knew nothing about chastity belts, on which someone—possibly the Berlin Peeping Tom, Rothe—has written a whole book.

"I can see that you're the suspicious type—just naturally," I countered, hoping that my laughter did not sound too artificial. No doubt our talk was unreal, like the dialogue in a play (I had dropped out of a play in grammar school because the lines I had to say were just too silly for words, or just too wordy for silliness —they thought it was stage fright, which it also was—but mainly I was being a drama critic, play-fright), but underneath it lay coiled all the tension of reality. Already, safely because banteringly, a momentous word, "love," had passed what Homer calls the barrier of our teeth.

There was an interval of silence during which we both seemed to be listening for the rain, but the night was still. There was just the faint tick-tock of the clock on the dressing table.

"I wish it would rain harder," I remarked.

"Yes, I love the sound of rain. But this is one of those fine drizzles that make no music. It started just as I came in."

"I was thinking that all we lack of the traditional comfort of the storybooks is that patter on the roof and a fire on the hearth. But it's nice here even so." By way of giving my last words the necessary significance I let my eyes (whether brown or hazel) rest gravely on her face. I hoped she made the most of every hint and understatement. As before, when complimenting her, I had said much less than I wanted to say. Somehow, when I wanted to be bold and ardent the words that came were invariably feeble and cold, and they backed up when I meant them to go forward. Surely she understood me anyway.

She broke away from my gaze as if she had understood me perfectly and the understanding embarrassed her. But perhaps she was only restless, for she arose and went past the end of the bed up to the dressing table, where she stooped before a square mirror—no larger than a shaving mirror—in an unpainted wooden frame. It was one thing in the room she had not dressed up, and I wondered why, for I understood that mirrors were of first importance in the life of a woman, and yet this one was hardly worthy of the elegantly draped egg crates it hung above. I saw her adjust a wisp of hair that had fallen out of the line along her brow. Then she put a hand tentatively to her cheek and drew closer to the mirror, whether in examination of her skin or her eyes I could not tell. But I was fascinated, and when she whirled around and faced me she caught me staring.

"I suppose," I ventured, as she sat down again, this time on the dressing table stool, "if I were not here you would be combing your beautiful hair at just about this time."

"No, not at all."

"Because you can go ahead. Pay no attention to me. Act as if I weren't here."

"But I don't comb my hair—hardly any, that is," she laughed. "Besides there isn't much that combing can do for it when it's as black and coarse and wiry as mine. I've been told, in fact, that when it's down it's like a horse's mane. I've even been nicknamed Horsie on account of it." With a quick motion she undid the knot and pulled her hair down over her face. "See?" she said, peering at me from underneath.

I sat up in bed and timidly touched her hair just above her forehead. "Whoever called you Horsie must love horses very much—or else he's very wrong and stupid." It struck me before I got the words out that I might be referring to her husband, and I emphasized the word "stupid" on the chance I was.

In the light passing of my fingers over her hair I was to my surprise a little reminded of wire, but that was probably attributable to the power of suggestion, and anyway the poets were always comparing the blond hair of their mistresses to gold, a metaphor that certainly did not bear close examination, as Shakespeare knew in one satiric sonnet. As for the nickname, it suggested in vain. It did not register at all. With her long hair down she seemed more beautifully alive than ever, but not with the life of an animal. On the contrary, she seemed more—not less—human; there was poignance in the disorder she had unraveled so suddenly and confidingly and now flung back from a face sweetly flushed like that of a child who has just parted with a secret.

"Let's drink," she said.

"Drink what?"

She disappeared behind the bathroom door. I heard the clink of glass and the running of water. Then she emerged with a tumbler in one hand and what seemed to be a bottle of amber-colored medicine in the other.

Drawing the stool closer she poured in silence. "I'm afraid I don't have two glasses," she said, when the clear liquid had come almost to the brim of the tumbler. "We'll have to pass it back and forth."

"But that will be nice. Only what is it?"

"Brandy. I just remembered it was here. It's part of the first-aid equipment." There was no smile on her face. Her carefree hair bordered on sombre eyes. Without making the gesture of offering me the glass first, she sipped, then drank deeply. Settled back in the bed I could see the rippling motion of her throat. Her silken shirred blouse, like her hair, was awry, a little over to one shoulder. There, where the sun had not touched her, she was fairer than I had known.

She handed the potion to me without looking at it, with the remark, "I'm glad to say it doesn't taste of toothpaste." I had been thinking of Isolde, and the words took me by surprise.

"Oh, you mean the glass!" I said, gazing down at what little brandy was left shimmering over the thick crystal bottom. In any case the acts were mixed up, for the drinking of the potion came in the first act and I was lying there like the invalided Tristan of the third—but nearly cured. All that was needed to crown the confusion would be the sudden second-act appearance of the husband. "By the way, what are we celebrating," I queried, "the opening of camp tomorrow?"

"Yes—the opening of camp tomorrow," she answered, taking the empty glass from me and filling it again. Her cool determined drinking struck me as outside the normal—she had again quickly passed the halfway point in the glass, for the brandy was not particularly good brandy, nor did she drink it as if she appreciated it. In fact she looked the picture of disheveled sorrow, her mouth quivered as if she were about to cry, and gazing with growing tenderness at her who did not gaze at me I realized, cursing myself for the slowness of my perception, that the loosening of her hair had been by no means the playful act I had taken it to be. It marked a total change of mood that now I fully understood. And with the realization there welled out of me, from recesses where it had been pent up, a kindred sorrow, sorrow for her, and for her marriage, and for myself, and for all the Tristans and Isoldes whose time, measured audibly in seconds, was short and might not come again.

"Now that's enough of that." I suited my action to the words, putting the glass on the floor at the far side of the bed.

"I'm sleepy," she murmured, turning her brooding eyes upon me.

"Yes. Well, lie here."

I moved over to make a place for her. Silently she filled it, her head sinking down upon the two lace-trimmed pillows that had just propped me and from which I had not yet had time to remove my arm, which was brushed against by her black hair. The moccasins she had been wearing all day she let slip from her sockless feet onto the rug where my shoes were. For a moment the sight of her lying on the bed, ankles crossed, her body relaxed in the single soft wave I had imagined, the crest coming at her blouse and sloping off to the head that was turned my way—for a moment this sight was mine, and then it was shut out by her reaching up to the bed lamp, eyes half closed, and putting the room in darkness.

I did not speak. Hunched on one arm, I waited, staring at the ghostly clock. My heart was not in time with its ticking. For some seconds the night brought me only this badly jumbled rhythm and the frail touch of her hair upon my forearm. Thereafter I made out the sound of her breathing.

Bending down my head I whispered her name. "Marjory . . . Marjory!" Everything depended upon her answer.

But there was no answer. There rose only her breathing like a periodic sigh. Desperately I waited, watching the forward push of the big hand of the clock. At last I drew away my arm, backed slowly off the bed, and groped about on the other side for my shoes. Having found them and got them on, still standing I called her again, all my senses strained for any sign or sound. When I had waited another minute or two, I tiptoed to the door. It opened with a creak that made me pause again before I went out into the thin rain, hurrying up the incline to my cabin, clutching my shirt to my throat.

9

The same truck that had brought the luggage brought the boys. The hay protruding through its lower slats, it careened down the road into camp, giving its cheering, fundrunk occupants a final jolt and thrill. After an exciting and indecisive moment when it looked as though it might go right on through the camp without stopping, it lurched to a halt in front of the lavatory cabin, into whose purlieus three of the boys hastily disappeared when the back of the truck was unhinged and they could jump down. Some made for other cabins. A few stood still and looked around. The majority headed in the direction of the lodge and the lake, skipping and shouting in unpent glee.

The director got out from his seat beside the driver. Within a minute the truck was followed by a station wagon, from which emerged, like late attendants at a festival, the counsellors—the counsellors and one boy. With this secondary spurt of life the population of the camp was complete.

I, standing self-consciously at the door of my cabin, wondered whether I ought to go forth and mingle, or just wait and let people come to me, as they could not help doing, I being where I was, conspicuous and near. Already eyes were surveying me curiously. I had never had to make the acquaintance of a whole population before. An imperfect comparison was the first day at school, about which the less said the better. If this was school, time had altered my role. I was now the nervous new teacher instead of the nervous new pupil. Not that it made any difference in comfort. In fact I longed for someone to tell me what to do.

I looked with interest at two boys who came close to the

cabin steps. One said "Howdy" and waved two fingers. The other only stared. Both passed on. The question with me was whether either of them might be eleven years old, one of my boys. Bob had been very vague when questioned that morning about the five names. Bryant and Combs were new boys; the others, whom he knew, he apparently could not describe: they were "good kids," nothing special one way or another. This I could not bring myself to believe.

The director had gone down to the cabin, his own cabin. The tallest of the men that had got out of the station wagon approached me. Hatless like the rest and clad in a long black mackintosh of uncertain vintage, he was obviously six feet something and his face was distinguished by a red beard, so that altogether he had the air of having just stepped out of the pages of *Trilby,* a book at home I had not read because the illustrations told enough. He stretched out his large hand.

"You must be the new music counsellor. Glad to see you. It's my misfortune to be the senior counsellor, George Gorman."

"Your misfortune?" I had given as firm a grip as I had received, glad to show that my hands were strong.

"I mean it's my misfortune to be the oldest. Nothing more, of course. You'll like it here. Come, let me introduce you."

The new music counsellor was then led over to the other counsellors, who were still standing in a group alongside the car. I did not on first hearing fix their names in my mind, but I observed that they were all very young—in their early twenties at most—and athletic looking. Gorman himself looked to be short of thirty. I wondered what counsellors did when they were no longer young. Did they go into other professions? Or did they become directors? And what did counsellors do in the wintertime anyway? Maybe they coached basketball, or went to college. Well, I wasn't sure of my future profession. I'd major in music, and then what? Meanwhile, as I looked up at Gorman, who was really quite handsome in the beard whose color I naturally admired—and he had a good nose—I kept thinking how appropriate it was that the oldest counsellor should also be the tallest. Life was not always so congruent. It fell down, for instance, in the matter of matching Gorman's beard and hair, for the hair that he pushed straight back from his forehead was, with the sun on it, close to the color of straw.

The introductions had passed the handshaking stage and were entering upon the exploratory question-and-answer stage, when the meeting was broken up by the pealing of the bell. A voice said, "That's assembly." MacSwain had come out of the cabin and was shouting through a megaphone in several directions, "Everybody down in front of the lodge!" Stray boys came at a run. The counsellors moved more slowly, as befitted adults, but still with an unmistakable urgency that showed that they were obeying a summons and that work was beginning and chatting would have to wait. One of them threw away the cigarette he had just lighted. These sharp divisions between the "on duty" mood and the "off duty" mood—or rather, the "not much on duty" mood, for a counsellor was always on duty, were to become familiar phenomena to me. But this first time I was caught by surprise, not at the swinging into action, but at the almost militant seriousness with which they swung, the hired men whose brief and arbitrary recess was over and who were now shouting words of admonishment to the sheep that, a moment before, had been allowed to roam at will and even fall into the lake for all the attention the shepherds paid them.

One of the younger boys had in fact fallen into the lake. He had slipped in only up to his knees, but he emerged crying, indicting two other boys for pushing. MacSwain had just sent him away to change. The director was fuming over the incident, and his greeting to the counsellors was a flat order that there must always be a counsellor at the lake when the boys were there. "Even if it is only one boy—this may seem extravagant but I insist on it—even if it is only one boy, and no matter who that boy is—it can be Tommy Ricketts even—a man must be down there to watch him." As the director spoke, tapping the megaphone for added emphasis against the palm of his hand, he eyed each of the group in turn, his beady stare ending with me, to whom he vouchsafed no flicker of recognition. I had to quell an absurd impulse to ask what was wrong with Tommy Ricketts. It later turned out that Ricketts—not at all rickety or rachitic (disposable as Spartans disposed of defective offspring)—but a tough wiry fourteen, was the best athlete and particularly the best swimmer among the campers.

His was the first name on the list of cabin assignments that MacSwain now began reading off. As he read, the counsellor in charge of a particular cabin—in this case Bob Coutts—stepped aside and his boys came over to him, one by one. It was the juncture that I had been looking forward to, without, however, guessing it would be so dramatic—something like choosing sides for a game, with the counsellors as captains. At my own name I moved only slightly, just enough to show who I was—the leader of Cabin Three. First Bruce Combs detached himself from the waiting group of campers, a fat boy with freckles, followed quickly by Jack Livingston, who wore a sailor's hat, Claude Bryant, who was blond, Ernest Vandevanter, a gnome with big ears, and Frank Case, who came at a skip and a jump and seemed highly pleased at the company—at the junior company—he was joining. I could only sneak a glance at my charges, for all were required to stand there in some semblance of attention until the director had completed reading the list. Other boys, I noticed, had saluted their counsellor as an old friend, wringing his hand or hanging at his arm, clustering delightedly around him like bees around a queen bee. This kind of affectionate pantomime and whispered greeting the new counsellor—and there was evidently only one new counsellor—naturally could not command. I was a thing apart. My boys whispered to each other. Only Ernest Vandevanter lifted up his ugly, mushroom-skinned face and smiled.

After the last boys on the list, the smallest, had flocked around the biggest counsellor, the assembly were told to go to their cabins, put on bathing suits, and report immediately to the docks. Away they scurried, glad for another chance to run somewhere. I was left behind by four of my group before I had said a single word to them. But Ernest Vandevanter proceeded part of the way at my side and insisted on taking my hand. "You don't walk right," he remarked, looking askance.

"No, do you know the poem about the old, old, old, old lady, and the boy with the twisted knee? I'm that boy grown up." Another morbidity come true.

Vandevanter screwed up his brows into a caricature of perplexity. "What happened to the old, old, old, old lady?" he demanded.

"Oh, she died at last."

The open door of the cabin loomed. Peering forward Ernest relinquished his counsellor's hand and hurried to get inside. When I arrived I found that the boys had already settled among themselves what bunk each was to have. Vandevanter, as the last on the scene, had no choice. He got the middle bunk on the right side, the cot that abutted on mine. The blond boy was keeping the cot directly across the aisle. He was fumbling with the blue hand-trunk, trying to open it. The boy in the sailor hat had taken off his shirt.

I, for whom the portioning out of the boys had been an unexpectedly formal and dramatic process, something I had failed to imagine, had supposed that the real drama would come with my entry. The boys would draw themselves up and look to me, probably, for a little speech, once they were gathered together for the first time under the roof that would contain us for seven weeks. I had been considering what I might say. Mrs. MacSwain's words to me would serve for a beginning: "Welcome to Silver Lake Camp." But I had to be careful not to sound formal. Should I next echo George Gorman? "I'm sure you'll like it here." But that would be silly, coming from a new counsellor to Jack Livingston, Frank Case, and Ernest Vandevanter—how often I had revolved the names in my mind!—who had been there before and knew perfectly well, much better than I, whether they liked it. I could not decide how my speech should go on. While I hoped they would be "good" boys, it did not seem wise to tell them so. Maybe I would have to rely on the inspiration of the moment. Maybe that would be better—look at them and say whatever their faces suggested.

And so the moment came, and to my best recollection I said nothing. It died without distinction. The boys, busy with their unpacking, did not draw themselves up, and their current of talk was not deranged by my entrance. The fat boy, Bruce Combs, did approach me with a proposal that we exchange beds. "I will sleep by the door if you want, sir, and you can have my bed." Before the counsellor could reply, Jack Livingston spoke authoritatively: "If you weren't *new* here you would know that the counsellor *always* bunks at the entrance." The fat boy, confounded, returned to the back of the cabin.

"I can't open this, sir" came from across the aisle. I stepped over to where Claude Bryant, back turned, was bowed in earnest struggle with the lock of his hand trunk. The hasps at either end had given no trouble, but the metal tongue that went down the center would not budge, and the round lock below it, though it wiggled, did not slide over and release it as it was supposed to.

"It must be locked," said I, irritated that my own efforts were no more fruitful than the boy's. "Where is the key?"

"There isn't any key. It's not locked. I know it isn't locked. It's just stuck." And Bryant, now that I had withdrawn my own hands, started jiggling the lock again.

"I am positive it is locked," I said, feeling that it was ridiculous to argue with a child, yet not wishing the contradiction to go unchallenged. "If you have no key, we'll have to fetch a hammer."

I sank down again on my bunk, strangely depressed. The others were undressing. Over in the diagonal corner Jack Livingston, naked except for his sailor's hat, was about to slip a pair of trunks over his thin thighs. In the opposite corner Combs had bared his fat feminine breasts, which quivered as he moved. The boys who occupied the in-between beds were at the underwear stage. I felt no inclination to put on my own suit. My gaze wandered back to Bryant, who, after a last jiggling of the lock, dropped to a sitting position on his bunk and looked ruefully at the stubborn trunk, as if it were the coffin of hope. Then he turned the same sorrowful eyes on me.

My first impression was of renewing an experience I had had before. I was considering this face really for the first time, yet the blue eyes, narrowly registering reproach, and also the lips, swollen into a just perceptible pout, were uncannily familiar. The association was not spoiled but rather made more poignant—as if in emphasis of the pastness of the past—by the blond hair, hair of an extraordinarily rich yellow, unlike Gorman's hair and the hair of so many children and adults, which might be called blond for its pallor, but from which the yellow was missing, as if the sun had drained it out and left anemia in its wake. Considered as a face and as a head, Claude Bryant instantly struck me as a thing of more beauty than any boy should be, and the promise of unusualness inherent in his name came to fulfillment at sight, at sight of him full face, that is, for his profile was rather undeveloped, the nose being even a little snub and serving as a timely reminder of immaturity and imperfection in the midst of the unimprovable hair and eyes and mouth. Mrs. MacSwain too had her touch of mortality, in the wiry texture of her hair, though that was something I would like to test again, something that was probably a matter of angle and circumstance, like the snubness of Bryant's nose, which vanished when looked at squarely. No, the circumstances had certainly not been right. Perhaps. . . .

"Cheer up," I said. "All is not lost. We'll get the trunk open. It is not a tragedy." And I got up and laid a hand on the boy's head. "Come down to the dock now with the others, and afterwards I'll borrow a hammer and force it open." Children were apt to take things too seriously. Their world lacked the leveling perspective of the adult world. "Look, I'm not going swimming either!" I added by way of final consolation, plucking at my polo shirt.

And so we all went down to the dock, the boys stepping gingerly in their bare feet. The confluence of boys and counsellors in trunks there was almost complete. They stood on the white boards, waiting, talking in groups, forming restless and never perfect semicircles. Some started hopping up and down on the two low diving boards, but were called back. The first person to climb the ladder of the high diving board in the center was the director who, still in his striped flannels, stood on the platform—it rose about four and a half feet above the dock—and looked down at the camp and gave them instructions.

"This is not a swim period," he explained. "This is more important than a swim period. This is a swimming *test*. I personally want to see you swim. You know, no boy leaves Silver Lake Camp without knowing how to swim. But some of you smaller boys and some of you new boys may not know how yet. You will learn. First I want all those who cannot swim to go over there to the wading beach. Go in up to your shoulders and then try to swim. Splash. Kick. Show me what you can do. I will be watching. All the rest of you stay here and you'll get your chance next to show what *you* can do. But first the nonswimmers. Over there!" He waved them off the dock to the beach and shallow water at the near corner of the lake, equidistant from the dock on the one side and the boating beach on the other.

Six or seven small fry, joined incongruously by two boys a head taller, proceeded to get themselves wet, squealing in skittish delight as the water climbed their bodies. The lake, which had become glassy clear after the all-night rain, was soon stirred in that corner to its muddy depths by the plashing the director had ordered, as the boys, in up to their chests, began to imitate swimming, an imitation which, however, did not include floating, for most of them were content to keep their feet firmly on the bottom and only move their arms. Those that did heed the shouted injunction to kick with both feet sank spluttering, intense and touching victims of the laws governing gravity and the elasticity of liquids.

After MacSwain had observed and checked off the non-swimmers, and when these were safely back on dry land, he had the others on the dock jump in and swim a few yards out and back. When they too had been checked, only Claude Bryant remained, standing off to one side on the grass beside his counsellor.

"Can you swim? What is the matter with you?" demanded the director. "Why don't you have your suit on?"

"I can't open my trunk."

"Well, son, you're among friends. Take your clothes off and jump in."

Silently Bryant slipped off his shoes and socks, his shirt and gray knickerbockers, his undershirt and shorts, and stood on the bank, cheeks slightly flushed, measuring the depth of the water before him like Narcissus viewing his own exquisite reflection. He stretched back his arms for a racing dive, plunged and swam, a sleek white form.

10

Six on either side, a presiding elder at either end, they filled three of the long tables at dinner and part of the fourth. The camp had drawn on hitherto hidden resources in the form of low stools for the counsellors to dine on, just as additional canoes and three rowboats had appeared, as if by magic, on the beach. I discovered both pleasure and pain in the contrast of sitting at a table which was a noisy world of its own, an aisle and another atmosphere away from Mrs. MacSwain, whose lovely back and arms, in a short-sleeved chiffon blouse, could just be glimpsed as she distantly faced her husband at the head table, that table where three had sat before, lately with some constraint on the part of at least one. Therein lay the present pleasure, the pleasure of escape in a crowd, a crowd which, though it made all kinds of demands on one's attention and shot "sirs" at one like bullets, did not involve under a neutral surface deep and delicate emotions and the problem of relationship, declared and undeclared. There was, for instance, absolutely no ambiguity of relationship between me and the small boy on my left—the same who had fallen into the lake—who was now systematically dropping half his tomato soup from his spoon onto his khaki shirt. It was clear what I should say to him, however often I might have to say it. But Marjory at breakfast and again at lunch—in between I had played Bach—I had not known how to face, and words and presence of mind failed me as they always did in a crisis. Marjory herself had seemed gay. Naturally I did not believe in her gaiety; I saw something unbalanced in the persistence with which she had chatted on about the expected arrivals, as if the opening of camp were her one true longing and zealous concern. The only direct allusion to the evening before had come from Bob, who asked me how my pain was, and that dangerous beginning was quickly smothered in a short reply and immediate change of subject. But what we had not said had been momentous. Yes, relatively simple it was to admonish the soup spiller on the left and to put on some semblance of attention while the third boy on the right told a long story about a pet turtle he once owned. The emotions were not involved. It was the sheer doing of one's duty, frowning here, smiling there, without in the one case being angry nor in the other the least bit amused.

At the other end of the table, restricting my view of Marjory's back, was the sturdy counsellor, Larry Walker, he who had been transferred, appropriately to all appearances, from music to track. At least I could not picture him playing hymns on Sunday, not that it was something I looked forward to resuming myself. There they sat, the far sides of a rectangle, the old music counsellor and the new, and the contrast again was inescapable. Strange it would be to take over duties previously assigned to those arms, swart with hair, those thick fleshy hands now crushing and halving a harmless roll. Instinctively, while the boy who had had the turtle paused to take milk, I glanced down at my own arms. They were not very thick, certainly, and they perhaps struck others as unnaturally white, just as Walker's hands seemed to me too raw and ruddy, like meat fresh from the butcher's, and the forearms too black. I wasn't going in for any baking either: I feared the heat of the sun, since I had already read in a magazine (no Merck Manual as yet) that people of my complexion are prone to skin cancer.

In the long run (this was a question as important as health) who would be loved more, and by whom? Failing the eyes of Marjory, I sought and found the similar eyes of Claude Bryant, where he sat diagonally across the aisle and happened to look my way. Or probably it was not chance that made him turn his head, with its hair still damp and sleek from the swim: probably it was the consciousness that he was being looked at. There was even an air of ironic inquiry about this return gaze, so full and unwavering. I felt the blood at my face. I dropped my own eyes in embarrassment.

After dinner most of the company went outside. The lights in the lodge were turned on. Two of the counsellors began to set up a ping-pong table which they had taken from the closet. I drew up a stool to the piano, which I had not touched since the boys came. As I was sitting down, Larry Walker accosted me.

"I hear there's going to be a songfest in about an hour," he said.

"Really? No one's told me."

"Yes. It sends them to bed in good spirits. Have you seen the music?"

While I strummed a few chords Walker brought from the closet two songbooks, a pile of sheet music, and a blue paper bag thick with mimeographed copies of choruses of songs.

"You see, we hand these sheets out—Sheet No. 1, Sheet No. 2 and so on. Each sheet contains the words of five or six songs. You of course have the music. Look." He motioned me out of the way, sat down, and jogged out, rather thinly, a jazz tune.

"Atta boy, Larry!" shouted one of the counsellors at the ping-pong table. Several campers drew near the instrument.

"Do you know what that is?" he asked me at the finish. "Probably you can't recognize it."

"It sounds familiar. Isn't it very old? I don't listen to the radio much."

"That was 'This Little Piggie Went to Market.' A favorite up here. Look." He fumbled among the sheet music. "Here it is. Do you want to try it?" He got up from the stool, opened the top of the piano, placed 'This Little Piggie Went to Market' on the rack, and, making shoveling motions with his hands, signed to me to sit down and play.

I had experimented with popular music only a little. I was used to reading music, playing the notes as they were written.

Jazz called for improvisation. Walker had been pathetic in his inability to supply it. I was not sure they would like my own efforts much better, but I couldn't be worse. I struck out the tune, employing in the right hand variously filled octaves, in the left a bass marked by unrolled tenths. And for the "breaks" I relied on my own harmonic intuition, making rapid sweeps from octave to octave. It was not after all so difficult. I was not being very "blue," but then it was not that kind of piece. Anyway the people around me looked interested. The ping-ponging had stopped. In fact the situation was ludicrously like that of the correspondence school ads of my childhood. They had doubtless been incredulous when I sat down, were ready to guffaw. "Ken, he a jazz pianist! You can't mean it. He couldn't even limp to the stool." Well, I was a wallflower no longer. I was the life of the party. I had only to swing my wrists up and down the keyboard with the agility and insouciance of a juggler. Yes, let them even have sour chords at the end, following Prokofieff's clever example in the March from "The Love for Three Oranges."

"Not bad, not bad," commented Walker, laying his raw hand in approval on my shoulder. And one of Bob Coutts's boys said that I sounded just like a player piano. Requests were made. One piece after another was set up before me. After a dozen years of playing I had come to this. Sudden popularity. The ads were right. I was surrounded by more enthusiasm than I had ever drawn on stray visits to Westchester parties, where the supposedly sophisticated people, on getting me to the piano, were sure to request the Second Hungarian Rhapsody, or the Moonlight Sonata, first movement.

My sagging ego needed this new experience in appreciation. If someone broke out into song, or whistled along the tune, or beat time on top of the piano, it was all to the good, a grateful acknowledgment that the tune was being played, that they recognized it and were irrepressibly pleased. Verdi had the same trouble with his Italian audiences. If they were not sure of the words they could at least hum, and they did, and still do, in the cheaper seats. Some of the older campers knew the words, or read them, with the result that I found myself the center of a small-scale songfest before the official one began.

Soon enough the MacSwains returned to the lodge, and the bell convoked the camp. With the boys seated on benches to one side of the piano, the counsellors behind them in the wicker chairs, everyone equipped with the mimeographed sheets, the first songfest of the season got under way and became part of a pattern that, once known, seemed immemorial. Animal spirits were at a peak. This was the glad vacation time; moreover—the delicious first day, first night, unique in the fulness of its promise. Every request met with a roar of approval. One song after another was called for until all those on the four sheets had been traversed. Even the boys of six and seven, who could not carry the tune, opened their mouths, swayed by the common impulse.

Such songs as "America the Beautiful" and "Old Folks at Home" were mixed in with the Tin Pan Alley successes of the past, often a nostalgically distant past. I found myself striking out tunes that I had heard, whether I wanted to or not, over radios and in record shops and under my sister's auspices, when I was small. I felt old at eighteen.

Maybe the traditional songs were for the younger boys. Maybe the others were chosen for the music rather than for the words. For the words did seem precocious. Voices not yet cracked by adolescence were ringing out "Under a Blanket of Blue," a title that might at first blush appear innocent and even highly suitable for a camp, but which was really not free of promiscuous suggestion as the lyric proceeded. And now they were loudly missing the sensual pleasures of "The Isle of Capri," with its message of *cherchez la femme*. Such sweet compulsion doth in music lie. "This Little Piggie Went to Market" was no simple nursery rhyme either. At the climax just before the end, without any hint that it was coming, the boys burst out with the hope that they would be breeders, that "dear, some day we'll have—a cute little Piggie of our own."

When there were no more words left to sing the director came to the front to dismiss them for the night. But demands went up that he do a solo. "Just one," he said, looking at his watch, which he wore turned in on his wrist. " 'Captain Mac' " he told me. The camp roared its approval: clearly this was an old friend too. MacSwain knew the piece by heart.

Back pressed into the curve of the wing of the piano, arms arched behind him in the classic pose of the singer, he released a voice that surprised me by its mellowness. The song itself was nothing musically, no test of a baritone's powers: it was a recitative in which the words, stringing out a whimsical tale, were all in all. The camp listened for these words, spending its laughter lavishly. A mere reading might have pleased the audience just as much and been easier for the smaller boys to follow. Yet MacSwain's voice gave out at least the promise of lyricism; despite the clumsy breathing of the uninstructed amateur, he sang better than he looked. I would have liked to tell him so. "MacSwain, you sing better than you look." I could imagine the little eyes widening with astonishment.

At the end Gorman called out, "Let's have a piano solo." MacSwain frowned and glanced again at his watch, but sat down on the vacant edge of a bench. I played with the purring rapidity that can be achieved only after years of practice, and often not then, the "Minute Waltz" of Chopin.

The instrument had responded well. They were leaving the lodge not unimpressed, I thought, and I felt a conqueror as I gathered the music together in one pile and closed the piano. In the slower middle part, the sostenuto, I had shown that the piano can sing too. Suddenly I was aware of her. Her ringless right hand bridged for a moment the indented edge of the piano top which I had just let down.

"That was perfect," she said. "Like pearls. The notes were like pearls."

"I'm glad you liked it," I answered in a voice that I did my best to keep light and casual. Casting my eyes down I stared at her wedding ring. There was no engagement ring, just the thin circle of gold. Had the marriage been very sudden? The wedding ring was new to me. Had she been wearing it yesterday? Perhaps in the cottage the pictures were out too—MacSwain in his Sunday best.

"Your husband," I went on, "when he looked at his watch, gave me the idea of what to play."

She was going. I could think of nothing to say that would keep her. I pretended to be busy with the music until she had passed out of the lodge with the last of the boys.

In the cabin my charges were undressing by flashlight. They kept playing the lights on each other and over the walls of the cabin, enjoying themselves fantastically. Ernest's father had bought him the biggest flashlight of all, one with five batteries. "Look at mine, look at mine," he said, focusing it on the same spot on the back wall where Claude was flashing his.

"Go away. You spoil my light," remonstrated Bryant, like another Diogenes.

"Oh Vandevanter, you're a bore," said the fat boy, who had just pulled on his pajamas.

"But he looks better at night," taunted a third voice from across the aisle.

The director came in. "Everything OK, boys?" His light flashed up and down the cabin. It stopped on Kenneth's bed.

"We don't use pillows," he said, picking up the pillow, which in fact was not mine but which Marjory had lent me, since I had neither pillow nor pillowcase of my own. "Pillows make for round shoulders." And, the pillow under his arm, he said "Good night, boys" and left the cabin.

My first motion was to turn and survey the other beds. I had not noticed that they all lacked pillows. But here was no warrant for MacSwain's action. My situation was different. I, a counsellor, had been wantonly humiliated before my boys. It was

124

calculated abasement. MacSwain could easily have explained to me, had he wished, in private, at another time, that the policy of the camp was that the boys should not use pillows and that it might be good for the counsellors, by way of example, to follow the same rule. This could all have been managed tactfully. As it was, I felt resentment raging impotently inside me like a caged beast. I was full of retorts now that it was too late to make any, now that the moment for retort had irrevocably passed (rejoice again, Miss Warren!). I could have wafted him a Shakespearean allusion: "You have two pillows soft, and I have lain on them, O Posthumus!" The blow had been swift. I had been too astounded to speak. Now a silence had fallen on the boys too.

"I will be back in a minute." I went out under the quarter moon. The light that came from the shaded window of the cottage etched a pale path on the ground. Without descending I passed along the front line of cabins in the direction of the entrance to camp. As I neared the first cabin, which gave, through its unshuttered screened sides, a dim skiagraph of movement within, the door opened and the director clattered down the steps like a man in haste. Done making rounds, he took a straight diagonal line to the cottage, looking neither to the right nor to the left but following the moving circle cast by his flashlight, his lecherous head thrust forward. He got there fast, faster than I could have, and with one step was inside. The light remained on for the further minutes that I stood watching before turning in with my boys. The lodge was lit too, but there was only one consuming bright attraction in all the wide night, but one cynosure of neighboring eyes.

The closed eyes did not stop seeing. I had strange dreams. First I seemed to be looking down a well at tomato soup. Its color was abhorrent: the blood of a man stricken with leukemia. The ghastly soup did not keep its distance long. As if a catch had been released, I seemed to be falling toward it. It broke against my face.

And at once the scene changed. I was alone on the top floor

of a country house at night, a house without lights. I saw nothing, but abruptly I heard footsteps on the cellar stairs. Hollowly reverberating they slowly ascended to the first floor. Then, plainer now, they came up toward the second floor, an echoing tread that paralyzed me with terror. The Unknown gained the second floor, crossed over to the stairs that led to the third floor, the top floor. Already they creaked under his weight, and staring blindly into space I could only wait. Something gradually took hideous shape at the top of the stairs—Mac-Swain, but not a man, a pole, a kind of battering-ram, armless, rounded at the end, with MacSwain's beady eyes in the midst of flesh. It pushed on, it butted against me, and the sleeper awoke to find a boy stumbling past his bed on the way to the lavatory. Which boy it was I never knew, but as one does on such occasions, I blessed the reality of the moment that freed me from (even while it contributed to) a nightmare.

11

Do children have a sense of humor? I fear not. Or maybe I'm just not funny. I made a couple of early attempts to be a hit in this way, before giving up. I spread orally over the camp, like scarlatina, Gelett Burgess's "Purple Cow" verses. Then when I couldn't stand what I was hearing all the time, I borrowed a box of water colors and outlined a purple cow, so that they would stop saying they never saw one. But the first camper to whom I showed my debut in art said it looked like a purple sheep, or possibly a buffalo. (Shades of the opening pages of *Le Petit Prince*, which, however, had not yet been published.) "That ain't no cow." Shocked, I wrote underneath:

> I never limned a purple cow;
>   It wasn't easy to paint it.
> But I can tell you anyhow,
>   You'd better not say it ain't it.

Another camper asked to see my painting, explaining, "I never sawed it." This was deplorable from boys whose parents had enough money to get rid of them for the summer, and I mounted my Pegasus again:

> I never sawed a wooden horse;
>   It wouldn't be easy to saw it.
> But I can tell you now, of course,
>   I'd rather saw than gnaw it.

If they had laughed, I'd probably have become that fright of frights, an English teacher.

The pattern of camp life was soon laid bare. I became especially familiar with it after serving my first day as O.D. I had come on a Tuesday, the camp opened on Thursday, and I was Officer of the Day on Saturday, the position falling on each of the eight counsellors by turn, just as the campers ("We all have our duty," said MacSwain), four at a time, took turns waiting on table. The O.D.'s duty was to see to it that the program for the day was adhered to. Seldom did the program for one day differ conspicuously from that of another day, though Sunday, of course, when the parents came, was a day apart, resembling only successive Sundays. Without Sundays the sliding by of the days (as distinguished from the carefully marked passage of the hours) might scarcely have been noticed, for the grooves on which they slid seemed to be the same, the bell doled out the inflexible periods of swimming and of meals and of bedtime, and the impression of one day became the impression of many.

The night before, the O.D. would receive from his predecessor, whose course was run, Gorman's community alarm clock, and go to sleep in the assurance of being driven out of bed by it around seven in the morning. Having dressed and washed, he would rouse the waiters of the day, who had to get down early to the lodge to set the tables. René, who led his own self-clocked life, would be up already, a busy and rather cryptic figure behind the serving window.

There would be a few precious minutes of waiting before it was time to ring reveille. This was the period that I most enjoyed on my days as O.D., when the morning lay sleeping at my feet, a still unravished bride of quietness. I had always liked getting up early, glad to have the night behind me. The other counsellors grumbled in adult or lazy unawareness of the romance and the power of it. You took the day by surprise, and she gave you what she never gave to a crowd. There was, first, the romantic sense of having the world all to yourself for a while: you could recapture the feeling that Adam must have had in the primeval, as yet unshared Eden. Only you were alive, and anything might happen because nothing had happened: promise had not yet been spoiled by performance, the slate was clean. On fair days I would stand outside savoring the stillness that was mine until I broke it with the bell. For the authority of creation was vested in me alone. I could make this earth, so deserted now, these inert cabins, teem with life by just stepping to the porch and pulling a cord.

The O.D. did not rely exclusively on the bell, however, to rouse the camp. It was his business next to make the rounds of all the cabins, pushing open the doors and stomping inside, shouting in cheerful tones at the campers and personally seeing to it that each one got up. The bedclothes were to be stripped back to the bottom: any boy who could not pass this test was forbidden liquids with his evening meal, as I had been. Boys could be typed as to whether they got up promptly or pretended that that was difficult for them, though of course they were not always true to form. But each time I served as O.D. I encountered the usual high percentage of cocoons, as I called them—boys who were reluctant risers, who hugged the bottom sheet, who lay crawled up in their pajamas even though their other clothing had been removed. It was often necessary and by no means unamusing to tickle these difficult cases, or pull them half out of bed by their legs. Pouring cold water on them, a common practice at other camps, was strictly forbidden here. Not only might it lead to colds: it spoiled the bed and might give rise, it was vulgarly imagined, to unjust accusations. Meanwhile, in the midst of all this rousing, the counsellor of the cabin would normally lie torpid, in an intermediate state between sleeping and waking, until that very last minute when he too would have to dress and present a drowsy face at breakfast.

"Cleanliness and self-reliance are lessons every boy learns at Silver Lake Camp," boasted the illustrated circular. And in fulfillment of this promise the first half hour after breakfast was spent in getting ready for cabin inspection, with the counsellor's encouragement but without his manual aid. The exception to this latter rule was Gorman, for whom this was a time of frantic activity, since his boys were too young and helpless to do more than gesture at making their beds and sweeping the floor: it became a stock joke among the counsellors to ask George how his "self-reliance" was this morning. Occasionally, for the sake of the cabin's morale, the O.D., when he came around with the marking chart, would find this cabin best. But it never was the best, for the competition was too keen. Some boys had the passion for neatness, and it took only one such boy to drive his mates in the same well-ordered direction. Jack Livingston performed this gadfly function in my cabin. He was always pointing complainingly to Bruce's sloppy bed, or to the careless arrangement of Frank's shoes. "We will *never* win inspection," he protested. But he, if no one else, would readjust the bed or the shoes, and they won quite often. The cabin with the highest score for the week were entitled to extra dessert on Sunday.

When they had stood at attention for cabin inspection, the boys, fifteen minutes later, had to face personal inspection. Thick-set Tod Wyant, who was in his second year at medical school and already had a gruffness, would seat himself on the steps of the cottage within reach of pills and first-aid equipment, and on signal from the bell the boys would line themselves up before him. He looked to see if their ears were clean, inquired after cuts and injuries, and asked them a question about their digestion. Answers were recorded in a book, and all irregularities given treatment on the spot.

The campers were now free to play according to schedule. A delighted few would learn that it was their turn to go riding. They would pile into the station wagon in their riding breeches and disappear with the director, who took personal charge of this activity. On rare occasions they could be glimpsed later in the morning skirting the camp on their steeds. A path that wound around the far side of the lake did service as a bridle path. Once, while out in a canoe, my eyes sharp because they knew what they were looking for, I discerned the gold hair of Claude Bryant between low-branching trees. Claude was an enthusiastic rider; he soon came to be put in Group I, the most skillful group, the group that MacSwain took out the oftenest. I, who found myself increasingly conscious of Claude's absences, only pretended to be glad when the boy triumphantly announced his promotion to this highest group. "So you will go riding more than before. Tell me, what do you like about riding? What is the thrill?" The boy did not answer at first, but on being pressed he said that he supposed "being high from the ground" was what attracted him. This answer stuck in my mind, especially as it pointed to a good reason, in my view, for avoiding horses. I kept wondering, but never asked, whether they could kick sideways.

There were other reasons why a boy might be absent. Almost daily Bob took a group down to the workshop, which was in a ramshackle barn a score of yards off the main road into camp. Opposite it was the shooting range, where the rifle counsellor led still others. On any morning or afternoon it was possible, too, that a hike would be organized. The owners of canteens having slung them, freshly filled, over their shoulder, the boys would set out in single file, a counsellor at front and back, all of the party carrying hiking sticks and on the alert for imaginary attacks.

But the mainstay—the proper heart and center—of the camp was the lake, there being a swimming period twice a day and boating at all times. It was by the lake that the O.D. stayed, keeping guard, taking the smallest boys out in his canoe, watching other canoeists and rowboaters, always with an eye to the possibility that even Tommy Ricketts might drown. There were collisions and upsets, certainly. Repeatedly MacSwain shook his head over the damage to camp property—the broken paddles and scuffed boats. The damage to the boys seemed to be minor by comparison, and, like the other, part of the inevitable pattern of camp life. At that closely guarded place the nearest to a "serious" accident came when one boy followed another too quickly from the high diving board and jumped on the other's head before the other had yet come up for air. The damaged boy was dragged out spluttering and bleeding. The excitement, however, died down when it was found that he was not drowned and that the blood came only from a nosebleed.

The boy who jumped too soon was docked from swimming for three days. This was a punishment that any camper would have found severe. The half hour of swimming at eleven thirty and again at four formed, along with meals and the Sunday regattas, the stable pleasure, the fixed event that no one willingly missed. It happened sometimes that the riders returned a few minutes after eleven thirty. They would rush from the station wagon to the dock, hot and eager, drop off their clothes, and plunge in. For Claude had set a precedent that first day, and more than half the boys habitually swam without trunks now, whereas in the previous season, George recalled, they had been nude only on the occasion of the Saturday morning bath. It became usual for many to step down from the cabins with only their towels around them, it being understood that at these fixed times Mrs. MacSwain was prudently inside her cabin and would stay there. Although there were those who clung stubbornly to their trunks, nudity gained more and more converts: the bodies, startling white at first, turned pink and soon in many instances so brown that they seemed to be clothed after all.

The counsellors wore trunks. This was the transitional era when at some public beaches men were still required to cover their chests. I had had an access of shyness, and at the store that I had gone to for supplies, such as gabardine slacks and sneakers, I had asked for a one-piece bathing suit. Partly, I was embarrassed because I had no hair on my chest, but I would also have been embarrassed if I had: at the moment I just didn't think my chest was anyone's business. The salesman said he didn't stock one-piece bathing suits or tops; he suggested, rather contemptuously, that I might use an underwear shirt. Murmuring that I would look elsewhere, I crossed over to the women's department and asked there for a plain black woolen suit. "What size?" the salesgirl inquired. "Oh, about my size," I told her.

However, after I had put the suit on at camp, I came to feel very womanish with my chest covered up, covered rather loosely at that. Call this the fear of being in the minority. After one day of it I could bear the distinction no longer and on the next day, the Saturday I was O.D., I rolled down my suit to the waist, strapping on my leather belt, which was the only one I had. Coming down to the dock had been embarrassing for other reasons too. I expected them to stare at my bad knee, searching for sores or deformity. Of course nothing was apparent on the surface, but men's knees always look peculiar anyway. To tell the truth, I didn't like to bare my legs either. But I had dived in quickly and begun to swim in my very best form, as if I were on exhibition, as perhaps I was. However, when I stopped cleaving the water and looked around, it did not seem that anyone had been watching my progress. An older boy who had sized up my bathing suit with a sneer, as if to say, "Oh, you're a maiden, are you?" was now disporting obliviously in the water with the others. Life was like that. It took you at your worst. My lameness and covered chest were stared at, but no one noticed how well I swam.

All in all the afternoons resembled the mornings, except that there was no horseback riding. But another mark of distinction and another fixed period of the day, another, so to speak, stake driven into the heart of time, was the rest period, which immediately followed lunch. The boys were required to lie on their beds without shoes for a least forty-five minutes. On exceptionally hot days this period was liable to be extended to two hours, when it met the swimming period, also extended. The O.D. again made a tour of the cabins, this time bearing candy, supplied not by the management, but by one or another of the parents, who easily averaged ten boxes a week. There was thus a margin of allowance for small boxes. No boy who received candy was permitted to get sick on it by himself; he had to relinquish it for distribution at this time, when all would enjoy it equally, with his compliments. And this was the only thing the recumbent campers had to look forward to, for, in contrast to the counsellors, they plainly abhorred rest. They fretted on their cots, impatient for the bell that spelled their release. All the napping that was done was done by the counsellors. Tuesdays were particularly painful, for that was letter-home day, and bell or no bell, a boy could not leave his cabin until the counsellor had read his letter and found it suitably long and cheerful. The minimum length depended on age. Three lines aslant the official stationery were considered enough from George's boys. Mine had to fill two sides. The counsellors were under instructions to collect the letters unsealed so that the director might look at them, if he wished, before mailing them. "There are always crybabies," said he pithily. "It's up to *us* to see to it that they don't cry in their letters home."

The evenings kept all within bounds of the lake and the cabins. Much of the camp clustered in the lodge, fleeing darkness as they fled rain. There would be ping-pong and checkers, and there might well be a songfest. To disperse chill a fire would be set going in the huge fireplace, and sometimes marshmallows were handed out, three apiece, for roasting. Each boy stood with stick thrust forward, blinking at the blaze, until the transfixed sweetmeat was a proper brown. When, on the contrary, the nights were relentlessly hot, a "moonlight dip" was granted before taps: a quick naked jump in and out, and off to the cabins and pajamas, but the hair must be dried before it could repose on the pillowless sheet. The O.D. would go around feeling the boys' heads.

That would be his last official visit, unless there were disturbances. Each counsellor, having got his charges to bed, would join the others in the lodge, but the O.D., while he too went to the lodge (for there was no other place to go), was still under obligation to scout the cabins now and then, reconnoitering outside to make sure that conversation was dying down, that the campers were gradually going to sleep and not doing anything illegitimate. An hour or so after the boys the counsellors would themselves trail off to bed, having spent the interval in ping-pong, letter writing, yawning, scattered reading or talk, while the radio gave out in an ill-suppressed voice dance music and advertising. René had sensitive ears, and when he put on his nightcap (which, being made of a woman's silk stocking, occasioned endless sly conjecture) at ten fifteen, he was likely to complain about the radio, and typing and ping-pong definitely had to stop. I, bent over my Proust, welcomed the increased quiet, but seldom could ward off sleep long enough to reap much studious advantage, and though commonly the last to bed—so that René called me "un hibou"—I followed the others all too soon.

All too soon, because when I had got my cabin to bed, the time I could steal from sleep was all the time I could call my own. It was precious little, precious *because* little. Really I had been wholly bought, but this time each night subsequent to nine thirty was graciously remitted, provided I was not O.D. As long as I could stay up I was relatively free and would be eventually alone. And being alone was freedom in its purest form.

On a night early in the season, when Tod Wyant and George Gorman and I formed a group in the wicker chairs and Wyant yawned, I expostulated at greater length than I had intended. Something in me seemed to break out rebelliously.

"There you are yawning! And you will start us yawning, George and me. And we'll give in and go to bed. But who knows what we might have missed because we failed to stay awake? Some great experience perhaps. A little bit more of life at least. Do you realize that a man of thirty has spent more than ten years of his life asleep? Ten years. Think of it! He's been alive hardly twenty years. I'm an enemy of sleep. It cheats us. I begrudge it. When we die at seventy we're really under fifty, yes, under forty-five since in infancy and old age we give even more than a third of our time to sleep. And it's mostly habit. You can live longer if you want to. You can cut the eight hours down to seven, down to six, even down to five. Gene Tunney said five was enough. And there are three more hours of life each day. To do with what you like. To know more, to do more, to *be* more. But what do we do? We yawn and go to bed, and don't care about life."

"Is 'life' that book you have in your hand and would go on reading if you stayed up three hours longer?" demanded Gorman. "Is that what you mean by life? I'll take sleep. Sleep is one of the legitimate pleasures of life. It's a part of life. You are making a false distinction."

"You're wrong medically too," said Wyant, whose large even teeth, under lips that drew back, seemed to be slicing the words that he spoke. "Cut yourself down to five hours, and you may go to your grave thirty years sooner. Then what would your gain be? Oh, the precise etiology of sleep is still, I grant you, somewhat mysterious. We don't know what immediately causes it. The physiology textbooks present different theories. The latest thing is Pavlov. You know, conditioned reflexes. Inhibition—after a while you don't get the expected response. The organism is tired. Inhibition here, inhibition there—when you have enough areas of inhibition, when it's spread widely enough over the cortex, you go to sleep. Or maybe it's poisons that cause it—the accumulation of waste products during what *you* mean by life, activity. Toxins. Hypnotoxins. (It's just a word to hide our ignorance, you know—like saying that yawning comes from intermittent spasm of the subhyoid muscles. What causes the spasm?) Anyway, we do know, and any fool knows that activity has to be followed by rest, a period of recuperation, of recovery. The organism refits itself for 'life' again. We have to submit to a kind of death each night in order to be reborn. And if you cheat the body one way, it's going to make you sorry another way, my boy."

"All right," I insisted, "die at thirty, if you've lived till then with some degree of fullness, with some intensity. That's better than sleeping until seventy. What I mean is you have to have a scale of values. Then you decide whether if you lose some sleep you are not getting something better for it. I mean it's a choice sometimes between sleep and something else."

136

"Oh, you mean *that*," said George, leering. "So *that's* the great experience you're talking about. Yes, of course. I thought you meant something higher, like Proust." And he winked at Wyant.

I sat silent, like one whose unconscious has betrayed him.

12

July 4th had come and gone without firecrackers. But there was an influx of parents, which established the day as a holiday. They strolled about the camp in their Sunday clothes, carrying cameras, trailing their boy beside them. A few came up early and brought sandwiches which they ate in picnic fashion on the little pebbled beach or on the grass near the tennis court back of the cabins. MacSwain's ironclad rule was that he never fed a parent, albeit some sought to buy the privilege of having a meal in the lodge with the boys, and others, more difficult still, thought that was their right, included in the fee. The official attitude was that parents were a necessary evil, to be tolerated on Sundays and this one holiday, but never to be positively encouraged. If they could get no food at the camp they would have to go home by dinnertime. And it was true that contact with parents made some boys homesick and therefore difficult for a couple of days after. There were little men who broke down and cried, not caring whether they were crybabies or not.

By that time I had met all the parents whom it was my particular business to meet, except those of Claude. For the mother and father of Ernest Vandevanter I felt something akin to pity each time I saw them. They were a timid and by comparison shabby couple, the father a bookkeeper who had obviously scraped hard to send the son to camp. They came up regularly as if to catch reflections of the happiness their money had bought. They did not know, and no one told them, that their son was being persecuted.

It was Ernest's cabin mates who were guilty, all four. Teasing him had developed into a game and a conspiracy. It had commenced the very first day, and I no sooner checked it one way than I found it cropping out in another. And—in that year of 1939—he wasn't even Jewish. No one at the camp was, for some reason or other.

I got them to say—at least when the counsellor was present—"Ernest" instead of "Sour-puss" or "Stupid," but they put such mockery into "Errr-nest" that the effect was much the same as before, if not worse. When they "Frenched" Ernest's bed, so that he could not get into it past his ankle, I simulated anger and told them fiercely that they were not to do that again. The next time it was a log tucked into the bed at the foot. When I took them to task, Claude said, laughing, "But we didn't 'do it again,' sir. This is *different*." Two nights later the conspirators secreted a bullfrog into the bed, but it spoiled the fun by moving and thus betraying itself to the suspicious victim before the two became bed companions. A titter went up. I myself found it difficult to look severe. That meant grace: they were encouraged. "I caught him," crowed Bruce. "It was my idea and it was me that caught him."

Their favorite trick was screwing up their mischievous faces in parody of the involuntary scowl that Vandevanter made when he was reflecting about something. These periods of abstraction were very frequent with him. At such times he looked his very worst: his sallow skin, with its black and brown blemishes, creased at the forehead, his sandy eyebrows beetled, and his mouth became one taut lipless line. Look wry he did, but you could not call him a crybaby, nor a tattletale. He suffered in silence, even retreating behind the tragic mask of thought like one who heeded not.

That silence bothered me most of all. I could not always be protectively present, and I saw what happened even when I was. What went on behind my back? What relation did the persecution that I knew about bear to the whole? How could I trust the others alone with Ernest at night or at any time?

Sometimes the counsellor, on entering the cabin, had an uneasy feeling that he was interrupting something. One or more of the others would have been near Vandevanter, and faces would assume innocence not quickly enough. But Vandevanter remained a sphinx. His parents went away each Sunday content that they had spent their money well.

"The terrible thing about this cruelty of children," I observed to the senior counsellor, "is that it is impersonal. Therefore it has no limits. They don't think of Vandevanter as having feelings, and they have no feelings about him. They don't get inside him—for them he has no insides. He's their game, their jack rabbit. They're watching for his reflexes like Tod's Pavlov. He's more fun than an inanimate object because he moves. Jump and entertain us."

George shrugged his shoulders. "Tell me, does the fat boy Combs take part in this persecution, as you call it?"

"Yes. In fact he seems to be the ringleader."

"Exactly. And do you realize why? If it weren't Vandevanter it might be Combs. He's keeping the pack away from his own dewlaps, delighted that they've found an ugly victim instead of a fat one. It's perfectly normal. I wouldn't worry about it. You may be sure that it's not nearly so terrible for Vandevanter as it is for you. You're giving him your insides. Most childhood suffering occurs when we're grown up. You're a bit on the sentimental side. I've noticed that before. Now me, I love children, but not sentimentally. I love them as a manifestation of energy, of which this teasing that you take so tragically is a part. Did I tell you, in the winter I keep an art gallery in New York which I'm glad to close every summer and come up here. To be surrounded by the young is for me the fountain of youth. As the calendar goes I'm not so young anymore, you know."

The large hand swept back wistfully a blond strand as if it would arrest a passing year. Obviously there was no help here. I had been a witness to Gorman's obsession before, and it had bored me (for why did not the man do more with his time if it was so precious to him?), but suddenly I saw the pathos of it. What was it Virgil had said in fourth year Latin? *Quisque suos patimur manis.* We each suffer his own shade. Gorman had his in his feminine and premature fear of growing old, of leaving youth even a little behind him. Not only did he take charge of the youngest boys: he played their games with them, as if shedding dignity were equivalent to shedding years. He seemed to hope that Father Time might mistake him for a child. That very morning he had played mumblety-peg just in front of the lodge, seated on the ground, his long legs forming a diamond well into which he flipped the knife from his nose, from his chin, and from the tip of his elbow, while three children of a smaller growth looked on, waiting their turn. At the track sessions no sense of distinction between himself and the campers could keep him from loping up to the high jump and leaping four and five feet. It was plain that he did this not to demonstrate, like the track counsellor, how it should be done, but to identify himself with the boys. His stock remark, afterward, as he stood puffing was, "Ah, I made it." And once he added, "But I'm not so spry as I was. It used to be easier for me." Yes, each had his shade— Gorman his, Vandevanter his, and their private sorrows (I sadly concluded) were capable of widening rather than narrowing the breach between men.

Though under questioning I had designated Combs as the ringleader, I addressed my protests mostly to Claude Bryant. There was a pleasure in taking him to task, a pleasure not unmixed with pain. I retained the fairy-tale association of beauty with purity. Each of Claude's derelictions seemed a betrayal. The others looked capable of teasing or of malice. Claude did not. Yet he had been found guilty even without accomplices. Once when just the three of us were in the cabin together Claude suddenly lifted a picture magazine he was looking at and smashed it down over Ernest's head. I sought an explanation. The first time the boy did not answer, but when I came nearer, repeating my question, he said, "It was a fly, sir. There was a fly on his head and I wanted to kill it."

This was worse. This was a lie. The counsellor had seen

that there was no fly. Without the faintest curl of a smile the boy was lying. He looked like a young angel, but he was lying. And I got the impression, without daring to test it, that no matter how often I demanded the truth the boy would give me this false-hood.

As it was, I contented myself, after Ernest with his usual air of insouciance had slipped out of the cabin, with simply asking, "Why do you tease Ernest so much? He has feelings, you know, like any of us. What's wrong with him?"

Claude seemed to be turning the question over in his mind. There went out now a faint smile which his eyes, lids narrowed —the eyes which were like Marjory's except that they were on more of an almond slant—mockingly enhanced. "What's wrong with him? Why, he's an ugly duck."

Further explanation I never got. And I saw no means of answering this. I could not lie in my turn and assert that Ernest was *not* ugly. The fact was too gross for denial. Children (at least according to certain sensitive accounts which had been rendered of them) never forgave adults *their* lies. Begin with false premises and the case was lost. The other approach, to argue that *though* Ernest was ugly, or *because* Ernest was ugly, he should be well treated, involved the elephantine mistake of treating an eleven-year-old boy like a grown-up. Did a child forgive adults their truths? A child was entitled to his world, and this would be thrusting another and alien world, a world of other people's suffering, upon him. What concern had the beautiful with the ugly? As yet none. Probably he could not be brought to understand. But if he should understand, would not that be worse, the greater of two tragedies? I had no mind to rob Claude on the chance of partially paying Ernest.

I knew all too well where my own inclinations lay. I was carrying around no clear conscience myself. Ernest in certain quiet but unmistakable ways early showed devotion to the counsellor whom circumstance—but only circumstance—had made his protector. He seemed drawn to me as emphatically as I was not drawn to him. It might have begun as gratitude, but it took on the lineaments of love, a love that was embarrassing partly because it made no demands. First there had been the episode of the flashlight, that enviable brand-new flashlight five batteries long. Ernest had straightway offered it to me when he discovered that the counsellor had none of his own. "But all counsellors have a flashlight. You must have one too," he had asserted. I agreed to borrow it for the time being. The boy handed it over reverently each night, joyous that the sacrifice had been accepted. For it was a sacrifice. I knew that. Though I took the flashlight only after taps, that was the very time when the others flashed theirs on and off, playing games of light and shadow before going to sleep. Also they liked to have it by them "for emergencies" during the night, an emergency apparently being any trip to the adjacent lavatory.

The proffer of the flashlight had come the third night. The next day at lunch—it happened so smoothly that there must have been prior arrangement—I found Ernest had replaced the red-headed boy (that one was called Red, which spared me) that had been on my immediate right before. There, at my right hand (counsellors are little gods), Ernest sat for all subsequent meals. Claude continued to be diagonally across the aisle.

When I withdrew into the lodge in the afternoons to practice, as I began to do with greater frequency as the newness of camp wore off, Ernest followed me there and sat wordlessly on a bench swinging his legs, or hovered near the piano with a look of absorption. I spoke to his parents about piano lessons, but the father at once inquired with such solicitude about the cost that the music counsellor retreated into embarrassed silence. I had indeed been thinking of being paid for the lessons, but now I had not the heart to name a rate that would not have been ridiculous. MacSwain had made it clear that of course any music lessons I gave were extra. However, the promised pupils had failed to materialize, though my purse needed them badly. To be sure, the campers were easy to captivate for two minutes or four when, at the end of a songfest, being called on, according to the precedent of the first night, for a solo, I played something sensational like "The Flight of the Bumblebee" or "The Ritual Fire Dance," but Ernest was alone in trying to imitate the chromatic flight of Rimsky-Korsakov's bee on the piano next day. I, curious as to who it was, had come in and found him patiently descending the keys with his forefinger, his mouth folded in.

On a memorable afternoon toward the end of the second week I had just got through the C Minor Fugue in the first book of the Well-Tempered Clavichord when my faithful audience of one approached from behind and observed, "You were playing the same tune again and again, weren't you, on different parts of the keyboard." And opening his mouth he clucked out the theme. He looked like some monstrous gargoyle come hideously to life, as he wagged his tongue and bobbed his oversized head from side to side in time. His mushroom face was fringed by hair so closely cropped that the sallow scalp showed through everywhere and his ears stood out mercilessly.

But he had the theme and had detected the structure of a fugue.

"You have a good ear. Sit down. I'll show you something." I put my finger under the first notes of the open book. "It is like three voices, three people singing. They all sing the same tune, but not together. First one voice sings it, then the second comes in, then the third. And you can put words to the tune. Someone did. Look. 'John Se-bas-tian Bach sat up-on a tack, but he got right up a-gain—with a howl!' And here it is in the bass. . . ."

I was proceeding through the piece when a sharp baritone voice called out, "Holm!" I stood up to face MacSwain.

Now the sound of my last name on MacSwain's lips offended me sorely. We had been living together at the camp for almost two weeks and had come into inevitable daily contact, and I was still the only person there whom MacSwain did not call by his first name. All very well to say that the other counsellors were by comparison old acquaintances and that the boys, even when they were not, had to be treated as if they were. The fact by now, and in the light of other circumstances, admitted of only one interpretation. This was the director's instinctive way of showing his dislike or contempt for the counsellor whose hiring he had come to regret. My desire to be "Kenneth" to this man was not very great, but the single and contemptuous monosyllable—in contrast to "Mr. Holm," which would have been cold but courteous—cut me like a lash. Everyone else was "George" or "Bill" or "Larry": I alone was "Holm." I did not ask friendliness, but this nice contempt—so nice, so deeply ingrained that MacSwain himself was perhaps not conscious of it, might have denied that any offense was intended—was a grievance that grew from day to day. "Holm" this, "Holm" that—leap and obey. The man was master; there could not be two "Misters" in this relationship. A servant, a hireling—moreover one who had turned out badly, what other mode of address could be used to him than "Holm"?

Having commanded my attention, MacSwain indicated some wisps of dust that lay near the wall to one side of the door. "Holm, we have to have a cleaner lodge than this. You are, you know"—at this point the beady eyes took me in full-length—"the indoor counsellor. The lodge is your particular charge. You'll find a broom and dustpan in the closet."

The riding boots turned and clacked out. I went back to the music lesson.

"Now let's see, where were we?"

Where were we before we were so rudely interrupted, I almost said. I had had an arithmetic teacher who was always saying that, who thought it was a good joke. Old Dr. Milvale, so small that he stood on a stool to teach. Whenever any boy who had not been called on by the doctor ventured to say something, Dr. Milvale (the only Ed.D. in the school) would stare at him impatiently until he broke down and then go on with the lesson. "As I was saying before I was so rudely interrupted—" He would send out his pygmy arms from his sides as he uttered the time-honored words, all the while tugging at his sleeves, which were too long for him, with three fingers of each smothered hand. The class invariably laughed.

"What I was playing is called a fugue. Let's skip from number 2 to number 26. This one is a full choir—four voices. It begins with the alto. And the soprano answers. . . ."

"But what are the words?"

"Bach didn't mean for words to go with any of these, you know. I don't know that he'd find them particularly amusing. Though he did make a fugue around the letters of his name. Anyway this can be nicknamed the Prodigal Son fugue. Look. 'He spent his mo-ney like a stup-i-d ass.' And the soprano takes it up—'He spent his mo-ney like a stup-i-d ass.' "

The mood of nervous levity would not down. Bach, the divisible polyphonic man, doing a contredanse on his grave. He spent his money like a stupid ass. The hireling had not received any money to spend. He could not even keep the flashlight stocked with fresh batteries—the lame duck's flashlight. No, pardon, the ugly duck's flashlight.

We were two of a kind. Neglecting all others, I was there to enlighten and amuse the ugly duck alone. The outdoor counsellors were outdoors earning their keep. I was earning mine, in the proper place and company. I was doing my duty as music counsellor, let the dust fall where it may. Duty or even justice was maybe no substitute for love, but I was giving the ugly duck his due, and one cannot always choose one's audience for the fairness of the human face divine. Hath he not copious ears to hear, and if you pricked him would he not bleed?

13

For days, in fact for weeks, I had not seen her except in the company of others. I was thankful for the regular assembly at mealtimes which vouchsafed me at the least a glimpse of her back when all were seated. Three times a day I could count on that much, and unless my lagging boys detained me too long there would be all the inner excitement of her entry. When I got down to the lodge before a meal, my outward self might engage in ping-pong, or chat, or be seated at the piano, but I was really waiting, and kept one sense open, for her. Best it was to be so situated that I could see her even before she passed through the screen door, while she was still on the path to the porch. My opponents at ping-pong found out that there was only one end of the table from which I would play. They might also have noticed that I lost my expertness before meals, sometimes sending the celluloid ball incredibly wide of the table on what should have been an easy return. Nor was it certain that I performed better when she had actually come, for then self-consciousness gripped me. If I was talking with someone, I talked louder in the hope that she might overhear, and strove for epigrammatic cleverness. When she had passed by me and was out of the line of vision, my back still felt her. And the ultimate in happiness in those early weeks was to be greeted by her, or for her to come up and join in the conversation for the brief while before the bell sent us to our respective tables. What she said at these times I could not afterward remember, perhaps because these were not things that she said exclusively to me. But I did remember one silent perfect moment when I arrived at the lodge just as she was ascending its porch steps, and our eyes met and rested on each other, and I held the door open for her like a perfect gentle knight, and with a little nod of acknowledgment she passed in before me. We were both late that day—the final warning had pealed forth. All too often *she* came this late, she and her husband together, and I, waiting inside, already standing at the dining table, was cheated of any chance to interest her in my talk, or my piano playing, or my erratic ping-pong. But that day that I, not MacSwain, opened the door for her, a thrill of possession and satisfaction surged unfamiliarly through my chest, and I felt like one of earth's favorites for almost the entire afternoon.

After meals she went straight to her cabin and was seldom seen outside of it. It was strange, not to say pitiful, how this creature who seemed to have grown on sunshine now shunned it, appearing only to go to the clothesline with her bucket, or to cross into the lodge for a conference with René on the menu. To be sure, there was a reason why she might not be present at the daily swimming sessions, but her conspicuous seclusion from the life of the camp could not be explained merely on the basis of her being neither a counsellor nor a boy but a woman, the only woman there. In the first place I did not take her to be the kind whom this fact would embarrass. In the second place her very complexion, at the first hour I saw her, had borne witness to her love for the outdoors. About her fondness for walking and for swimming we had once talked. Now, however, she grew detectably pale, like the dungeoned princess who has married an ogre.

I longed for an occasion to speak with her. In the mornings when MacSwain had gone off with the riders the counsellors were supposed to be at the lake or elsewhere supervising a play group. Eight counsellors were not too many, whatever the division of their work. All the boys took me for granted now, and I was surprised how easy it was to get along with them. I even fancied that I possessed a certain popularity, especially with the younger boys, who flocked around me at sight to be taken out in a canoe, since they might not go alone. Normally at this time mine was the most heavily laden canoe on the lake, plodding cautiously through the water with two or three boys squatting on the ribbed floor besides the boy at the bow. Else I was a useful umpire at horseshoes or at volleyball. Nevertheless there were naturally intervals when I would have been free to knock on Marjory's door, could I have thought of an announceable reason for doing so.

At last there came to the forefront of my mind an inquiry that I might plausibly take to her. The question would serve as a wedge, but it was also a question about which I had a genuine curiosity. When the third Sunday came without bringing any answer I resolved, that night, that the next morning I would go to her and ask her. It would be a casual question, of course. I would saunter in and say, "Do you happen to know—" No, better this: "I was just wondering, and perhaps you can tell me—" Or ought I first to apologize? "I hope you're not busy." "Am I interrupting?" The problem of exact approach kept me awake Sunday night, and resumed its tortures very early Monday morning. I envied my charges their innocent sleep. At breakfast I was still coining phrases and rejecting them as counterfeit.

Anyway it looked as if it would rain. In that case the riders would not go out, and the bold enterprise would have to be abandoned for that day. I would have at least twenty-four hours more in which to plan and to still my raucous heart. While the cabins were getting ready for inspection I kept staring through the open door at the questionable sky. Postponement would be both a torment and a relief. "I'm not at all sure you'll be going out today," I told Claude, who had his riding breeches on. "It looks like indoor games to me."

I left it to fate. Fate freely showed its hand. The rain held back. The station wagon drove off as usual. Then, as I stood hesitating on the ledge of my cabin, I lost my footing and stumbled forward down the steps. That was fate's pat of encouragement. I was out in the open now, no longer skulking Hamlet-like upon a threshold. Probably she had already seen me from her window. At any rate the boys had seen me, and I would have to go either to them or to her. I had previously determined that the best way for me to be free to choose between these alternatives was to linger in the cabin until the station wagon had departed, and then go straight from my cabin to hers as if I had business there, as indeed I had. That would give me the maximum time, and I would not be abandoning any boys because I would not have yet become involved with any. . . .

Nobody drew near. There were campers and a counsellor at the far side of the lake, evidently hunting for frogs, but the approaches to the lodge were deserted. The beach I could not see.

That dark morning the cabin in its isolation had a sinister air, not for the first time. The curtains framed only emptiness, impenetrable to the passing eye. What prisoned her there? My visit took on the aspect of a rescue.

With tense hand I knocked, knocked more loudly than I intended. The door behind the screen door was wide open. I stood there, my head cast modestly down, playing the self-conscious game of pretending that the barrier before which I waited admitted neither of my seeing nor being seen.

She did not answer. Maybe she was asleep. I knocked again, gently. Arouse her from sleep I would and must, there was no turning back—but gently.

My sidelong glance caught a movement at the clothesline.

"Oh, there you are! Hello!" I was hearty and enormously surprised.

"I'm just taking these in. At the very last minute, it looks. I forgot them last night."

Forgot them? It was not like her to forget. I studied her face sympathetically.

"Let me help you," I said, reaching for the basket of clothes.

"No, it's light." Before I could open the screen door she was inside with it, and while I was wondering whether to follow her in, she reappeared, shutting the inside door behind her.

Looking up into her face, into the eyes the blueness of which never failed to take me by surprise, I blurted out, "Has he any parents?"

She knit her brows for one perplexed instant.

"No. . . . You mean Claude Bryant. No, I don't think he has parents. At least they don't acknowledge him."

"They don't acknowledge him?"

"You're interested in him, aren't you?" She moved down the steps. We turned our backs on the cabin and began to walk toward the dock. "It's strange—only last night I was asking Harry about him."

Some campers at the landing beach had caught sight of me. One of them called my name and waved a paddle.

Waving back, waving them away, I reversed my steps, indicating to my companion the path between the lodge and the cabin, where it joined the road out of camp—the road of escape. For a minute the only voice was that of the gravel beneath us. When we had passed the last cabin I looked at her inquiringly.

She returned my glance, but dropped her eyes before she spoke. "It seems that he's a, well, a love-child."

I had never heard it put that way. "A love-child? What a beautiful word. I mean interesting, that is. It implies that the children born of marriage are not born of love. Was love-child what your husband called him?"

"No." She bit her lips. "No, that was not what he called him. Anyway this is all that is known about your Claude. A man—whose name is not Bryant but who called himself his guardian—made all the arrangements. But—as you too have noticed—he doesn't come to see him. Of course he could be an orphan. But Harry said the man resembled the boy."

"Then he is very handsome, not to say beautiful. Did your husband describe him?"

"Not really. I didn't get a picture. But you're right about the child's beauty. It's a shame."

"Yes, too literally."

The walk into which we had drifted was a delight, but an anxious one. I was afraid that any moment rain would cry halt, or some other prudent consideration against which I had insufficient charm, or none at all. The going fortunately was downhill to begin with; I could husband my breath for talk. Silence, now that we had passed the last outpost, might cause her to question where she was, what she was doing. I began to pour out words in nervous haste like one to whom seduction is new. I took without forethought, without art, the next subject that occurred to me, not reasoning that I was drawing her attention to the very fact I wished her to overlook.

"This road—this is the first time I've been on it since I came. Except two nights ago. Did you hear? We borrowed the station wagon and went to town for banana splits. That was a treat, a major event, nothing less. Bumping eighteen miles through the darkness. Something exhilarating about it. We had to close the windows to keep the shrubbery out. Then a square of neon light—the drugstore, the only drugstore. Astonished to see us. They gave us the large size—*two* cherries, extra whipped cream, a whole banana—forty-five cents. We all had two. Tod said three would be unwise. Not everybody can do that on a Saturday night. I felt sorry for Larry, who was O.D."

"And me—did you feel sorry for me?" she inquired with a smile and a toss of her head.

"Yes, I felt sorry for you, too," I said soberly. The road was looping up now. I let a pause sink in. It was no time to feel heavy and awkward. If ever there had been a signal of distress her question was that. I recognized and appreciated as of old the brave façade. One might smile and smile and still be villainously used. No one could tell except for a certain pallor on the crest of the cheeks. The eyes, measures as they were of her spirit, were unconquerable, and the tilt of the face still spoke defiantly. How to proceed? Sooner than I had dared anticipate we had reached personal ground. It called for the utmost wariness, but it must be clung to, just as when there were acclivities to climb, one foot must somehow be dragged after the other.

"On the way back," I resumed, "Tod began to make one of his killing scientific analyses. He's brimful of facts, you know. If you juggle him, out they come. And they invariably destroy the beauty in life. The very words he uses do. This time someone ventured to say that somebody's eyes were blue. That, it seems, was a crass fallacy, and we should all go to medical school and learn better. In medical school all human irises (except those of albinos) are brown, whatever else they may seem to the lay observer. The differences that strike us ignorant folk, and are important to us, including all the poets and painters—are mere differences in *brown* pigmentation. Eyes that look black are the most heavily pigmented; eyes that look blue are deficient in pigment. The other shades—meaning not only brown—brown-brown—but such romantic delusions as hazel—I've been told I'm hazel, what do you think?—gray, green, and so on—oh, what short shrift he made of them!—are likewise variations of brown between these extremes. And so with a sweep of his hand and some polysyllables I can't be expected to remember, our nascent scientist got rid of a disturbing variety in the human species and made us uniform. Yes, blue is just a deficiency in pigmentation, and moreover such people will pay the penalty for their fairness by being more liable to eye trouble. For a dark iris is a better deflector of light. Ah, I can just visualize him telling his blue-eyed sweetheart (whom he will call brown-eyed) that it's too bad nature didn't give her more pigment, for she'll be needing glasses pretty soon. I told him he ought to read Aldous Huxley's *Brave New World*. But he said he had no time for fiction. Of course not. He'd probably love Huxley's scientific Utopia anyway, including the test-tube babies. But *I* am one of those who would hang myself there."

I finished, surprised at my own fluency and passion. I hoped she didn't think I was obsessed with eyes, because I was. Something had loosened even my hands, usually so reticent, so bound.

153

What their varied activities had been earlier in the speech I had only dim awareness of, but with the final sentiment on reaching the personal pronoun "I," I had slapped my right hand against my chest, and there it was, to astonish me at the end. It all went to prove what I had never to such a degree tested before, that walking, even when scaling a hill, was by no means incompatible with talking, given the strong impulse to communicate and a sympathetic listener who showed no sign of interrupting if I rested between sentences or between phrases. At the beginning I had hardly turned her way, my eye had slipped off to the landscape in front of me. But as my confidence rose I had stolen more and more glances at my audience and been reassured of her sympathy, of her undoubted interest in what I was saying. It was of course no accident that I had chosen to expatiate on blue eyes, on the wrong attitude toward blue eyes. I would not have taken oath that the original discussion in the station wagon had not started with black eyes, that I had not changed the color and the emphasis for obvious reasons (and some she didn't know about). This was not a courtroom (nor a paternity suit), nor was I a man of facts. Yes, my enunciation of the word "sweetheart" had been unmistakably satiric, scornful of the man of facts and not a little scornful of the word. Yet, that word, once it was out, embarrassed me, as if no intonation could disguise its naked, native softness. I had taken breath before going on and was indescribably glad that at that particular juncture she had presented me only her profile.

But now we had both stopped by the side of the road and she was facing me squarely and there would be more words of hers to remember.

"About blue eyes—what you say is very interesting. I wear glasses."

I leaned for support against a tree. "You? Glasses? But of course you don't. It's obvious." I thrust the joke aside.

"I wear glasses when I read," she insisted. "Tortoiseshell

spectacles. I do read, you know, even if you haven't seen me. And when I read I wear spectacles."

I felt the need for movement, pushed myself off from the tree, and started limping down the road.

"It's the blue-eyed curse," she observed after an interval. "Aren't you glad you're normal?"

"Normal?"

"Yes, brown-eyed. Brown-brown-eyed."

"Oh. Don't be so sure. Can you be sure without your spectacles? Some say I'm hazel-eyed. Anyway, I'm not glad, not glad at all. I wish I had blue eyes. The most beautiful people have blue eyes."

"Such as Claude Bryant?"

She was looking straight ahead. Was she teasing? Had she been teasing about the glasses? Did she mean it about my eye color? I could not fathom her. Her childlike voice could maintain a tantalizing neutrality of tone.

"Incidentally," I answered, "since you mention it, do you know there is some resemblance between you? I don't mean just the eyes—though it *is* the eyes. But it's the whole face—yours and his. Something in common. I wonder if you feel it."

She released a little laugh. "Why, in a moment you'll be saying that I'm his mother."

"Now you *are* joking. But I'm serious. I've never seen anyone who looked like me. My sister doesn't look like me. Of course a perfect resemblance is dull. Twins are dull. Too much like a mirror. But to run into someone who has a partial resemblance. Like you and Claude. You and yet not you. The eeriness of it. What's it like?"

"Well, you will have to become a father."

I felt my blush. I could not keep it down. I arched my neck and began to take elaborate notice of the surroundings. A few yards ahead stood straight and unblemished the sign, the reassuring sign, where two roads intersected before the one that we were on crossed the railroad tracks.

"Why, there's the sign!" I said and went on to tell her what that heartening symbol in freshly painted red and black had meant to me the first time I saw it.

"And who do you suppose painted it?" she demanded.

"Of course. I might have known. And you had done it the very day I came!"

I was savoring the poetic justice of this when great drops of rain began to fall. Two shelters offered themselves, the railroad shed and a lone tree that stood on guard at the crossroads. We made our romantic choice, standing close together under the barbed hearts of the leaves and looking out in silence upon the drenched world. There was the sound that I loved, I was thinking, the patter we had been cheated of on a certain previous occasion. Again thanks to rain, I was next to her, our shoulders touching. It did not matter that the green roof, with its twisted gray rafters, let some of the rain through. Or rather it did matter—it introduced a new pleasure. Without losing the sensation of shelter I had added to it the titillating effect of cool moist kisses on the face and neck and arms, the rain being a furtive but persistent lover. Nor was I closing my eyes to imagine this, for the sight of her was the reality on which I built.

We had been lost for some time in perhaps intermingled thoughts when she looked up at the boughs and informed me, "This is a plane tree." I was admiring the profile of her throat, that challenge to the plastic art of the sculptor, and I did not immediately turn my attention to the tree. When I did there dawned on me recognition of an old acquaintance.

"A plane tree. How marvelous that you should know! I never can tell anything but an oak, and then I wouldn't swear to it. I'm not observant. Nature is something new and strange. But this tree—I think they have plane trees in Philipse Manor. I've seen them all my life without knowing their names."

A sense, hitherto dormant in this place, a sense of home—what had once been home—stirred within me and caused me to

156

lay my hand in appreciation on the scabrous bark. "I'd like to show you parts of Philipse Manor," I added. "We would—"

But she had suddenly stiffened and turned her head. A vehicle was coming down the road toward us, crawling over the ruts, its two windshield wipers working in furious unison. The station wagon stopped abruptly at the tree. The man at the wheel leaned back and opened the rear door. Two boys slid over to make room for us in the back seat as we got in.

We drove on, on into camp, in forbidding silence, broken only by two or three interjections thrown out by one of the boys, to which none of the adults responded by so much as a turn of the head. I had what seemed a very long while in which to contemplate the thick butcher's neck of MacSwain and the contrast of that thinning black hair, dandruff-powdered (now I have dandruff, which will be cured with baldness), beside the soft, silken, and on this day immaculately combed and watered-down sheen of Claude Bryant. During that same period of suspense I could not help regretting the tree after all and wishing that we had taken refuge at the shed instead. It was not the luckiest of trees.

14

Hours later the director accosted me on the path between the cabins. The camp had just emerged after rest hour. The sun had cleared away all traces of rain. It glinted on MacSwain's face, causing him to turn as he spoke.

"Holm, I'm afraid you were laying down on the job this morning. It was raining: your place was in the lodge entertaining the boys. We have thirty-seven boys, in case you don't know it, and only eight counsellors. Nine, counting myself—I think I work as hard as any. It's enough, a better proportion than at most camps, but not more than enough. We all have to work. That's the point. Not a single counsellor can be spared any time. There can be no vacations on the job. If we go out in a canoe there should be boys in it. If we take a walk boys should be with us. That is why we are here. That is what we are paid for."

MacSwain was always saying "we" when he meant "you." An oily hypocrite he was, but this time I had an answer for him.

"But I'm *not* paid."

MacSwain stared open-mouthed.

"I haven't *been* paid."

"No, of course not yet. At the end of the month. When you have earned it—not before."

And to this there was no answer. I stared in dark defeat at the broad brown-shirted back of my opponent, who was striding off toward headquarters. Even with words I could not beat this man. The surge and passion of the morning, of the walk with her, had gone out of me. I was empty, dejected, impotent. I told myself that MacSwain was jealous, that it was obvious that he was jealous, jealous with reason, but though the mind relayed this fact to the heart and bade it rejoice, bade it gloat, it did not. The very thought of that marriage was a grief without a pang. How to rescue Marjory seemed a problem impossible of solution, except by fate. If only MacSwain would get sick and die! But he looked as if he had never been sick in his life, as if it would never occur to him to be. He would outlive me, and his wife too. Wasn't that always the way? Beauty perished; grossness was immortal. Likely she would die giving obscene birth to the ugly and ponderous image of MacSwain.

But out of the wasteland of despair rose a new intention. It seemed advisable to skip a day—one should not be too obvious— but on Wednesday I was at her doorstep again.

"I seem to be free for a while," I said in mock surprise. (I had darted directly from my cabin to hers the moment the station wagon had dropped over the crest of the hill.) "Wouldn't you like to walk a little?"

"Just a minute." I wondered what she was fetching, or perhaps she was adjusting her hair, but she was outside in less than the promised time, not noticeably altered, all the more tantalizing for those few seconds offstage. Backstage I myself never went now, I was thinking. What was it like? What were the changes? What was it she closed the door on? What went on there? Was MacSwain above even physical cruelty? She was not the girl to cry out, though I had often lain listening on my cot at night, or brushed close by the cabin window at odd hours. I was a night roamer anyway because of my embarrassment at the open-stalled toilets. Once, unable to sleep and seeing by Ernest's flashlight that it was 1:25, I had got into bathrobe and slippers and gone down and stood just back of the window, leaning there for twenty-three minutes, until a shiver went through me so strongly that I was afraid it was audible, louder than the obscene snorts sent out into the night by MacSwain—swine, not swain— which in fact ceased. That was not the only time I had reconnoitered, but it was the longest time. On another occasion I had opened the door to find the full glare of the risen moon upon me and retreated like a culprit on whom the police have turned a searchlight. A moonless night was best. You could not trust the obscuring clouds which had a way of suddenly unswathing that evil eye.

"There's one thing," I said. "We ought not to go alone. We ought to take at least one boy with us."

"Chaperone?" she jested.

"Well, the fact is I *am* supposed to be on duty. I think there'd be less chance of somebody's objecting if we took a boy along. Objecting to my wandering off this place of duty. It becomes a hike, you see. You and I and a camper." My eyes were scanning the tennis court back of the cabins. "Just one second."

I climbed up to the edge of the steep, bumpy court—it slanted like a warped deck—where, at the permitted hours, a game of doubles was in perpetual progress (singles being a luxury too great to be countenanced, since there was only one court). It was the oldest boys who played. The tennis counsellor stood alongside, shouting corrections, and among the other spectators were two from my cabin.

"Come down. I have a surprise," I admonished Claude, putting a hand on his shoulder.

Ernest looked up eagerly. Claude was inclined to question.

"What sort of a surprise? I'm next in line here."

"You will see. Come on." Others were showing interest too. I began to move away, taking the chance that Claude would follow. But Claude hesitated, looking doubtful and even petulant. It was Ernest who detached himself from the group, who skipped forward, his face a horror of delight.

"No, Ernest," said his counsellor, frowning and freeing his arm from the boy's affectionate grasp. "You had better play tennis." I pointed to the court as one would direct an inconveniently effusive and disobedient dog.

And Ernest put his tail between his legs—that is to say, the smile vanished from his face.

"The surprise?" he faltered.

"The surprise this time is for Claude." I looked back at Claude as I named him. He was coming, he had decided to come. Something almost painful happened to my heart. Meanwhile those questioning brown eyes were raking me. I had no time, no time at all, for my sympathies to be played on: this mock sorrow was absurd. The boy was an actor. "Besides it isn't much of a surprise anyway," I added in a low voice. "You will hear about it. Now go and play tennis."

I moved on. Claude caught up alongside. He was alone, thank God.

"You *are* difficult," said I.

"I didn't play tennis in a long time." But there was acceptance in his tone, and he was not going to be inquisitorial about the surprise after all, though it was safe now to tell him.

"You mean, you *haven't* played tennis. Now the surprise is this. . . . But can you guess?"

Claude was waving to Marjory.

"She seems to be waiting for you," he said. "Is it another walk?"

"She's waiting for *us*. You're going too."

We joined her, Claude standing for a moment in between. I faced her smiling, my fingers playing with the boy's hair. It was, as I had noticed before on occasion, the softest hair in the world.

"I thought so!" said she gravely.

"All right. I don't seem able to surprise anybody."

There is an age when children lag behind, and an age when they march on ahead. Claude was at the latter age. He walked on a little in front of his elders without passing out of earshot, so that our conversation was modified by his presence. Yet he himself did not speak. He accepted, he understood, he was serenely aware. His straight little back within the knitted polo shirt, the shoulder blades charmingly apparent, the head that never turned round, the resolute swing of his arms and legs—

entertained no doubt that we were following. Throughout the walk he was the center of our vision, and knew it.

In between our fragmentary talk I played a game. I would narrow my eyes until all the irrelevant world was excluded, leaving only the bright blur that was Claude's head. "What are you doing?" Marjory asked on the third of these occasions.

"I'm experiencing yellow," I replied.

"The heat—it's gone to your head," she laughed.

What we said was preserved from triviality by the intonation we gave it. Intonation *is* meaning. The Chinese know that, and lovers find it out.

We went as far as the intersection at the railroad tracks where the plane tree spread its shade in vain. That was a comfortable distance so far as I was concerned, enough to exhilarate at a saunter without fatiguing. Instinctively we wandered off the road here, passing through weeds to where, back of the railroad shed, the grass was stubby and the ground looked good to sit on. A brook tunneled through under grass. Claude in fact slid into it as we were choosing a place to sit. I watched with amusement while Marjory insisted that the wet sneakers and socks be removed at once and sunned. "Dampness has nothing to do with colds," I informed her. I had just learned this from Tod. But at the finish of my sentence I shuddered, hot as it was, remembering my rheumatism. It was not that I was experiencing a fear of its return: I feared the reminder I might have stirred in her of the last time it returned. "I mean," I hurried on, "you're not his mother."

But this was not fortunate either, and she frowned, and glanced at Claude, who was leaning back on a mound, his stripped legs already docilely offered to the sun.

"*Pauvre garçon!*" she murmured.

My eyes and the boy's met, and, as had happened before, it was I who was disconcerted. Certainly the boy showed no signs of hurt feelings at the reference to his seeming lack of parents. On the contrary, he was regarding me with sardonic amusement, as if I had just proclaimed my own illegitimacy, not his. Or was it the slant of his blue eyes that made him look sly, a slant as unintentional, as devoid of planned meaning, as the infinitesimal curling of his parted lips? Another impression which gathered strength that day was that while in activity, as when walking or swimming or seen in the distance on a horse, Claude seemed masculine, completely a boy, a very athletic boy, his personality changed in moments of repose. Leaning back, his legs arched, he was almost coquettishly languorous and feminine, as if he were bent on carrying almost to caricature the resemblance between himself and the woman yet girl who was not his mother.

But to say that she was not his mother was to betray grossly a higher reality. I did not understand Claude, but I understood my own mistake. Man cannot live by facts alone, and besides, this fact was getting staler all the time. I never served it up again.

It was an idyl, an idyl of which these who have experienced only a city park can form no adequate conception. I felt sorry for—and superior to—the cliff dwellers, the benighted people of New York and all their tribe, climbing their stairs or waiting for elevators, mounting without aspiration, facing a bleak stony enclosed existence without impulse from a vernal wood, without the chance to become Wordsworthian sages. The trees, railed off in regular rows, and the tracts of grass with the signs barking at trespassers—these satisfied no longings, though they stirred them. I leaned back on my elbows and cast a dreamy and appraising eye on the scene now before me. It was of course not the most distinguished scenery. Too many straight lines. There were telegraph poles, but no immediate trees, and the railroad shed, of a putrescent gray, uncompromising in its naked rectangularity, was considerably less attractive from behind than it had been the day I descended to it. For then at least its ugliness had served a purpose. And there were no flowers except the ubiquitous dandelion. I could not recall a single poem about this humble flower, though it was said to be good for soup. Nevertheless there was something reassuring in knowing its name, as I might not have known the name of a daffodil, for instance ("I wandered lonely as a cloud"), had I come upon one.

But the sky, the sky at least, was unimpeachable. I stretched out flat, my head on my hands, the better to consider it. Its blue was a rinsed blue across which floated a shifting pageantry, where white radiantly answered for all the colors in a Mardi Gras of the most shameless magnificence. That connoisseur of painting, George Gorman, would have blushed at such display, would have said that God was imitating Maxfield Parrish or some other calendar painter, but what was vulgar in a painting became ineffable as the thing-in-itself. I sighed, and tried to think of a rhyme for "dandelion."

An ant skirted my ear, causing me to sit up, and, had I been alone, I would have screamed. She was sitting up too, and seemed to be given to reverie, her face worked on by thoughts I would have given much to be able to read. It had been so quiet, all three had been so contemplative, that the gurgling of the brook a yard below our feet had become distinguishable as the one rhythm of the universe. But the sudden roar of a southbound train broke in upon our consciousness. She started, then looked at me with a smile—it seemed a brave smile—as the train crashed past.

We waited for speech to be possible. "It gave me a shock," she said.

"Yes, it comes like a profanation. I *hate* all loud noises, don't you? They are especially out of place here. I think this is the basic fear. Or rather, there are two. The fear of loud noises and the fear of falling. We're born with them, and we never get over them. Shall I confess—I used to run to the hall closet and shut myself in whenever there was a thunderstorm. It wasn't the lightning I was afraid of—it was the rumbling, the horrible rumbling. The voice of wrathful God. My great-aunt is the same way."

"Tell me about your family."

"Well, I have no—" I was going to say "mother," and if we had talked long enough I might even have added "father." But Claude, across whose prone body we had been talking, stirred, came to a sitting position, a blade of grass dangling meditatively from his mouth. I was diverted, and probably it was just as well, to trying to make out whether he was eating the grass or just chewing on it. "By the way, what rhymes with 'dandelion'?" I inquired, my eyes on the blade of grass, which was disappearing.

"You do have a grasshopper mind, as the ads say. How about 'mandolin'?"

Before she had finished I cast down my head, as there spurted foully through my brain the French word for "dandelion"—*pissenlit*. Would she think I was being dirty, or even guess my soiled past? How much French did she know? Gosh, I couldn't even hold a clean conversation anymore, and yet I hadn't remembered the French till that moment. Dirty those French, and what really were they talking about, *pissenlit* soup?

With scant courtesy I changed the subject. "Won't do. I can't write my poem. Claude, is it good?"

"What?"

"The grass you've just eaten."

The boy shrugged. "It makes juice."

More indecency.

"I think in that case," she said, reaching over and feeling the socks and sneakers, "we could try the brook."

This returned us to the romantic, as distinguished from the Romance languages. She showed me the precise cupping of the palms that would work. Her hands were wonderfully delicate, and though the fingers were not long they were slender. I told her it was a pity she had given up the piano. As for the water, such coolness never came from faucet or refrigerator. I drank with small brooding over the question of invisible pollution. I was carried away—would risk germs and all in that company. If Nature wasn't pure, who was?

Then we headed for home, what had to serve as home,

Claude again in the vanguard, military in his bearing and in his silence. *"Il a une beauté orgueilleuse,"* I commented, but she did not understand me. I did not repeat it, just waved in the direction of Claude's back. Either my pronunciation left something to be desired, or her vocabulary was as small as I had hoped.

I kept thinking with every conquering step how much better, all in all, this walk was than the last. We made a perfect combination, tied in a union that required no words. We must have struck an observer as not different in kind from, though nobler than, those groups that strutted so proudly about the premises on Sundays.

And the irony was that I was carrying out MacSwain's instructions. MacSwain could see us, for all I cared. To be sure, he was not likely to, since we would be back well before eleven even. That was really too bad. It would be a pleasure, a sweet revenge, to be overtaken on the road, to refuse a lift, to say curtly, "No—we *like* to walk, thanks."

By the entrance to Cabin Three she asked Claude, who was turning to go, whether he had another pair of sneakers. "Those seemed fairly dry to me, but now that you're back you had better change."

Claude made a moue.

"Go ahead. Change," his counsellor commanded.

I turned to her. "You do take care of him, don't you?"

"But it's only natural."

"Oh, is it?" I said. And laughed.

15

On Sunday July 31st the director gave one of the most sickening of his weekly talks. What the camp apparently needed was a minister to conduct the Sunday services. Once, the preceding Sunday in fact, it got one. He drove up in a battered Ford, and listened to the hymns in the unadorned chastity of his cassock and saved his voice for a sermon in which he told the boys that the conscience was the Holy Ghost. That at least looked and sounded official, whatever my personal reaction. He had a Bible and read from it, and advised the boys to do likewise. After the singing of the recessional—it was "Onward Christian Soldiers," but they did not, of course, move from the pews formed by the benches in the lodge—he signed out over their bowed heads a formal benediction. But the next week we reverted to MacSwain.

"Boys, do you sometimes think of God, on weekdays I mean?" he said. "The other evening I thought of God. I saw two campers fighting over a paddle. One of them tripped the other up. The one who fell was smaller than the other, a good deal smaller. Otherwise I'd have said, 'Go and put on the gloves, both of you. We'll have this out here and now, have it out fairly. There was no need to fight over the paddle, but since you started let's see it through properly and to a finish—with gloves, and I will referee.' That is what I would have said if these had been campers of the same age and size. But they were not. So I thought, if only the small boy had a big brother to take care of him, to give the bullies a punch in the nose!

"Now boys, that is where God comes in. We call ourselves Christians, and on the whole we live in peace and happiness here at Silver Lake Camp. We give the other fellow a chance.

Fair play is our motto. We share alike, and we do not bully. That is, most of the time. God watches and He does not frown. But we have to realize that He is watching, that He is on guard. And then the thing, the ugly thing, that happened the other night will never happen. Never if we think of God, think of Him in these moments of weakness when we want the other fellow's paddle, or do not feel like cleaning out the cabin, or listening to our counsellor, or think we can conceal our box of candy in our suitcase and have it all ourself. But the thing that gets me maddest is bullying, hurting the other fellow who cannot hurt back. That is not manly. Just remember, everyone smaller than you has a Big Brother. That Big Brother is God Himself. He looks down, and He will come to the rescue in some form. And the bully will be punished. I give you my word that he will be punished!"

He looked around defiantly, his face red, as if he dared someone to contradict him. The campers stared back, awe-stricken.

He resumed in calmer tones.

"The bully of the other night I myself refrained from punishing. But perhaps by now he has been punished. He is here—I do not name him—and I think if he was not punished before he has been punished now. And those of you who ever wish for someone to protect you, remember the Big Brother who looks down is all-powerful, more powerful than Tarzan or the heavy-weight champion of the world! Let the bully watch out. At Silver Lake Camp we are men, and Christian men. We know that God is looking. Never do we forget.

"Let's have 'Stand up, Stand up, for Jesus'—Number 17."

It was arranged that Gorman should always be O.D. on Sundays, since he was known to be "a good man with the parents." His tall form in white flannels moved with easy bearded grace and without lapse of memory from one group of visitors and patrons to another on those populous afternoons. After serving as a welcoming committee along with Mrs. Mac-

Swain, who came out of her seclusion on this one day of the seven, he took charge of the regatta. This afternoon the feature was a series of canoe races according to age groups. First the boys of six to ten, the few who were eligible to get into a canoe alone, zigzagged across to the other side where MacSwain stood as judge. The next race, for those from eleven to twelve, was won by Jack Livingston, whose sailor's hat seemed to make the victory appropriate. Finally the campers of thirteen and fourteen got into the red craft at the landing beach and waited for the signal to start. George, in a rowboat that was much too small for him, was at the center of the course. He dropped a red flag. The canoeists sped toward him, amid shouts such as I had heard at a horse race, and I wondered whether any of the parents had made wagers. But they should have known that Tommy Ricketts was sure to win. Already, going straight as an arrow—no easy thing to do in a canoe—he had taken the lead and was alongside of George at the halfway point.

Then a strange thing happened. The man in the rowboat had maneuvered it so that its prow was exactly pointed at the goal where the judge was waiting for the winner. The rowboat began to race the canoe. It caught up with the lead canoe, which had no chance against those oars and those long arms. Under the sun that day the race went to the swift, but not to the right age group. George bounded in a yard ahead of Tommy Ricketts.

Yet another event was to mark the day. Although, since the last of the month had fallen on a Sunday, he was perhaps under no immediate legal obligation, the director paid the counsellors half their salaries. He went around at dinner just before the dessert was served passing out ten- and twenty-dollar bills like Fortune distributing her bounty. "Yop, it's payday," he said jocularly, with a wink at Ernest, as he came up to me. It was like him to be ostentatious about it, and not to care if the whole camp saw how little the counsellors got. Perhaps the witnesses were to take the place of receipts, for he counted the money out carefully. I pocketed the thirty dollars quickly, shamefacedly, but with a feeling of satisfaction that made me keep touching the money with my fingers as I bent over the jello. Money was sordid, but it was more sordid still to be without it. And besides, this was the fruit of five weeks of responsibilities. We ought really to have got more than half our salaries, since only fourteen days of duty remained. There would be only two more Sundays; Sunday, August 14th, would bring the season to an end.

We had just passed through what the senior counsellor had predicted would be the most difficult week psychologically. "The first three weeks it's all novelty and excitement," he explained. "Then that wears off. The fourth and especially the fifth week may be deadly, despite all their divine energy. Comes their second wind, as they realize that only two weeks are left, and they make the most of everything and wind up in a whirl. So the fifth week is our problem." But I had not noticed anything unusual, except that the barbers came for the second time, and Frank Case developed a cold which kept him isolated in one of the vacant cabins for three days. I had visited him to help him pass the time. The first day I brought along a rotting leather volume of Edgar Allan Poe's poems that I had unearthed in the lodge closet. (His tales had haunted my early teens.) It was apparently the only book that the camp owned, and it owned it inadvertently. I had meant to read to the sick boy "The Raven," but Frank's attention had wandered so after three stanzas that I perceived that this was not the time and place for poetry and shut the book. I had tried very hard to be dramatic, but all my elocution was wasted on this boy with the stuffed-up head.

"The whole trouble is there's nothing here, George, for their imaginations to feed on," I complained afterward. "Where's the library? No wonder the rest hours are an inferno of ennui. Yes," I savored the phrase—"an inferno of ennui. And take the cabins. Number One, Number Two, Number Three. Song Sheet One, Song Sheet Two, Song Sheet Three. It's all arithmetic, cold barren killing numbers. (Oh, to get to that Berkshire music festival! Rubinstein is playing.) I'm proud to say I always got poor grades in arithmetic. Thirty-seven boys aged six to fourteen. How can you appeal to a child that way? Why not give each cabin a name? Some of the counsellors go to college. Call the cabins Harvard, Dartmouth, Princeton, Yale. Hang up banners and stir up loyalties. How can anyone be loyal to Cabin Number Three? I'm surprised we ever win at inspection."

George had been gesturing impatiently. "Like so many innovators," he broke in, "you are only suggesting something which has already been tried and failed. Do you know why? We couldn't get anybody to go to Harvard, which was your cabin, because it had a rotten football team. And Navy got an inferiority complex because it had lost to Army the preceding season 21 to 0, and Army kept telling it so. But the worst complication was when we consented to create Michigan. We hadn't thought of having Michigan but a popular demand went out for it, since *its* football team had been neither defeated nor tied. So we created it. What happened? The whole camp wanted to get into that cabin. Before we had feuds. Now it was a miniature civil war. That is why this summer 'Michigan' is Cabin Five. Numbers give peace. Don't you know H. G. Wells's theory that personification of nations is behind all our modern wars?"

I would not have gone to the Berkshire music festival if it meant leaving camp for so much as an afternoon. I was being insincere. I did not really care whether the camp had a library or what the cabins were called. It was a matter lately of looking down from a height at the misfortunes of others without any sense of participation. Euphoria lapped me. A high and secret poetry had entered my life, rendering me immune to ordinary things. It was independent of and better than books, this new and mostly wordless poetry. It brimmed over from certain morning walks of three.

Two nights after I had been paid I bought myself a flashlight, at the drugstore, and also got fresh batteries for Ernest's. That debt was now discharged. About time it was, too. I glanced around at the wares in the showcases as I put away my change.

Should I buy Marjory something? Perfumes with come-hither names lay ensconced in velvety caskets. Boxes of candies were pyramided high, looking glossy and stale. The probable staleness of the candies hastened my decision. A present—a present, moreover, bought at a drugstore—no, I would not vulgarize our relationship by so conventional and overt an act.

We had got good at conveying meanings by intonation. On the average of twice a week we strolled down to the brook, always now with our "chaperone." We joked about him, but we took him, and, if for no other reason than that he was flattered at such attention on the part of the grown-ups, Claude seemed glad enough to accompany us, provided it was not his turn to go riding. So that on mornings when Claude was among the riders, there was no excursion, just as, for other reasons, there was none on Saturdays and Sundays and when it rained. Even so we could have averaged more than twice a week, were it not for some unspoken sense of restraint that marked our whole relationship, some common agreement not to push a happiness too far, mingled, on my side at least, with a feeling that rarity is of the essence of preciousness, and anticipation not the smallest of pleasures. This fear of excess laid its hand on me at the drugstore. I never had the courage to put my feeling into words on the walks, nor the sense that this was necessary. Was it not enough to say "Good morning" in the tones of a lover? I caressed her by the way I uttered her name. We understood each other perfectly, and the presence of Claude proved a help rather than a hindrance. Our interest in him stood, in some way not yet explicit, for our interest in each other. Is it that the inarticulate need an intermediary or a symbol? I wasn't ready to call myself inarticulate: I was just careful about words.

Music served as an intermediary on one occasion. This was on a rainy afternoon of the next-to-last week. Indoor games were being played, chiefly and most boisterously "musical chairs." The wicker chairs had been lined up in a row, their seats alternately facing east and west, and the accompanied parade around them got steadily shorter and shorter, if not quieter. I ordinarily did not reflect on the degenerate use to which music was put by this game, but today, for some obscure reason, I was more bored than amused. Perhaps I had been asked to play for the game once too often. At any rate I was inclined to compare myself to a giant in chains, or to a Hercules who has been asked to lift up a pin. This was the nadir of music, when its value depended entirely on wondering when it would stop.

At last the game came to an end, in the usual way, with two boys walking warily around one chair and me interrupting myself for the last time. Released, I felt the need to express my freedom, to prove to myself, if to no other, that skill and sensitivity were still mine. Accordingly I went into the slow and expectant beginning of the Liszt Sonata in B minor. Though the piece was a prize show piece of mine, I had not played it for months. There were two quiet thumps in the bass, like some great power bestirring itself, an impression that gathered through seven measures of suspense, when these pairs of G's were touched out for the third time. And then, allegro energico, the power broke out in brilliant octaves, scorning bounds.

I was hammering home the staccato bass that, after another dramatic pause, follows the octaves, when I became conscious that Marjory was standing by the wing of the piano. Evidently the grand declaration of the theme had drawn her to the lodge, even as it had quieted the ping-pongists. All seemed to have stopped what they were doing to listen. I sensed this without looking around, and thought it entirely proper. I did not nod to Marjory, though I lifted my head and was dreamily aware at the edge of my vision of the green of her dress; it would have been impossible for me to speak and play such music at the same time. For now I was in the schwärmerei part, the part which, restrained at first, soars in a crescendo of wild, swirling notes and then maintains that height for measure after measure in an astonishing mixture of legato and staccato until the octaves for the two hands breathlessly return, winding themselves up into a frenzy that threatens to quit the keyboard, for it seems to leave no part of it unstruck.

The romantic music was best. This part, which billowed out now in a different tempo, grandioso and fortissimo, resembled structurally some of Liszt's arrangements of Wagner. But it was far better than these, completely pianistic and as genuine as the sea. No borrowed passion this. It surged; it hesitated; it came and went in waves. It gave the sign of yielding, dolce con grazia. And after some hovering, some tantalizing delay and preparation, there came that theme which is Love itself, strung out with such fragile lyricism as cut my heart to play.

This was it—the sense of touch—the only reality—it had come to this. Take her up tenderly, young and so fair.

The accompaniment was trickling off far up the treble. She had taken a seat by the window, was looking out, her profile a shadowed glow. I watched my hands, my own dear hands, as if they were somebody else's, darting over the keyboard with exquisite assurance, incessantly at home there, these fleet strong fingers that built worlds and could take them down at will. Even a deaf man would have loved these black-and-white patterns that shifted like the kaleidoscope. I was often possessed by a quite impersonal admiration for these hands at their beautiful work, and would follow their reflection—indirection was best—in the polished panel. The sight of a mechanical piano, playing away without any hands, was unbearable, and once when one was on at a party—a very good one, Duo-Art—I had gone up and sat at it and sheltered it. Now these hands, they were my hands after all, released, were ardently telling her what nothing else could say so well.

I had lingered over the theme which is the lyric expression of Love itself. Happily it came back again and again, but never, perhaps, with such agonizing sweetness as the first virginal time. There were fierce outbursts of passion in between, and other

174

resting places of calm. This sonata had much in common with the "Tristan" music, I kept thinking.

The thought of MacSwain came like a bolt as I stormed down the keyboard for the final climax. I lifted my head ever so slightly. MacSwain was not there. I could tell without directly looking. In a different way I was as sensitive to that presence as I was to hers. But he might come. There was need to hurry, to finish. I swung into the prestissimo octave melody. First the right hand carries it, then the left. The eye could not follow my flashing hands. Now as loud as possible those heavy B-major chords.

The piece ended calmly and quietly. Liebestod. The calm after the storm of passion. Like death the satiated sinking back. As quiet as possible. After the key tone not a sound.

Boys had been hovering restlessly around the piano. One passed between my face and hers. When the space was clear she said from the chair, "It's like *Tristan and Isolde.*"

"It is, it is!" I answered, getting up excitedly. "But what made you say that? Have you seen the opera? We had the same thought."

She came up to the piano and touched its tilted back. "I'm not an ignoramus," she pouted, looking at me. "I've seen *Tristan and Isolde.* Once at the Met—as we habitués say. Well, to be frank, it's the only opera I've seen except Gilbert and Sullivan. Tickets are hard to get. But I've heard others and parts of others. I like music."

"It can say things." My right hand made a silent pattern on the keys.

"You play magnificently. Is that what you're going to do—I mean for a career?"

The wonderful simultaneity there had been between us was something I half wanted to go off alone and consider. But her question opened up a beloved subject, one that no one else had touched that summer. It was further proof that we were kindred spirits, or better still, one soul in bodies twain. The others seemed to think that I was a perpetual music counsellor. They did not know that I was a giant in chains.

I cast certain doubts aside. "Yes, I'm going to be, that is, I want to be a concert pianist. Of course being a composer is more glorious in the long run. I want to be both. I've written pieces, you know. I've been playing them lately at the end of songfests. Nobody knew any different, apparently. I take that as the highest compliment. They've been compared to Schumann. I don't mind that either."

"I'm sure you will be very successful."

"Of course it takes money, at least a thousand dollars, maybe two. For the debut at Carnegie Hall. And only a few at the very top really make a living playing. The rest teach. Yes, the competition is tough. One doesn't get to the top overnight."

I spoke as one who, already there, was reminiscing.

"And then you tour the capitals of the world," she responded. "London, Paris, Rio! What a future! And I, I will be in the audience—a mite, another face. Down front, I hope."

Her gaze shifted to the door. I knew who had just come in. She went casually out, without a glance at her husband. They were in different orbits. But I suddenly wanted MacSwain to notice, and I shouted after her, "Marjory, I will send you tickets! Down front!"

Now we had a secret. Let the director make what he could of that.

MacSwain half turned and regarded me with a faint disdain, with a slight lifting of his upper lip, as if I had just made some sort of foul noise. I hated this man, who had no right to exist, but who made absolutely no apology for existing, for being near or present at all times, like the pestilence.

That hatred came insidiously out that night. The rain continuing, we had a songfest, and of course the director had to comply afterwards with the popular demand for a solo. He stood up, and they knew that was the signal for the request, and they never failed to make it. Tactful they were, knowing which side their bread was buttered on, little diplomats, clamoring for their master's voice. Well, you Scotch nightingale, what's it going to be? It was going to be "On the Road to Mandalay," a piece that I had accompanied him in not more than a dozen times before. I could not immediately find the music. The director glared at me with impatience and scorn while I fumbled.

It was as if bile was poured from one into the other. My jaw set as I opened the music on the rack. Alla Marcia, C major. Then Voice, C minor.

The accompaniment was marked by triplets, foolish bouncings on the part of the piano without equivalent in the line of the voice. The voice was to be steady, but how steady would it be if these triplets were dragged—not much, not grossly much, but just enough to throw the singer off balance. I indulged in these and other ritardandi, drawing the fire of my enemy's glances by the top of the second page. Yet it was delicate sabotage, a matter of split seconds. MacSwain could not be sure that he was not himself wrong. Yes, it was jujitsu versus brute bull strength. "Ship me somewheres east of Suez, where the best is like the worst." They thought that he, my mortal enemy, was out of time. They were looking at him more than at me. And he darts worried eyes at me. "For the temple bells are callin'." Slop the arpeggios out a trifle carelessly.

It was a long piece. But MacSwain tripped through to the end. And tripped was the word. He heeded the piano as he never had before, tried to follow it: which was as it should be. But it did not work. Nothing worked. I relented only at the last words of the chorus, where the title comes in, "an' the dawn"—rumble—"comes up like thunder out of China 'crost the bay"; and I relented then only to make conviction more difficult.

"That's all, boys. No, no more. Off to bed! No, good night!"

The fist came down on the rack. "What the hell was the matter with you, Holm?"

"I thought we weren't *quite* together in some parts."

"You're damn right we weren't!"

He fumed off and out.

But it was a bitter, a bilious triumph. I felt the need for purging as I lay listening to the booming of the frogs and the insect voices. Bungled rhythms jagged through my mind, rending the thin curtain of sleep each time it drew near.

In the sunshine next morning, even on a walk with those two, I carried Poe, as if to fortify myself. She wanted to know what the volume was, naturally, and when I launched into praise of "The Raven" for its mellifluous, mesmeric capture of a mood, she begged me to read it. I read it out loud above the brook, with Claude sitting between us munching grass. I tried to enunciate the "Nevermore" a different way each time, and when I said it for the last time I said it in a whisper that had my soul in it, as if I would never lift my voice again.

16

She had concealed from me that she was ill, but now I knew. Now I knew why she kept within her cabin so much and looked so pale.

The first episode came on one of our walks when she had suddenly gripped me and sat down by the side of the road. She had buried her face in her hands, while I pleaded with her to tell me what was the matter, what I could do. Claude began to cry. I sent him running back for water. It was like being shut off from life, kneeling there beside her and waiting for her to speak and show her face. Actually, though, it could not have been many seconds—Claude was still in sight—before the spell, the attack, whatever it was, passed, and she lifted her hands and said it was nothing, it was the heat, and all she needed now was to go back to the camp and rest.

On the way back I was more silent than she. I was thinking how I hated MacSwain. There was no question but that Mac-Swain was behind this sickness.

She was chatting with forced gaiety about some flowers she had planted, when I broke in to ask her if she was going to see a doctor. That made her silent too.

Another morning toward the end of the season I came to the screen door and she was lying down. I hastened in. She got up right away. She said there was no reason why we should not walk. But anxiety was planted now in my mind. This once I had happened to see her lying down. But all the other times, when I had not been there? How far back did it go?

"You have to see a doctor," I said. "Right away." I reached for the phone book and turned to the yellow pages in back, under Physicians and Surgeons.

She intervened between me and the phone, leaned against the desk, her face flushed with determination. "You will do no such thing. If you *must* know, I *have* seen a doctor."

"Who?"

"Dr. Cummings."

This name brought my questioning to an abrupt end. This was the fabulously prosperous doctor who had given the piano to the camp. I remembered Tod's words: "Why, he's the camp's sugar doctor. A Park Avenue specialist. Women's diseases. Lads, that's the way to make money."

Dr. Cummings regularly came up on Sundays to see his spoiled son. It would be perfectly natural for him to make a professional visit to Marjory on the same day. But had he been called in his capacity as a specialist, or simply as a physician, the only physician on hand? It was impossible to determine.

There was a certain constraint between us as we went out to meet Claude. She seemed to be annoyed that I had forced this revelation from her, and I myself had the old feeling of my clumsiness, my monstrous irrecoverable clumsiness again. I had a right to know, whatever was wrong, but it was a right I was blunderingly ignorant of how to exercise.

About the marriage I had long since learned the little that the counsellors knew. Marjory had gone to the public school where MacSwain was employed in the wintertime. "He was her instructor in physical education," said George, making an indecent joke out of it. Eight months after graduation she became his bride in a weekend ceremony that some of the counsellors had attended.

My theory, not, to be sure, based on much experience, was that MacSwain was the first man (for schoolboys did not count) that had come to her adolescent attention. In all (and now regretted) innocence she had taken him. Now she was paying. "And me—did you feel sorry for me?" she had asked. MacSwain was the direct or the indirect cause of her disorder, and certainly he persecuted her in ways that I had as yet been unable to get direct evidence on.

My practice of reconnoitering about the cabin in the hope of making some decisive discovery was no longer something to be ashamed of. It became a duty. I kept wishing, however, that she would confide in me. Of course this should be mutual. Perhaps she was waiting for me to start. But what could I say—to inaugurate a new stage of intimacy—that would not repel her? Just in case, to be prepared, like a Boy Scout, I should inform myself about the divorce laws.

On the Monday of the last week of the season I stayed up late, as usual, with my Proust and then stood a while on the lodge porch, my hands on the railing, getting the wistful feel of the night. On this as on most nights, the cabin that I stood facing, always with expectation, always with disappointment, was dark. The only light came from the stars; it made the sky clear, nothing else.

I had lingered and listened in vain and was about to leave the porch at last and move slowly, reluctantly, toward my cabin, flashlight in hand, when I heard a sound that I recognized as that of a screen door being opened and a figure that I took to be her went stealthily down the cabin steps and toward the lake. I followed quickly, afraid of losing her, for there was now no sound to guide me and, clad in something dark, she was already merging with the trees.

At the farther edge of the grove before the dock I caught up. I came on so heavily that the figure heard me and turned. The first thing I was conscious of was a man's bathrobe and for a moment my heart sank, I could see nothing else, imagine only that I had stopped before MacSwain.

Then she spoke.

"Kenneth? What are you doing still up?"

"I saw you from the porch of the lodge."

"I couldn't sleep."

The words were low—only the confiding night could have

imparted them. She moved to the dock and sat down with a long sigh, almost a moan. "Oh, Kenneth, I hate it. Sometimes I hate it." This burst from a frightened child. Depths of instability were sounded that went far beyond my thin imaginings.

A part of me was full of pity, but another, dominant part was glad, thinking of the joy that would come out of this sorrow. It had come to an issue. It was time to speak frankly of divorce. Yes, that was certain. She would become legally mine, mine alone. I raised a hand to her as she sat there, her face white, the rest of her huddled in the bathrobe that did not fit. I raised a hand and touched the coarse garment, the garment that ought to be torn off. Fantasies darted through my head. How wonderful life would be—our life together. The spark of her was all that was needed to keep my genius burning. I would work tirelessly for her, would go on to brilliant success as a pianist, and then, gradually introducing my own pieces, would triumph as a composer. That theme for a concerto that entered my head that last time we were by the brook—I must write it down, develop it. Yes, she would sit in the number one box, where I could look up at her, and, after the manner of Rachmaninoff, my first bow when I came on the stage would be to my wife. Her black tresses would hang loose over her shoulders, just meeting the soft silver gown. And when I was offstage she would come to me, come to me in those nervous intervals between pieces. But of course I wouldn't be nervous anymore.

"I know," I said.

She put her hands down and gripped the dock. "You know?"

"I know how your marriage is. Does he hit you?"

"What gave you that idea?" It was too dark to read her face. She reached down and picked up something, probably a stone, and turned it over in her hand. "No, you don't understand, Kenneth. The fact is—I'm going to become a mother. Already I'm going to be a mother."

She paused as if expecting me to speak, but I was stunned,

powerless to find a single word. This was one revelation for which I was totally unprepared. All other forms of cruelty, but not this.

"I owe you an apology," she went on. "For that night when I fell asleep. I hadn't been feeling at all well myself. And it had just come to me what was wrong. I should have been glad. But I wasn't." She bent forward and her tone changed. "Anyway I was a good nurse, wasn't I? You didn't notice that the nurse wasn't feeling so well herself?"

Her gaiety almost broke my heart. "You shouldn't have been," I answered thickly. "You shouldn't have been glad. Why should you?"

She recoiled. "I mustn't go through that again," she said, all her false élan gone. "Day after day I felt awful, good for nothing but lying down. I wouldn't always have been up for meals if Harry hadn't said I should, I must. Harry said it wasn't normal. He got very—very hurt. Said it was a sign I wasn't accepting the child. I would feel well as soon as I really wanted the child. So I've never missed a meal."

"But that's monstrous. He's inhumanly cruel."

"Cruel?" She weighed the question as if it were one of great delicacy instead of the gross unmistakable thing it obviously was. "No, he's not cruel. I think you don't know him, Kenneth. You're opposites, not able to understand each other. Harry's not cruel. What's cruel is the situation."

There was a long pause before she resumed. "I'm eighteen. That's young, I can't help thinking. Too soon for this. I was entitled to other things—first, anyway. So, in the midst of the terrible revulsion I've hated everything, at times. Including him. Yes, I think I hated him the day I first knew." I felt her eyes upon me as if she were contemplating the recklessness she had escaped. "Certainly I've gone through revulsion since."

"And now?"

"Now it's better—with some lapses, such as the other day,

183

or tonight when I couldn't sleep. Better mentally and physically. I owe much to you."

"To me?"

"You and Claude. Our walks. They've shown me the good side of it."

I was startled, as on another occasion, by the conjunction of our ideas, for I had played a similar game. Only mine was, now, completely and inalterably a game. Time it was, now, to put away childish things.

"So that's what you meant," I observed, "when you said that taking care of Claude was natural?"

"Yes."

"I'm sorry," I said, making no effort to keep the bitterness out. "I thought you were referring to an instinct, not a fact."

Facts were always against. No wonder I did my best not to face them. Would it ever be otherwise? Would I ever have a single important fact on my side? I stared dismally at the lake, which had never looked blacker or colder, the embodiment of the Everlasting No.

"And you, Kenneth?" she said at last. "What have the walks done for you? It's time to take stock." She laughed. "To confess. They've come to an end, you know. Claude rides out every day this last week in practice for the exhibition on Sunday. In what direction have your thoughts gone?"

"You know, Marjory. What's the use of asking? In one direction only."

"In one direction only?" Then, with an abrupt shift of subject, as she stood up and started to go. "He's beautiful."

As I limped beside her she said only one more thing. "Balance—balance is important." I couldn't make out whether she was saying this to herself or to me. She was facing straight ahead. Probably it was her formula: she needed one to carry her through. What was mine? Or was she giving me this? I had to admire her, her strength.

Neither of us risked a "good night." After she had gone in I stood alongside her cabin following her in my imagination. She would doff the bathrobe, that mark of possession which she wore without a second thought, and lie down. It was quiet. MacSwain was quiet. Maybe that meant he was awake, expectant, the expectant father. I, Kenneth, had actually been instrumental in bringing about what might be described as a reconciliation. I had her grateful word for it. It was good, such a satisfaction (like a lump of ice in the pit of the stomach) to know I had helped. I was glad to do any little thing I could. Of course—anything to bring man and wife closer together. Whom God hath joined. But, unfortunately, there would be no more walks; MacSwain would have to depend upon his own charms from now on.

That there would be no more walks I had been informed with mock sorrow by Claude when the boy came back from a meeting of the Group I riders. "Nevermore," he said, parodying "The Raven." "Nevermore! I go out Monday, Tuesday, Wednesday, Thursday, Friday, Saturday—and Sunday!" It was really just as well, now. I would not be called on to adjust myself to—to the fact.

MacSwain's bathrobe ought to have been sufficient warning that things were not as I had imagined. One did not wear anything belonging to one one hated, no matter how cool the night. It was the sign—if I had given it a second thought. The mark of possession—the mark of the beast.

I blundered into my cabin, having forgotten that my hand was grasping a flashlight. The springs creaked ever so slightly as I sat down at the foot of the bed and held myself still, concentrating for some seconds on the familiar adenoidal gasps of Frank Case. As if, incredibly, I had got my directions mixed, I was sitting not on my own bed but the bed across from mine. When I was certain that all were asleep I turned on the flashlight, focusing it not on Claude's face, for I did not want to wake him, but just below. The boy was lying on his back, one arm wantonly flung across his forehead, shutting off many, though not all, of his curls, the other arm down, almost off the cot. His head was turned away from me, his neck under the rays an exquisite intaglio. It was a favorite posture of his, both at night and in the early morning. Beauty and innocence, I had often thought, ought not to flaunt itself so. It was past all discretion. Sleep shamelessly unloosed the last restraint.

I snapped off the light and, as hastily as was compatible with stealth, moved to my own bed. Night after night, after whatever vigil I had kept, I had returned to the cabin that was, after all, however temporarily, home, with an excitement that never failed to quicken my last steps. Repetition could not kill it, and indeed there was comfort in having one thing that could be counted on. I would close the door behind me, knowing that no matter how the horizon changed elsewhere and at other times, there was during the sleeping hours one fixed star that, if it was not luminous of itself, could be made luminous. But, whatever I was, I could no longer pose as the fond parent.

17

It was the last day. In the afternoon, after an equestrian exhibition by the best riders in a field back of the tennis court, the campers would be taken home by their parents. For any who could not be so accommodated, the truck was coming. Everybody was in a festive mood. MacSwain at the head table beamed like a man whose fees, payable in advance, had at last been earned to the satisfaction of all. His hearty laugh played bass to the other merriment. This noon meal was in fact a party, a birthday party.

During the season a number of the campers and two counsellors had had birthdays, and each time the occasion was celebrated with ice cream and cake. They would sing the birthday song while July's child, or August's child, cut the cake. It seemed only fair, then, that all the others, Claude and I among them, who had not had a birthday, should have a party too, on the last day of camp. René had brought a monstrous cake to the director's place. They were singing, without benefit of accompaniment, "Hap-py Birth-day to Us," swaying on the benches and waving spoons.

I looked at Claude, who was on my left, the second one down. A general reshuffling of meal companions had been ordered at midseason, and Claude, without anyone's asking him to, had come to my table. Nothing, however, could budge Ernest from his place at my right. Marjory also remained fixed, opposite her husband. Now Claude would not be near anymore, and I would have to worry about college. He looked serene as ever, seeming to condescend to the festivities, like a visiting angel whose gaze was ever one of irony.

When all had had seconds, the director tapped on his glass

187

and announced, "No rest hour today, boys!" They whooped and cheered and stampeded out.

This was truly the end, for Sunday had never brought any such exception before. The fact was, the exhibition had to be put on promptly if the boys were to get home (home was New York City for most) in time for a late supper. The equestrians were getting into the station wagon now. Bruce—he of the seismic breasts—was leaning over the back window, giving last-minute reassurances to Claude. "You can't fail us, boy. It's the honor of the cabin."

For days now in Cabin Three a certain Judge Lindquist had been mentioned. He was an unknown power. Before turning up at the Danbury Fair, Judge Lindquist was to pick out the best rider in Silver Lake Camp. Claude, although the youngest of the five select competitors, seemed to have a good chance to win, even over Tommy Ricketts and Theodore Ralston Cummings. It was the latter who always sat at the director's table, who assiduously cultivated the counsellors rather than the campers, who in fact had gotten out of the station wagon with them the very first day. Straw was not good enough for him. Nor did he pay any attention to the music counsellor, who was just a newcomer, the man who played on his father's piano. "You know this was mine once" was all he had ever said to me. The rumor was that Dr. Cummings had gone far beyond the piano in backing the camp. There had been dark hints among the gossiping counsellors of steep mortgages, first and second, of endorsements and counterendorsements, of finances that would crumble at a puff.

I sincerely hoped that Judge Lindquist was above politics.

The camp was swarming with parents. Ernest had joined his, and was explaining something to them with happy, exaggerated gestures. I felt isolated. I looked around for Marjory. She was talking to one set of parents, and others were coming up to her. I didn't like it. This universal friendliness of hers made me despondent. I did not want her to smile, when the smile was not for me. I wanted to take her away from all the strangers and walk down along the brook with her, where we could sit down, hidden from others, and listen, and hear no unloved voice. But there she was, giving herself to others, and I stood alone.

To regain contact seemed only a dream. I had glimpsed, two days before, that which ought to have removed the last doubt. My vigilance had received a wry reward. MacSwain, whose public relations with his wife had always been an impenetrable model of decorum (perhaps he was capable of shame, the identical shame that kept him from letting out the secret of his expectancy and forced his wife to keep up a front), had not—as if for my special benefit (though he could not have seen me at the window of the lodge, he probably thought they were quite alone)—completely restrained himself on the steps of the cabin after the two had crossed over from the noon meal. Close behind her, he said something that made her laugh, and thereupon he playfully reached out a hand to her chignon and loosened it and down came her hair, and that made her laugh all the harder, without protest, except maybe from her hands, which pushed back the long black hair as they went in together. It was a little flourish from the possessor specially designed to be memorable to the observer, and I relived it now as I stood there and watched her beam on strangers. I slowly made for the road, turning to look back for a moment when I reached it, my hands in the pockets of my slacks. There's a divinity that shapes our ends, and this end, whenever it came, would have to be shaped in order to be recognizable. Even popular songs had a shape. One sank into my mind as I walked, pursuing me unbidden from the last songfest that had been held the night before. The basic tune, the basic tune repeated, the digression, and back—it was banal but it was a pattern—back to the basic tune ending on the basic note. AABA. How was the digression? "Summer time was nearly over. . . ." Then something about "rover" and "love." Anyway the piece ended, "She wore a plain gold-en ring on her fin-ger. 'Twas good-bye on the Isle of Capri." Was this the way divinity spoke, now that miracles were past and nobody read the Bible except in church? Capri—it was near Italy. "Blue Italian skies above." It was linked with something else—something I had read about and could not quite forget—an emperor—orgies. Silly, these tricks of association! There is more silliness than is dreamt of in your grave and reverend philosophy.

I came at length to the familiar boundary of the railroad tracks. In all our walks we had never crossed these tracks nor sat elsewhere than on the swollen ground back of the brook, with the shed squatting to the right. It was as if we had been tied to a leash that came to an end here. This far and no farther. I looked for the print of our bodies on the short, silent grass, and while testing flatness with my lame foot I was suddenly reminded of hair, of an argument about hair I had had with Tod the week before. Tod had said hideous things, things worthy of Jonathan Swift. He had compared human hair to the claws, feathers, scales, and hoofs and horns of the lower animals. He had gone back to the embryo and traced keratinization and the multiplication of the epidermal cells around the papillae. With his large even teeth slicing out the words so that he looked like Balaam's ass, he attributed luster to the sebaceous glands. He had said that black hair was the coarsest, and had shown by what hundredths of an inch it was coarser than flaxen hair, the finest. I flinched. "No, stop!" I had shouted. "Such an attitude, such language is immoral. Yes, obscene. You scientists make us beasts. Sebaceous glands. Follicles. Figures on thickness. I suppose you have counted the hairs on the head too." (He had. It depended on natural color. Blondes may have as many as 140,000 . . . but I was too revolted to let him go on.) "Why, hair, which sounds like no more than dead skin, as you describe it, is the very soul and determiner of human beauty. It does everything to the head. And the proof is that if the heads of women are shaved they look exactly like men. I saw a picture in the paper once of four girls who had been initiated into a fraternity—no it must have been a sorority—by having their heads shaved. And they looked exactly

190

like men, like men in dresses. You could not tell the difference. That's how important hair is."

"I would tell the difference soon enough!" hawed Tod.

All this returned to me now, and I had no time to wonder why, for I looked up to see the riders. They were coming down the road at an easy trot, Claude leading the way and looking like a young prince with his cortege. Imperiously he bestrode his horse, his beautiful head and shoulders bent just enough forward for grace, the reins loose in his hands, a picture of lithe, effortless control from his spurs to his radiant hair. I had not been privileged before to view so near so proud a sight.

But around the bend sprang a train, bearing down on those sleek steeds, who reared and whimpered in terror. Claude's horse stood on its hind legs for a moment, then veered off to the plane tree and slammed its rider against a projecting limb. One foot stayed in the stirrup a second longer than the other and in falling the boy was shunted off the flank of the maddened animal and kicked. Low on the ground he lay, face forward.

For a moment I stood there. For a moment I could not move. I stood there, my arms rigid, staring at Claude, and hoping he would get up by himself. But Claude did not move. Then suddenly I saw the director advancing upon the boy. But before he reached him I was there, to turn him over and to support him in my arms. The face was pale flesh except for dirt and a trickle of blood down the side of the mouth.

I bent my face over Claude's. "Are you hurt—do you have pain? You aren't very much hurt, are you, Claude? We'll bring you to the hospital and everything will be all right," I went on speaking to the lifeless child in my arms.

Then as in a dream I saw the big red face of the director, and saw the director's tufted and clumsy hands next to mine on the boy's body, moving up and down there. Then they withdrew, the director stood up and his voice came from far away. He was sending a rider for Wyant. "Don't tell anyone else what has happened." Now he was saying "Damn!" over and over. I could see his boots and hear the repeated slap of his fist against his hand. Then the machine that was making these monotonous sounds stopped.

"The boy is dead. We are ruined!" This was followed by sharp instructions. "Put him down—don't touch him. By God, you're rocking him, and he's dead. Didn't you hear? Put him down and don't touch him."

Slowly I relinquished the body beside the tree and turned away. I had had a strange desire to clean the face of the dirt and the blood, with my tongue, if necessary.

The first I met on the road was Tod, running. I shook my head in answer to the question, and looked up the road to her, whose agitation, before I could see her face, was plainly visible through a certain wild and clenching motion of her hands.

"Don't go on," I said, when she was a yard off. "There's no use. It is better to stop here."

"He can't be dead." Her voice was almost a whisper. "Twenty minutes ago I saw him riding away. It isn't possible."

I did not know what to say.

Finally I said, "I know what he was." I looked steadily into the face on the cheek of which she had laid a hand as if she had been struck or were afraid of being struck. "He was the child we will never have. Do you see? This is the end."

Her eyes lighted with tears, tears that words of mine had brought forth, for they were not there before. She had never looked more beautiful.

"Oh, my poor Kenneth!" She stretched out a hand toward me, then let it fall. "Yes, it is true, isn't it," she resumed after a pause in a voice without tone and looking away. "This is the end." She seemed to be considering something. "I don't think that's what he was," she added thoughtfully and slowly. Her eyes, tearless now, and very somber and mature—not at all those of a child—cornered me. "I think, Kenneth, you were a little—a little divided."

Though I had bidden her not to go on, she went on, and I

192

had nothing to say that would stop her, nor any kind of strength except the strength that pulled me in the opposite direction.

All ways out of camp were intolerable, but I had thought the train would be least so, until as it ground to a stop for me and I climbed up the iron steps with my suitcase I wondered whether this was by any chance the same train that—no, it could not be. But the noise hammered at my brain and it seemed to me that I would never sleep again. This was the thought that ran round and round in my head on a mad little track of its own—that I would never sleep again. I did not believe in the drugged miracle that could make me sleep . . . and even so, what dreams would come?

Part
III

Part
III

18

That, twisted and small, was my first corpse. And my last or latest—I'll be coming to that. But what am I myself coming to, and how long will it be?

But the unseen body of my mother has dominated my life. Everyman's first woman. The body that, when alive and young, was too accessible. Or so I was led to suspect. You must understand—in fact *I* must understand—this matter has not been cleared up. I still ask persons I get close enough to, what color eyes they think I have—and I receive different answers, including green. The big questions are always in doubt. Talk about the quest for identity! Here I am still searching for my father. Half my heredity is in doubt. (What abnormality, physical or mental, was passed on? Do I refuse drink because *he* was alcoholic—or because he by far wasn't?) Was he a musician—or a milkman, or a traveling salesman, or a mail handler? Or just a gigolo, a woman handler?

I once overheard my mother remark that when she was in her twenties she took singing lessons from a Russian named Sokolov. It was something that just popped out—as from an open fly—when she was chatting with a visitor. It was never mentioned again, as far as I know. Which could mean that it was of unspeakable importance; or it could mean that it was of no importance at all. Even if it took place (what piece of furniture fostered me?—Florence and I did a lot of experimenting with an armchair) it might not have been important—a mere one-shot incident that happened to result in me. Anyway Sokolov is my favorite candidate—I feel stewed in Slavic melancholy. I picture him with bushy hair (sign of virility) and an accent like Mischa Auer, if you're old enough to remember him. (I'm almost old enough to remember Leopold Auer, the violinist. Say, maybe *he* was my father. No, I've just checked—he would have been too old. I refuse to have an elderly father. Indeed, the trouble with mothers—as D. H. Lawrence well knew, see *Sons and Lovers*—is that when you're old enough to make love to them, really slam it in, you don't want to, because they're too old—nature's safeguard against incest. Boy, you just can't beat biology, can you?)

Suspicion, like that spilled by the biology teacher, is a disease. You either catch it or you are immune. You can always ask why I wasn't immune in this particular case. Do I derive a perverse pleasure out of libeling my mother? Am I having my individual variation on an archetypal fear—the fear of a child that his parents aren't his, that he has been adopted, that he is a changeling, or a bastard? Those nasty fairy tales, with their uncertain genealogies (are you a frog or a prince?), could have started it all. The only consolation is being able to disown my sister. Mere half-sister. That's why we're different. Or, in other words, has there ever been an affair that lasted the difference between her age and mine, seven years?

Maybe Dad would have been nicer to me if he had been surer I was his. Did Mother give me less affection because I reminded her of her mistake?

These are thoughts I drag around like a clubfoot.

The higher truth comes from Blake, as usual. "Everything that is possible to be believed is an image of the truth." I sensed a coquettishness in my mother (I must have witnessed instances of it that I've protectively forgotten), and she has to pay for it, and I have to pay for it, a sort of penalty for being attractive, instead of fat and ugly. Love and jealousy are born at the same moment, because you cannot believe that a woman who is attractive to you is not attractive to others.

While being so astute, am I to analyze that summer of 1939? If you're simple and crude, you'll say that I ought to be in jail for pedophilia. You wouldn't trust your son to my care, not if he was pretty, anymore than you'd trust your little girl with the Reverend Charles Lutwidge Dodgson.

Well, far be it from me to deny—what is said to be normal at a certain young stage—latent homosexuality. I've even heard that a man who goes for another man's woman may be concealing an unconscious feeling for the man. In other words, my true love was MacSwain. Only I didn't know it. I sure didn't. Me and my boyfriend. Mac, you are my Swain. Browning enthused, "O the wild joy of living!" We translate it now as, "O the wild Freud of living!"

In my view, what I was hovering over, mother-doomed, was adultery. Finally my feeble, wounded libido didn't care about sexes, because it didn't much care about sex, which in me had gone into a deep freeze, revulsion.

I had a weak impulse to reenact my whole situation, which of course also included the boy that was I. My interest in Claude was narcissistic. (Associaton with *claudus,* vocative *claude,* Latin for "lame"?) I was suffering from sexual indifference, unaggressiveness, impotence, psychological—but never physical—action. I just didn't have the gumption—or to put it more sentimentally—the heart, for anything. Just hovering in my repression, watched by the moon (that white and yellow eye) and MacSwain, but never caught. A soul in limbo.

Rest assured, parents. And rest assured, camp directors. I never went to camp again. And that goes for the army, too, that hotbed of buddyism. I sat out World War II, thanks to my "PN" classification. My lameness, my physical lameness, my limp, I got over by my sophomore year at Dartmouth. I took a risk in not nursing it through the war, but, you see, I have a basic honesty, if not a basic health.

What a frustrating place Hanover was, with no girls' colleges for miles around. Every boy pretended to have had much sexual experience, and the more he boasted the surer you were that he had had none. They were so frustrated that they giggled through all the love scenes at the local movie. Two of them shaped a phallus for the big snowman at the Winter Carnival. I remember the dizzy blonde that someone had at last found; she looked up dubiously at the blatantly naked giant. "You don't like it?" said her boy. "If you don't like it, melt it with your mouth." And they got her on a chair and pushed her face toward the offensive protrusion. Thus I was almost introduced to fellatio, but instead she knocked it down with her arm. "Just like a woman. Always the mutilator," growled another of the desperate students.

I don't know what I got out of that rah-rah, Colonial place for four years except much interruption of my piano practice. That, it turned out, didn't matter. I gradually realized that I didn't have what it takes to be a concert pianist, and my composing was just a flash in the pan. I abominate traveling, and I couldn't see myself flitting from one country to another. I'm scared to fly. I get lost easily. I would worry too much about missing connections. Besides, your luggage is constantly misplaced. I don't sleep well in strange places. (In fact I don't sleep well anywhere.) Exotic food—such as fried ants—makes me sick. I'm afraid to practice the foreign languages that I've studied: the natives would be baffled or would laugh in my face. I hate deciding when and where I'm going to carry my own suitcase—or yield to a porter. Shall I take a bus or a taxi, and is the taxi driver going the long way around or otherwise bamboozling me? I dislike being cheated, but I'm embarrassed to argue. I never know how much to tip. (The Parisian waiter explains to the poor dumb—literally dumb—tourist, "service" is included, *compris*, in the bill, in *l'addition*, but the *pourboire* is extra.) I'm poor at arithmetic, and foreign currencies are overwhelming. All the flunkies intimidate me by staring at me as if there were something visibly wrong with me, which there probably is. Like Rousseau, I can't handle their arrogance and their greed. I have never lived with servants, and I can't stand them, because I'm always projecting myself into them.

Also, I have heard *great* pianists. Well, we can't shoot

ourselves, can we, when we reach a certain age and have to admit we're not geniuses. It's an illusion for the young, who always feel they're going to do great things because they haven't yet proved they aren't.

But there was the stubborn problem of earning money, even for the summer following my freshman year. Most of the Dartmouth boys are rich and spoiled. I myself came to feel that I was meant for early retirement, say at age twenty. But Dad, I knew, had different ideas; he was the old inner-directed, laissez-faire businessman.

So I actually did something on my own, and a bright something at that. I found I had a knack for the epistolary style, or rather, various epistolary styles. This began with my personal situation, as I had to write home explaining why I was out of money, or why—according to the transcript of grades—I was having trouble with Oral French. ("You see, Dad, the natives have clogged sinuses, and I don't. To make an 'un' sound different from an 'en,' and either or both from an 'on,' you have to be born nasal, and all I've got is a trick knee, which, by the way, accounts for that (temporary) D in Medieval History: I was late (slow) climbing the steps in Reed Hall for the test on the Children's Crusade, and the instructor—would you believe it?—locked the classroom door.")

Like so many tragic figures, I am also a bit of a clown. I contributed in my Freshman year to *Jack-o'-Lantern* the following:

Mary Witty
"Advice to the Lorn"

Dear Mary Witty:
I am having trouble with my cat. There is a pleasant middle-aged man, a former chauffeur, who lately has been very sociable with me, has in fact spoken of getting me to change my state. I've been unable to find out yet whether he means by this that I oughtn't to live in New Jersey—

he's from Massachusetts—or whether he has blessed matrimony in mind: he probably means both. I'm thirty-four and hopeful. But the trouble is that he can't get very near me. Whenever he comes and we sit in my little parlor, the cat insists on leaping to my lap, and there it stays arching its back and swinging its tail back and forth and digging into my dress, and, though Bill says he likes cats, it interferes with everything—conversation and everything. It has a very loud purr: in a dog it would be called a growl, and no matter on which side of me Bill sits it refuses to face him, which is bad manners that I have never seen in it before. I like to receive Bill with all hospitality, but this is a real dampener, and if I put it out it makes a terrible fuss, and I do owe it something—it's been my main companion since the day, three years ago, it was born in my linen closet. It sleeps under my blankets every night.

L.K.

Dear Miss L.K.:

Old ties must be cut when new are formed. Your problem is the old silver cord one, or whatever your cat's color is. The cat is blatantly jealous and feels insecure. What sex is it? It it is female it may be Lesbian, unless it is really out to lure Bill and neither of you realize it: that presenting him with its rear—you do mean that, don't you? —is significant, but can be read either way. *Altered* cats often get confused. It may be, or think it is or was, a male, and is drawn to you. I really can't judge from the imperfect data whom it is drawn to, but you are going to have to make a decision between Bill and the cat. The cat knew you would, eventually, and, unable to bear uncertainty, is forcing a break. It faces up to things, that cat, even when it is rearing. You would be well advised to do likewise, unless, of course, you are planning to have kittens.

Mary Witty

My fame spread through the dormitories. On the spur of the moment (and my need) I suggested to a classmate that, for a consideration, I could produce a successful letter to his well-heeled father for an increase in his allowance. "If it works, give me 10 percent of the increase—that's all I ask." Another needed to get off something fast to a disgruntled English professor. I batted out a note a good deal sooner than I could do the César Franck Prelude, Fugue, and Variations in D Major. "Dear Professor Jensen: I deeply regret that personal difficulties (very personal, unspeakably difficult) impeded my work during the first half of this semester, and prevented the prompt delivery of my papers, etc. Not only as a student of a teacher, but as one person of another whom he has offended, I humbly beg your pardon for any inconvenience or annoyance I have caused you by my untoward behavior. I sincerely hope and believe that my better half will forge its way through in the remainder of the semester and that, meanwhile, you will reserve judgment. We were all young once, perhaps, but we do get over it, don't we?"

We chuckled over "forge its way through," since the letter was a forgery and the not very bright lad was proposing that I also write the compositions due in the course. He flashed bills at me, but I drew a line. I would confine myself to letters, and there would be a certain honesty. For C students I would produce C letters, or just a notch above. I would be faithful to the person and the occasion. He would explain the situation, and I would produce what sounded like himself. It was playacting, without the stage fright. I threw myself into the particular role. I believe I belong to the Stanislavsky school. (Was *he* my father?)

I branched out, as a consequence of placing signs in shop windows and an ad in the local paper: "Having trouble with that personal letter? Letters written to order and in just the right tone." That reference to tone betrayed the musician. After a couple of bad experiences, where people tried to get out of paying by claiming they didn't, after all, like the letter, I worked on a time basis (for who can guarantee results?): five dollars per hour or fraction thereof.

In snow-bound Hanover, where people can barely wade to the mailboxes, a lot of letter-writing goes on. It is surprising how many wanted my services. I foresaw the occupation of a lifetime. No more songfests, no more unpublished music, no frustrating piano lessons (listening to some child miss the G in Beethoven's Minuet). Fortune would come to me, especially as, with growing reputation, I raised my fees.

My first outside client was a man riled over a Christmas card his wife had just been forwarded from a spinster friend of hers. The man and his wife and two children had moved the year before, just before *that* Christmas, and in the turmoil had skipped sending out Christmas cards, including the usual dutiful one to Myrrha, who resided with her widowed mother on Martha's Vineyard. Inside the card, which had a shaggy dog on it, Myrrha had written:

Dear Eunice:

Three bags of mail last year, just before Christmas, got burned up on the island—incoming mail—and I have a hunch that if I didn't hear from you that may be why.

I got a very secondhand rumor last summer that your household had split up. I was awfully sorry to hear it—and hope you'll write me what's happening.

I'm going to stay on the island this winter until March when I'm driving Mother to Florida for the month.

Let me hear from you—

Love, Myrrha

In the husband's name I replied:

Dear Myrrha,

I got a very secondhand rumor last summer that you and your mother unfortunately had had a terrific quarrel and haven't spoken to each other since. It is said that you are occasionally seen in each other's houses but communicate only by notes. I was awfully sorry to hear it. Do send me the details.

Eunice and Johnny and little Sarah, who to my surprise moved right to this address with me and still speak to me, said I shouldn't get out on any limbs and write on the basis of what admittedly is only a rumor. They say it would be awfully embarrassing if I were wrong. But I don't think I can be wrong. I've always felt a tension there, sensed that you two were incompatible the moment I met you. In fact I've been telling our mutual friends for years that this couldn't last—that you were headed for a split. You know how the statistics are—and not only in Reno. The rate at which mothers and daughters are separating in this country is appalling. Sometimes it's glossed over, of course. The mother is driven to Florida or some such place. But the great point is that she's *left*.

Well, I can only wring my hands this family season. Don't spare me the worst.

Yours, Harold

It's rather fun meddling in other people's lives. Or participating. Like being the family lawyer or cleric. Of course it may ultimately lead to adultery. I gathered that Harold was very, very displeased with Eunice as well as her spinster friend. He may even have been resisting a conjecture that had some truth in it. What was Eunice like? Was she pretty as well as discontented? Well, I wasn't ready for the future yet.

As I looked to a lifelong living out of my letters, it is proper that I give two or three more samples from my Hanover years.

To the Bank on being notified that One has overdrawn One's account.

Gentlemen:

To my unspeakable embarrassment I received a phone call this evening from the chief accountant of the Hot Oil

205

Heating Company informing me in no uncertain terms that you had declined to honor my check for $44.56 made out in good faith in return for 335 gallons of oil. He apologized, as well he might, for calling after business hours, but he knew I would wish to attend to this matter immediately.

I have checked my account. I am familiar with the popular view that it is the banks who are always right, and the customer who has always overdrawn. In fact I mentioned this, sarcastically, to Mr. Ektopius of Hot Oil, but I don't think he realized that I was being sarcastic. This is the age of machines, of automation. You perhaps even have a robot there, a mechanical brain, grinding out humiliation. Its gears never slip. Oh, no. Of course it couldn't make a mistake. It couldn't be that I still have $1.13 in my account *after* you have honored my check (*and* charged me ten cents for your services). Oh, no. You have bookkeepers and comptometers, and it is of course inconceivable to Mr. Ektopius that *you* could be wrong. Who am I, a mere citizen armed with a lead pencil and high high-school grades in mathematics (Brenner Medal, 1927), to correct Hanover Corn? Oh, no. Better a thousand times that I be humiliated than that a robot be found wrong. Better that I be fined $2 for Insufficient Funds and my wife look at me strangely and Mr. Ektopius address me as a criminal. Who am I against an institution like Hanover Corn, I with my lead pencil?

I tried to call my lawyer, but he was out. I know what he'd say. He'd say file suit for defamation of character. You have damaged me irreparably locally. I'm the man that makes out checks that bounce. Isn't that against the law? Either I'm a criminal or you owe me a pretty sum for libel.

I've checked and double-checked, and I'm about to call Mr. Ektopius and tell him to redeposit. That's what I'm going to tell him, and I'm going to swear that he mustn't think I'm sneaking in money to cover the check. I am not depositing a cent. That check is as good as it ever was—as good as my arithmetic, and as bad as yours.

And tomorrow I'm calling my lawyer. This is a country where the individual still has a few rights.

Yours,
John Greggs

P.S. I've noticed that what I read on the stub as a "9" is an "8" (the ink in my pen is lousy), and so I am overdrawn less than two dollars, and so you've had a narrow escape, and I'm sending this letter anyway on principle, because I'm really shocked. The way you've handled this is inexcusable. The bank where I used to live used to cover me. To be sure, it was a bigger bank than you are, much bigger. I don't want to be drawn into personalities, but the assistant manager there was a gentleman, who knew a gentleman when he saw one. They had lots of assets, much bigger assets than you have, and he wasn't a robot.

A fiance's complaint:

Dear Maud,

It is with pain I write to you in aught that can seem like a strain of reproach, but I confess that your conduct last night both surprised and disturbed me. You received Watson's attentions with so little resistance that I feel it due to yourself to offer, in between sips of black coffee, my comment. It is undeniable that your name is Maud, but it was by no means incumbent upon you to respond when he said, "Come into the garden, Maud." In the first place, this left me alone with Miss Fennimore, who was entirely Watson's responsibility. In the second place, there is no one more to be looked askance upon than the player around with quotations. No seduction is baser than the literary. You came back after twelve minutes giggling, positively giggling, and I wondered what further quotations had been applied during that painful interval when you left your intended—I *hope* intended—husband's side. O much deceived, much failing, hapless Maud! Did he next say, "It may be we shall touch the Happy Isles,"? Were you his lily maid of Astolat? Believe me, I am in no way given to unprofitable jealousy— if I gave you a handkerchief I would do my best not to notice what happened to it; still less am I unconfident enough to wish to deprive you of society—good society. But this man belongs to the Triangle Club, and it could scarcely escape anyone's observation that although he was wearing white gloves when he took you out, they were off when he returned. Fingerprints, Watson? What fingerprints on the promised maid. Oh, I am sick, and this coffee burns me to the heart. Too hot, too hot! Paddling of palms! Break, break, break, on thy cold gray stones, O Sea!

From a girl engaged:

My Darling,

I can't tell you how much I love you. You are the air I breathe, the ground I walk on. You are my life. I can't wait for the day of our marriage. Imagine the jealousy of Mrs. Rice because her daughter is nineteen, one year older than I, and she hasn't even been able to find anyone to take her to two dances in a row. Mrs. Rice said with a twisted face—you know how neighbors are—that I am getting married not out of love but just to leave my family and the hard family life I had. What a spiteful lie! You know my family and how happy I am with them. It is true that my parents quarrel sometimes about money and one or two other things. But I am intelligent enough to know that everybody does. We will too. As a matter of fact we did already, but this has nothing to do with love. If it weren't for you, and you being what you are, and meaning what you mean to me, I would never leave my parents and my little brother.

Then Mrs. Rice said you have nothing to support a family. Of course she is not so wrong here. But I have my good job at P. T. Filene, and Mr. Filene, who likes me very much, has promised to move me up to be his private secretary. Don't get jealous now, but he found out from one of the girls when my birthday was and sent me a lovely gold bracelet, right to my home. You must have forgotten my birthday, which was March 3rd. What *will* you do when you come out from the service? You said something about going to college. But that takes four years, and even then you may not be fit for anything in particular—like typing. Do you think I will support you? I suddenly have a headache: that darling brother of mine has "God Bless America" on too loud. I better not write anymore.

Kisses,

I put my heart into that one. If there recurred in this professional writing of mine a jaundiced view of romance, don't necessarily blame my mother or Miss Warren or that experience at Silver Lake Camp. It was my clients who dictated the contents and gave the cue for the style. Still, I came to feel that there is, at best, something cowardly about writing letters.

19

With San Toy, a not to be underrated female, I had slept. With another man's wife I had bundled. When would come my first copulatory experience? One wants it and one dreads it.

For years I had not wanted it, or was not conscious of wanting it. Lamed in body and in psyche, I compensated by glorying in the mind (as if that were what college was for!). No, I never made Phi Beta Kappa, never came near it. I was lucky if I got B's. I was too disputatious, and in Baker, that excellent library, I pored over too many books that weren't on the reading list, that I had heard about in a roundabout way or just stumbled on. Or I spent hours in the piano room, or worked for my epistolary fees.

They wouldn't let me take as many music courses as I wanted. I had to resort, as an upperclassman, to English literature courses, in which my views were never the same as the professor's. The seventeenth century was all the rage, but I preferred the rational and satiric eighteenth. With enough boldness I'd have thrown myself into the role of Dr. Johnson. I had his view of Donne—a gnarled maker of riddles. That big bad novel of Hemingway's came out, and I never finished it. I went around proclaiming defiantly, "I am an island." If it had been the late 1960's, instead of the early 1940's, I'd have sported a button or two.

In class I sailed into "Drink to me only with thine eyes." I argued it conveyed a homosexual dislike of the woman.

" 'But might I of Jove's nectar sup,/I would not change for thine.' This clearly says that if he could get Jove's nectar he would keep it and let hers go. And what's the association with

Jove's cup? Who is Jove's cupbearer? Ganymede. I remember Rubens' painting of the fat, squalling, but unmistakably male infant being raped to Heaven by the Eagle that is Jove. Didn't Jonson write a play about a man who marries a man? . . . The second stanza is equally plain. Why did he send her 'a rosy wreath'? Wouldn't the wreath be full of thorns? In fact, there's the admission, 'Not so much honoring thee.' Celia, recognizing his true nature, sends the present right back. And what do the last lines tell us? Only that she 'smells'!"

This did not sit well with the professor, who, instead of refuting me, merely sneered, "Why are you so bent on perverting the poem?" Professors are the petty tyrants of the classroom, brooking no opposition. He taunted me with a B-minus for the course. I'd have preferred the overt hostility of a C.

By that time my trick knee had ceased to be tricky, and, shaking off self-loathing, I branched out to parties, where there was always a good chance of picking up some business. You know, when people are slightly tipsy they start talking about their problems, and you offer to write a letter for them. The summer, of course, was the great social season, with all sorts of summer people coming up from New York. You've been confined all winter, ice-bound, and now you melt. I was rattling off the A-Flat Polonaise at parties years before a film about Chopin made it a national bore.

It was in early June, 1942, just after the completion of my junior year and just after the Battle of Midway, that I met Angus.

He was a ruddy Irishman whose face got still redder over the bloody English. I was drawn to the bloody English, myself, especially at that juncture of history. Indeed, one of my complaints against my English professors (I had got only a B-plus for my paper on Swift) was that they weren't—and naturally should have been—English. I hurled back at him, at the very first party, that even Cromwell was not without his provocations. "The curse of Cromwell on ye, then," stage-snarled Angus, who never let you forget that he had done a bit of acting in his youth. He wore a toupee that shifted on his scalp. He carried a shillelagh but was born in the Bronx, and had never got nearer the old sod than Central Park, though, at fifty, he had intentions, if his mother ever handed him the travel money.

He was unread, and I didn't bother to tell him that "ye" was wrong both in number and in case, that he meant "thee." He had a hearsay education, was a familiar figure at the Joyce Society in that city that I had been so pleasantly avoiding for years, dropped frequent clichés about *Ulysses* without ever having read *The Odyssey*. A perusal of the New York Sunday *Times* gave him all the allusions he needed for the week.

Yeats, he was now asseverating, was no poet, because he had deserted the cause. On the other hand, Pound was a great poet. I bore my tomato juice elsewhere.

But Angus proved difficult to avoid. We had too many acquaintants in common who, inconsiderately, without giving a thought to how incompatible we were, kept inviting us to the same parties. Angus was a social butterfly, and I was bent on drumming up business. The result was collision, but also a helpless feeling on my part that, despite his uncontrollable belligerence, he took to me and was unable to conceive that I did—or could—find him resistible. He would clutch my shoulder with his rough-hewn hand, without being at all drunk. Like a hypnotist he went after me with his watery blue eyes, pushing so near that I could see myself in his dilating pupils. Sometimes shaking his head so vigorously that I expected his yellow toupee to drop on my shoe, he wore me down. There is no use pricking a bull with wit. That wide upturned nose of his put me in mind of an adze hacking the opposition thin. Knowledge was wasted on him. If he hadn't seen it in the papers lately, it didn't exist. I gave up and just listened.

Others, too, seemed to think I wanted to hear about him. Soon I was in possession of these shabby domestic facts—that he had once had a wife (of course rich, the only kind that he would go after), who got rid of him in record time, and that for twenty years—with vacations being given him in the summer—he had been keeping house for his mother, the house that she owned in the Bronx. His two brothers had gone out into the world and been business successes, but Angus had never worked for his living. Most of the year he swept, dusted, shopped, and cooked for his invalid mother, a service that was financially recognized by his brothers as well as her. He and his mother were now living in the Hanover Inn. He had permission and allowance to go to cocktail parties, with change left over for ice cream cones, which he doted on, he said, even in winter. (The Bronx had the best.) Whether he had one before or after the party, it kept him from inebriation, he claimed, and this seemed to be true.

In a half-hearted way he was a skirt-chaser, as I heard from some of the skirts he chased. One of them even wanted me to write a crushing letter to him, but it was against my professional ethics to write to anybody I knew. Whenever he was alone with a married woman, it seemed, he would drop instantly to his knees and declare his undying passion. "Give up this lonely sorrow," he intoned above his arched hands "—you know you don't love your husband—and away with me." Of course he was never taken up on his offer, and did not expect to be. Rebuffed, or laughed at, he got up, brushed off his knees, and reached for the cheese tidbits.

At one party he circulated nude photos of himself, with the object, no doubt, of whetting the appetites of future lonely sorrowers. I must say he had a good figure for his age, a remarkably trim waist. Bending over the broom and vacuum cleaner, maybe it does more for the abdomen than Vic Tanny (who went out of business).

Sophisticated women tried not to blush at the unexpected exhibition, passing the photos daintily to their neighbors. "Oh, Angus, you're a card!" tittered one. I thought of certain playing cards, obscene Latin-American importations, that circulated furtively in the dorms. They were multisexual shockers.

Which brings me to the outrageous manner in which I learned a hitherto hidden domestic fact about Angus—namely, that he had a grown daughter.

Without subtlety Angus had been displaying interest in my sex life. "You Dartmouth boys, with the rich daddies, get all you want, I wager. I wager you've broken the heart—and cracked the box—of many a lass, begorrah! Tell me, who did you seduce last week?"

He chucked me in the ribs.

"Oh, you don't have to answer," he went on, his eyes continuing to interrogate.

"Thank you," I said. "Thank you very much." I started to slip away, but he followed me and pulled me into a bedroom where coats and hats were piled. He closed the door conspiratorially, pushed me to a vacant spot at the foot of the double bed, reached into his inside pocket. I half expected him to draw out a weapon. I am as scared of weapons as King James the First of England. But it was his wallet. "Kenneth, I'm not just blathering," he said, shoving two coats aside and sitting down so close that his femur ground against mine.

"You're drunk. Go get a cone," I was on the verge of advising—when I felt something in my hand.

It was a nude photo, but not Angus. A young woman with plenty of breast lay on her back on a chaise longue, one leg coyly arched. The face looked oddly familiar—Angus with real hair down and all the crudities softened, a nose more of the Grecian sort, dimpled cheeks.

"How does she strike you?"

I stared at him. I wondered if my mouth smelt as strongly of what each of us had been drinking. If your girl eats onion, take something strong yourself. It didn't work with gin.

"Maureen. My daughter. Five foot two, eyes of blue."

He held me transfixed. "Anyway, it's Maureen's head," he added. "I don't guarantee every detail of the body."

I looked down, turned the cardboard over. It was one of those old-fashioned French post cards. I passed my finger lightly over the picture. Yes, to a model's body he had pasted his daughter's head, a perfect amalgamation so far as a stranger could tell.

"I'm not considered worthy to see her," he went on. "Her mother doesn't let me. But I come up every summer to be secretly near. We only talk over the phone. But this is a good approximation, surely. I know she's well developed above the waist. The poor girl has to be. She had paralytic polio when she was eleven. Has been in a wheelchair ever since. She just had her twenty-first birthday. I told her about you, made a proposition."

Did he tell her—did he know—that I myself had been lame, was just a year over it? Did he think it appropriate to bring two lame ducks together?

"You mean you want us to—"

"She's never had a man. Imagine—twenty-one and never had a man. If necessary I'd—well, no woman should die without it. Not that there's anything wrong with her except her legs: she has the normal life expectancy. But life expectancy without life—Kenneth!"

He was standing before me now. "You'll do it. Of course you will. Think what you'll be doing for her, for me, for yourself. Now there are two ways of going about it. I can show her your picture first—"

I pretended to fumble in my pockets. "I don't think I happen to have any nude portraits with me."

He didn't flick an eyelid. "Better by all the saints is you presenting yourself in person. She lives in Woodstock, Vermont. She's not apt to refuse you. But woo her, talk to her. Be gentle. Be gradual. You know how. You're an old hand. I've picked you, Kenneth. I'm counting on you."

He wasn't the sort who made bad jokes intentionally. I shook my tomato-juice-befuddled head. "No. It's cold-blooded. And what about the long future? How many—uh, visits—are there to be? What may I want, what may she want?"

"Who can say now? Can you ever say ahead of time? Ken, I know you're thinking there's no fool like an Irish fool, but I've lectured to her on this till I was blue in the face. I've toiled and moiled to get her to see the light, and you can't let us down now that she sees it. You can't, man. Man!" He put his fist into his palm in a sort of imploring gesture. "An emergency situation calls for emergency measures."

I was prepared to see him drop to his knees. But like a cunning orator he suddenly veered. (Or was it lust coming to the fore—lust that in Angus never had far to travel anyway.) He tapped the French postcard. "Just think. A willing woman. Waiting for you. A beautiful girl tremulous for life's greatest experience. Prepared to be grateful. Charity? Charity means love. God, if I wasn't her father—"

I had to escape his lick-chopping urgency, get out of that muffled room. Putting the nude in my pocket (because I knew he wanted me to), I said, "Phone me—" and rushed back to the crowded, stimulatingly smoky living room, where I was so upset that I sipped champagne under the impression it was ginger ale.

My thoughts drove me away before the party was over. I walked the considerable distance to my two-room apartment (the newly acquired glory of a senior and successful letter writer).

It was Angus I thought of more. To pimp or not to pimp—what other fathers had that problem? In some ways simpler, in some ways harder than finding a husband. Marriage had carefully not been mentioned—but were there secret hopes? He seemed blithe enough. How long had he been carrying that montage around? Had he made it just for me—or was it also for himself? To pore over incestuously. The girl of course wouldn't know about it, the bait, the lure. I must make sure not to have it in my pocket when I visited her. Now what complex did this superficially simple man have—was he Narcissus or King Lot?

And who was I, who already knew I was going but hadn't explored the reasons why? Not to be a cad? A wholesome answer. To be kind? A noble answer. But true? I had been feeling more and more the burden of sexuality. There were several things it wasn't greatly relieved by, including pictures. Nudist magazines never meant much to me. Girlie magazines were worse. The group tableaux on the dirty playing cards were disgusting. So was my late friend Jonathan Swift. What he did to Ben Jonson's Celia—never mind what I did, it pales by comparison. Remember how "Cassinus and Peter, a Tragical Elegy" ends? Who, having once come upon it, can ever forget. "Nor wonder how I lost my wits;/Oh! Celia, Celia, Celia s—ts." He was patently stuck, that man, in the anal-erotic stage. But he had a nasty influence on me, and I went through a period of— whenever I saw a half pretty girl—which was seldom: I went through a period of invariably imagining her on the throne, yes, a real queenie, and using toilet paper. Such, still earlier, had been Robert Burton's cure for amorous thoughts. Picture all that's foul that goes through a woman's body. This was the sour grapes—the sour gripes—attitude. Diarrheaed by such sick productions of the 1730s as the aforementioned verses and "A Beautiful Young Nymph Going to Bed" and "Strephon and Chloe" and "The Lady's Dressing Room," all the evacuations of those years when Swift was slowly going mad.

Of course a prostitute could never have tempted me: dirt upon dirt, much too unhygienic.

So I had been left with very little beyond the Arthur Machen translation of Casanova, whose love affairs in twelve volumes came to seem exhausting. I had to go back to memories of Agnes for something real—both real and pleasantly passive. I hadn't had to do anything. That's the advantage of voyeurism. Look, but don't touch. You don't have to face up to a relationship: if you're skulking at a window she doesn't even know you exist. Could an orgasm be brought on just by looking, or was a little manual assistance always necessary? Anyway, the solitary did have its timid advantages.

Still, if I were to break out of my virginity, as Angus thought I already had, the Maureen proposition seemed ideal. (Would she have taken provision for birth control? I was determined to assume so, if she didn't say anything, because I just couldn't worry about that on top of everything else, I mean on top of Maureen.) The easy conquest—every man's dream. A paralyzed woman's slavish gratitude—a titillating thought. I fingered the postcard in the side pocket of my blazer as I strode down the pale street. I managed to locate, just by touch, the exact spot where Maureen's head joined the other woman's body. I ran my finger over that infinitesimal edge. . . .

A week had to pass. Angus's telephoning resulted in arrangements for the next Saturday morning. The mother, a society gadabout, would be at the hairdresser's, and then had an appointment with a dermatologist. She was out most of the time, it seemed, though Angus never dared to come near. The maid would be gone. The daughter would let me in. I associated sex with night, but it seems that polio patients get tired with each hour of the day, and it would have to be a morning.

I took a taxi from Hanover to Woodstock, twenty miles, a pretty penny. A pretty penny for a pretty girl. She lived in one of those massive Colonial houses of mottled brick that must have been at least a hundred years old. It had the ivied elegance to which Dartmouth had accustomed me.

The mahogany front door was ajar by a tiny crack. As a gentleman, I knocked, but after some seconds realized I was meant to enter, in the spirit of permissiveness and prearrangement that pervaded this whole enterprise. "Yes. Close the door," called a voice as I stood in the shadowed hall. It was a voice that I immediately liked, something like fine china. It was a good mezzo-soprano voice, artificially cheerful perhaps, but what could be expected? "All the way down the hall," it further directed after the door had snapped behind me. It was sort of like visiting the invisible Wizard of Oz: the long deep-piled runner was green. Would she be in her bedroom or in the parlor? Of course she had to appraise me first. I put my hand to my tie to make sure it hadn't slipped.

At last, at the end of the long hall, I emerged into sunlight. I stood on the edge of a voluptuous Bukhara. She had backed her wheelchair into the wing of a Louis Quinze grand of ex-quisite fruitwood lines. I came forward and she gave me her hand. Ah, the lovely miracle of heredity. How different—the deep blue eyes a stunning change, how different the Grecian nose, the attractively overpale skin—how different from coarse florid Angus. And yet she was unmistakably his daughter. I had to restrain myself from babbling some wild romantic effusion such as, "You, love-at-first-sight Maureen, colleen of my dream, you have renewed my faith in evolution and progress and irreplace-able womankind."

Her stockings and sandals matched her chestnut hair. One leg was resting slightly higher than the other in the adjustable chair, which had cushioned armrests. Her skirt was gray. Through her white blouse her brassiere was easily traceable.

I glanced at the piano. "Do you play?"

"Yes, but not well. I can't work the pedals."

"Haven't I heard that Horowitz was in a recording studio, or maybe an auditorium, where for some acoustical reason he couldn't use the damper pedal. And he performed the feat of playing without it—just as well as ever."

"I'm not Horowitz."

I stooped down before her, being careful not to touch the wheelchair, which I was afraid would move. "I'm glad you're not Horowitz."

She stared at me. "Want a drink?"

"No thanks."

"I've had three already."

I sat back on the rug. "I suppose your father advised you that alcohol was an aphrodisiac."

"Oh, I've read," she said. "Don't think I'm a complete ninny. I was in love with a young doctor once. But we aren't here to talk, are we? Mother will be home at one. If we're going through with it—"

Her arms went to the wheels. She was halfway around me before I arose. She led the way down the hall to a room on the left. She angled the wheelchair alongside a double bed that had the cover turned down. She bent over and slipped off her sandals. Without letting me help her she made a quick maneuver, principally by means of her strong arms, that transferred her, sitting, to the bed, which was the same height as the seat of the wheelchair. With her hands she picked up her legs—each one separately, at the calf—and placed them straight on the bed. Then she lay back on the big pillow and looked at me.

"If that," she said, indicating the wheelchair with a flip of her hand, "bothers you, you can remove it. But don't forget"— she smiled palely—"in case of fire—"

"It's fine," I said, sitting alongside, my arm a bridge over her waist. "Everything is fine. You're very lovely. You're a brave lovely girl."

"Don't say brave. I'm sick of that. Say bold." Her hand went to her blouse, undid the top button.

I moved my hands toward the rim of her brown stocking, to pull it down. "No, not them," she panicked, her hand coming down defensively. I must have looked my astonishment, for she added, more calmly, "I mean, is that necessary?"

"Absolutely."

In moments I was in possession of the unspoken reason for her hesitancy. Under each nylon stocking was a thick woolen one, worn to flesh out her emaciated legs. From the waist up she was a fully developed woman, as perfect as any I have ever seen—and I speak in considerable retrospect. But her legs had been left behind: they belonged to some scraggy child. Those thin still legs that I had to help her to move, they made me feel as if I were ravishing a little girl.

For a first time it could have been worse. On the other hand, it could have been better. Kissing her brandied mouth and then weighing in the palm of my hand one of the locks that curled so charmingly into her throat, I murmured, "Next time will be better, dearest."

Her eyes held mine. "There won't be a next time. Not with you."

I could feel the change in my complexion. "Maureen, listen. We began cold-bloodedly. That was my first reaction to the whole idea. We have begun brutally. But I have truly fallen in love with you, I *am* in love with you. Give me time to prove it."

"Love," she said. "No. Go now. I can't get involved." I stared my incomprehension. "Don't you see," she went on. "I can't tell love from pity. I'll never be able to tell. And you, with your male confidence, what is it you can tell? Can you tell love from sex?"

She closed her eyes and shut me out of her life.

In the ensuing weeks I skipped parties. I lived ascetically. I didn't want to be on hand for probing by Angus, black Angus. I kept being surprised that he didn't call me, with that prurient curiosity of his. I kept hoping she would call me. I lived in hope and fear. I suppose lots of people do but I never did before. I mean, not with both emotions coming at me simultaneously. Every time my phone rang I lifted it up in hope it would be she and fear it would be he.

20

That kept me chaste for a year. Then I fell into the hands of an older woman.

My life has been extremely episodic, with no lasting relations of any sort. In fiction this is considered bad form, as in the picaresque novel. The critics deplore the lack of unity. It is just a string of episodes loosely attached to a titular character. There is no rounding out, no well-conceived plot; the story could stop anywhere, or just drop from exhaustion after several hundred pages. There should be, these aesthetes argue, other characters besides the titular figure, who stay and interrelate and are developed. Now is it my fault that people just keep dropping out of my life, to be followed by other people, who also drop out? Did I want my mother to go? Or Agnes? Or any I may have loved at camp? Or Maureen? The only one who turned up again, after some years, was, irony of ironies, Sis.

Is the solution to get married? You know what a price to pay that is. And to produce the red-haired likes of me? Not if I know all I've been taught about birth control.

Maureen, presumably, continued to live twenty miles away, but I didn't take a taxi and peek out for her wheelchair. How could I? Rejection such as she delivered to me is a total knockout. Unmanning. "Man," Angus had said to me. I was supposed to be proving that I was a man, and technically I did lose my virginity, and Maureen, bloodlessly, hers. But I couldn't even win, or satisfy, a cripple, one who reminded me so much of myself that it felt like masturbation. As I say, I lost my nerve, such as it was. I never saw her again.

I did see Angus, not that summer but the following, when I had my B.A. I stayed on in my apartment in Hanover, in good condition from the financial standpoint. Besides my letter-writing income (I was getting quite a few mail orders from rather distant places) I added another. In that region of millionaires I would appear at parties as just, seemingly, another one of the guests, who, on being coaxed, would sit at the grand and play, but in fact I did it for a prearranged fee. I would get up to a hundred dollars for a couple of pieces, with all I could eat thrown in.

Angus, on being encountered again, said nothing about the past, not a word, but did me the favor (did he feel a certain responsibility for me?) of introducing me to the future, a married woman before whom he had doubtless knelt in vain. So there's your unity for you.

"She's the Circe of Wilder. You know Wilder, where the dam is. Man, they don't come any wilder than her. By St. Patrick, the snake-chaser, some of your classmates must know her. Dartmouth boys she collects."

He licked his middle-aged chops.

Angus had evidently reached the age of vicarious pleasure. Well, I was willing to be collected, sow a small oat. And there she was, I was told, over at the corner, at that very party.

At first I didn't know she was married. There was no one around her who could possibly be her husband. At academic teas, couples stuck together in smug self-defensiveness (as if anyone would want either of them), never leaving you in the smallest doubt as to who drably belonged to whom. At these more sophisticated places, couples strayed far apart, in every sense of "strayed." The stories that I heard, but couldn't personally vouch for! Talk about wife-swapping. I heard about an orgy where husbands lined up naked swathed from head to toe in a sheet, except for a strategically cut circle you know where, where you know what was danglingly exposed. And each wife was invited to pick an immediate lover on that basis, of course avoiding her husband, whom she presumably recognized but might comment on to one of her neighbors. "That's George, the third from the left, and I *don't* recommend him, Ethel dear, but if you want to find out why I'm here in the first place—"

But the hosts and hostesses that paid me were too elegant for that.

Her straight black hair, down to her shoulders, had something on it that made it shine as much as her black eyes and black satiny Rita Hayworth sheath. I had to keep my eyes off her décolletage. Boy, no wonder she didn't move much. She didn't dare. Her age could have been twenty-five, or it could have been thirty-five. It was my first promising encounter with the dark demonic type. Satiny, Satany. Time I was weaned from blue eyes?

She looked you straight in the eyes, as hypnotic in her own way as Angus, who was now mentioning her name for the second time. "Katharine Beers."

She held out a hand with three rings on it. I hadn't yet developed the habit of looking at a woman's left hand, which is now the first thing I do.

"I'm very fond of Ambrose Bierce," I murmured fatuously, saying the first thing that popped to mind.

She said only, "My name is spelled B-e-e-r-s, and if you don't like it blame my husband." I could see she had had a lot of drinks.

I looked around uneasily, while she watched. Then she enunciated slowly, as if to keep a grip on each word, each syllable. "Ha-rold is in the Pa-cif-ic."

Oh. That was like not being married. I mean, if you haven't even seen the husband. She might just as well have been a widow. In fact she might be, the way the war was going in that year of 1943. Men were getting to be in short supply, and well, we 4-Fs were left to keep the home fires burning.

"Don't tell me," she pursued, "that you've had enough *beers* already. I've heard that one before."

"No, I don't drink beer. I'm afraid I don't drink anything. Real dull."

"And what *do* you do, besides play Chopin waltzes?"

As a matter of fact, it had been a mazurka, but I already saw I wouldn't get anywhere by being pedantic. I tried to think of something agreeable to say, and fell into another pedantry, by way of some suddenly remembered dictionary.

"Katharine, that's a nice name. A very nice name. I believe it means 'pure' in Greek."

That brought a throaty laugh. (Angus, the old pander, stood by, ogling, fazing neither of us.) "I never heard *that* before. Why didn't someone tell me that before? . . . But if you don't drink, what *do* you do?"

"You can't expect me to show you here," replied I, bawdily.

Angus intervened, "Milady, he's *bachelor*—fresh bachelor from Dartmouth."

An invitation was duly extended to visit her at her hunting lodge on Wilder Lake Monday evening, after dinner.

But that turned out to be a fiasco. In the first place, when I got there I found another Dartmouth man already installed, a fellow graduate of '43, whom I knew but slightly and didn't want to know better. He had been there for dinner (possibly even breakfast); they were sitting around the remains of it when I was let in. I could see they were old acquaintances, she and Harris, whose sallow attempt at a moustache I deemed ridiculous, but maybe it tickled her. They kept talking about people I didn't know. Angus had said she kept a "stable." Underrating the Irish penchant for metaphor and perhaps mythology, I had understood that to mean horses. That she should invite two men for the same evening, that struck me as crude and outrageous. Even socially. I'm good only for conversations involving two: I can't handle three. Of course that was the drooping end to expectations that she had teasingly raised high. I had spent a sleepless night fantasying what she and I were going to do. In the grip of what the author of *My Secret Life* would call "a letch," I had even practiced certain postures in my bed.

There was another dampener in the form of a curly-headed

three-year-old offspring of hers that didn't go to bed. This creature ran around barefoot with a half-eaten piece of rye that dripped honey on its pajamas and everything else. Its name was Leslie, which was no clue to its sex. Eventually I learned it was a boy, but it was so long-haired and unbelievably cute in a dark-eyed Georgy-Porgy way that you had to be told. Even if Harris weren't there, there would still be this lively problem.

In fact I was left alone with it while Mrs. Beers and Harris went out in a motor boat. "You'll be a good baby-sitter, won't you, just for a few minutes?"

"Oh, yes," I said, with false joviality. "I used to be a camp counsellor."

I would have really given it to them, but I had been soothed by learning one nice fact about Harris. It was his last day, his last night. In the morning, at six thirty, he was to be inducted into the Army. I suddenly felt charitable. Whatever last fling they could have, more power to the outboard—or was it inboard?

Taking hold of Leslie's sticky hand I went up to the three canvases that Katharine had proudly admitted doing and that had left me speechless. I like short cuts to people, such as speculating over their handwriting. This is the precaution of the timid, who don't want to find out things the hard way.

I have no notion what George Gorman, camp counsellor and art dealer, would have said of these abstract paintings, which had fine frames. I don't know what a psychiatrist would have said either, but they impressed me as crazy, and posed the difficult question of whether I liked crazy people. They consisted mostly of up-and-down undulating lines in shrill orange and green that could have been vomit. One painting suggested—it could have been my natural conditioning—thin couples moving toward—there were some horizontal lines too—copulation. I think now Katharine was an early abstract expressionist, without knowing it (which is exactly what the abstract expressionists recommend). Anyway I have since associated the movement with sex, aided by the fact that a leading exponent of it is named

Motherwell (too young to be my father). Jackson Pollock confessed, "When I am *in* my painting I am not aware of what I am doing." Translate, "When I am *in* [name the right woman] I am not aware of what I am doing." Baziotes repeated, "What happens on the canvas is unpredictable and surprising to me." Read, "What happens on the woman is unpredictable and surprising to me."

I was left alone with lively Leslie for an hour and fifteen minutes. As soon as they came noisily through the back door, I headed for the front door, scarcely saying good-bye. I would have been glad to express doubt as to whether I ever wanted to come again, but she, her arm around Harris, didn't give me the cue.

Hanged if I would call her. After three days she called me. Did I care to come around teatime? *Tea*time? She drank *tea?* "I will gladly *come* anytime," I said, mollified. I don't know whether she got the pun. It was morning and she probably hadn't been drinking: even Miss Warren didn't drink in the mornings. Being tipsy sharpens some women's wits as well as their libido.

My ring at the front door wasn't answered. This is one of life's little problems. Having rung (and having heard that the bell works—some bells aren't audible from the outside and if no one answers you *never* find out if they're working), how long do you wait before pushing the button again? If you ring too soon, you will be criticized as impatient if she's there and in the bathroom or putting on her girdle. On the other hand, if you wait too long, you may miss your last chance to get her, which can change your whole life. Being in the backyard or the attic, or running water or the radio or the vacuum cleaner, she had dimly heard the first ring, stopped, approached, heard nothing, and decided it was her imagination and went back more thoroughly to whatever kept her from hearing you the first time. In fact, because, not wishing to offend her or hurry her, you didn't ring quick enough and often enough, she gave up on you and went boating for the afternoon.

I screwed my courage to the sticking point and rang again. Nothing. No patter of female feet. It would be a point of pride not to ring a third time: that would be begging. I was starting to turn away when the door jerked open and she, naked-shouldered, put her head out.

In daylight I saw that she was nearer thirty-five than twenty-five. Thickness of applied cosmetics is directly proportional to age, a truism so well known that if I were a woman I would try the thinner layer of one ten years younger to see if I could practice some deception that way. Katharine had done too much to her eyes, and her face was slightly puffy. But my eyes did not stay on her face, for after a momentary hesitation she let me in, and I found she had rushed—if that's the word—to the door in bra and panties only.

The bra was not transparent, though insufficient. The problem was to keep my eyes off the panties, for through their white rayon her black triangle gloamed like part of a witch's pentagram. And she was as insouciant as if fully dressed, saying only, "I wasn't expecting you. What time is it?"

I apologized for not having guessed correctly when teatime was.

Without throwing any more on her that sunny afternoon, too negligent for a negligee, she endeavored to leave me in her sunken living room, but I followed the creased white panties like a beacon to the kitchen. And whom should I encounter, seated at the raspberry jam, but Georgy-Porgy Leslie? He not only didn't go to bed; he didn't go to school. Here I was in the midst of a strip tease—a burlesque show, for she had the radio on, and her bending over the stove or into the refrigerator or reaching up for cups (she shaved her armpits) was an andante version of bumps and grinds. Her breasts were rolled bursting tight, and her shifting triangle not only smiled at me behind its thin veil, but there was also an outcrop of pubic hair high up on her inner thighs past the constriction of the panties. Frankly, I thought it indecent that she walked around Leslie that way.

I wanted to devote myself to lust, but this third party stopped me cold. I had written facetiously about a cat getting in the way of a wooing. Now life took its revenge, as indeed it had done before. Leslie was an obstacle I wanted to get out of the way, like Helen's little brother and unlike Claude. Don't call me a corrupter of children, or I wouldn't have cared. Believe me, I wouldn't have slipped him a sleeping pill. I only wished something would render him unconscious, our curly chaperone. I supposed if he went out and played, this wouldn't be as good: she'd have to keep watching out for him.

A further strain was that I was expected to speak to him occasionally, because she did. She smiled at him, and I would simper too.

"When does he nap?" I asked finally, crudely.

This was over the cups, the teacups, on the formica table. Leslie had his too, with milk and honey.

She had been talking about a painting she was working on but hadn't finished. How could she tell when one of her paintings was finished, I silently wondered. We discussed titles for abstract paintings, and I suggested opus numbers. "If it doesn't represent anything, why give it a representational title? On the other hand, if you think of it as program music—"

She didn't know much about music, and I didn't know much about art. But now, with my question about the nap, she beamed again on her offspring, whose forefinger she gently emptied his nose of.

"I was twenty-nine when I had him. I am thirty-three, would you believe it? I hope you wouldn't. I count it as thirty-four, for I count from the month of my conception. This helps me to get adjusted for the coming year."

Another time-conscious Gorman? How repetitious life was.

But the rest of the afternoon had some difference. She led sticky Leslie upstairs, and I followed with a remark about how much I wanted to see the rest of the house. We all went into Leslie's nursery. She pulled down the dark green shades, placed him on the bed, put on his Mickey Mouse radio very loud, and locked the door from the outside. Then she led the way into her twin-bedded room, ostensibly to show me a fourth painting of hers.

My God, the most vomity of all! And right over the nearer bed, where it could fall on somebody's head. Did it really come from a paintbox? Keep your nose at a distance. I sank down on that bed, a little sick. Joan Baez has confessed, "The overriding and most terrifying bogeyman of my life, which has been with me ever since my earliest memories, . . . has been the fear of vomiting." I'm so afraid of that uncontrolled attempt to turn oneself inside out that I don't dare get sick to my stomach. Anything but that. I'm even afraid of other people's vomiting (which of course can lead to one's own). Barbellion said that the true test of love is being willing to cut your beloved's toenails. Not at all: the true test is holding your beloved's head while she pukes. And yet you'd better hold it, in self-defense, or else she'll do it all over you. I have never undergone that. The challenge has fortunately never presented itself. But that painting was a challenge. She was standing with her naked side at the level of my chin, and expecting me to say something, while I rocked with my arms folded over my queasy belly. Swift would have roared with laughter.

"It has an effect—it really does," I finally got out.

But my eyes slipped down to between her legs, to that beckoning bushy haven of restlessness and rest, and the conflict was resolved as Swift never resolved it. I took her arm and mutely invited her to sit beside me, and when she did, my mouth moved toward the uncovered part of her right breast.

But she lifted up my chin. "I'm years older than you."

"Yes, *Mother*," I said, and went back to my goal. I nuzzled down the half-bra, exposing one pink forbidden fruit. Then the other.

"Did you nurse Leslie?" I asked.

Without answering she lay back and drew me, fully

dressed, with her. I was fumbling at my shirt when the lower part of the painting intruded on my vision.

"Over there," I said, getting up and going to the other bed.

It was a risk—it could have broken forever her languorous mood, and I walked in a ridiculous hunched-over way as if that would conceal the bulge in my pants—but I just couldn't take the chance of having that thing shaken down upon us. Talk about flinging a pot in the face of the public!

So now I had to reach for her hand all over again, and—I now know—after such a breaking of contact many a woman would have burst out, "To hell with you." But evidently she was tolerant of—or even relished—inexperience. Teaching was a pleasure. When I was down, like her, to just my shorts, we got under a sheet (like Agnes and her man), and in unison our hands worked down on each other, from chest to what the Elizabethans call the fork. That step-by-step mutual caress (she taught me to press the umbilicus, which results in a pleasant bladder pressure) to the climactic spot was the most thrilling experience of my life to date, but was soon surpassed by three others. Within an hour she milked me dry three times in the standard copulatory way, expressing admiration for my virility ("Is it your red hair?"), which was not so much that as stored-up frustration. I gathered that I did something for her, too, at least once, but she was no moaner.

How far it all was from the rather stoical encounter with Maureen! How sorry I am for the monogamist, the man who, having known only one woman, can never make comparisons. Fidelity based merely on lack of experience (and very often lack of opportunity) is meaningless, saith the Sage.

A couple of mornings ago I accidentally stepped on a bath towel that had fallen down in my bathroom, and there rushed back—as with Proust's tea biscuits—memories of Katharine's shag rugs, which she had all over the house, different colors for different rooms. Naturally her bedroom was scattered with blue, blue for boys. There confronts me too, despite all that has intervened (or perhaps I should say, all that have intervened) these twenty-five years, her own personal black shag, and its warmth. I'll bet a thermometer, inserted, would have registered over a hundred.

The times we had—how many times was it? It was an interesting, dwindling summer, in which my gratitude took on the appearance of love. I felt pathos, too. At twenty-two I had a number of fears and peculiarities; it was she who added time-consciousness and made it stick. This was partly because all the paint around her eyes didn't stick. She would never let me kiss her there, but in our perspiring wrestling matches, now I on top, now she (what conflict there is in the effort to be one!), the mascara and eye shadow would get smudged, and I would be confronted sadly, even grotesquely, with change—or mortality. She looked remarkably young much of the time; one could foresee, but scarcely detect, the beginning of a double chin.

Of course when I reached my forties I thought women in their thirties young, at least a good many of them.

I strongly suspected that, despite the departure of Harris, I was not the only young man in her current life. I was the afternoon man. I think someone else visited her at night, someone who was free only at night. "Youth is catching," she once said (instead of "Youth's a stuff will not endure"), after I had run over with my hands and mouth, and praised, her lovely legs. She cautioned me never to come without phoning, and became precise in appointments. I mean at their other end too, telling me when to leave. You would think her husband was about to walk into the door, poor "A.P.O. San Francisco" man. We never discussed him—I had had enough of that with Marjory. But once, at a perhaps pardonable moment of absent-mindedness, she called me Frank, which was not his name. I could have done some snooping around; it was tempting on a mere curiosity basis; but I wasn't about to commit the mistake of begrudging to another what he—and she—had as much right to as I had. To tell the truth, I felt better at the thought of the guilt and the responsibility, if any, being spread around.

She was not one of those chatterers in bed. We proceeded to the fulfillment of our needs with only little complimentary interruptions, a word or phrase of appreciation now and then. Afterward we lay back silent, not afraid of silence. She closed her eyes a lot. But like so many women, she loved talking on the phone. Sometimes I would have to point out, "I'm going to be late seeing you if you don't let me hang up and go." What makes me uneasy about the phone is that I can't see what effect my words are having. That disadvantage is by no means balanced by the fact that my own consternation or other emotion is invisible. This throwing a voice into the void is as scary as any other abyss if you reflect upon it, which you probably don't. Twice I've been tricked by voices, mistaking the high voice (never heard before) of a husband for the deep-throated one of his wife. Hanging up doesn't do much good when you've already said, "Will three thirty be all right, Mary dear?" So I have mixed feelings about the time when the Tom Swift audio-visual phone becomes a widespread reality. If you can't turn your own image off, adultery and kidnapping and blackmailing won't be what they used to be, and the phone company will lose a lot of money.

Speaking of kidnapping, Leslie, that kid who didn't nap, commenced to prey on my mind. I kept thinking of him, locked in his room, with that trash blaring, every afternoon that his mother occupied herself with me (double entendre!). "Why does he have to have the radio on? How can he sleep?"

"That is the only way he can sleep, darling. If he goes to sleep and I turn Mickey Mouse off, he wakes up. And if he's not asleep, but just lying there, you don't want him listening, do you?"

I didn't believe he could hear through two doors. *I* couldn't. Nor did I like the idea of his being locked up. Suppose he started to vomit? I wouldn't want to be in a room locked from the outside, and I never was.

While in bed with her, the speculation would paralytically seize me as to whether Leslie was, at that moment, asleep or awake. If he was awake, exactly what was he doing, mentally and physically? Where did he think his mother was, and what did he think *she* was doing? If his door *were* unlocked, would he be likely to hop up and push open our door, which wasn't locked? Couldn't we try the experiment of not locking his door— surely that would make him feel better—and locking ours?

I didn't dare suggest this to her, as my inquiry about the radio had met with a certain tone of impatience.

But my red-haired virility ceased to be what it had been. Finally she took note. "Are you tired? Writing too many letters? Playing the piano too hard? Playing me false?"

The spoken words flattened me completely. I wanted to expound all my broodings, and tell about my life. But she wasn't the sort who gave or received confidences. She wasn't interested in analysis. She called psychologists "psychos."

I would have told her that I identified Leslie with myself. I would have explained how I had gone over in my mind that afternoon when I committed that first act of adultery (as distinguished from fornication). Why had I changed beds, leaving hers (that was the one with her night table by it) for her husband's? I was reenacting the presumed circumstances of my own conception. If I couldn't find my father, I would *be* my father, make it real. Of course I gave (my cunning unconscious) a credible reason for moving: no painting on our heads. But I had said, "Over there," and that gave it away—"Over There," the World War I song ("The Yanks Are Coming"). My mother's husband had been in World War I, and so I was referring to his bed, which a stranger usurped.

But not only was I the adulterer. I was also Leslie, my mother's child.

And you couldn't, Katharine pure, expect me ultimately to be any more potent than Leslie.

We dwindled apart in embarrassment, and the warm summer ended in September, and we met only at parties. The end came round to the beginning.

Ken, who kens too much. I had sicklied o'er with the pale cast of thought a nice robust relationship. These healthy animals—I wish I could be one.

The logical extension would have been to get her with child.

21

My life pattern was set. Most that has happened these twenty-five years since I was twenty-two and a resident of Hanover, is just a matter of detail, and who wants to go into that? We're done for at an early age, as the psychoanalysts expensively tell us. The only difference is between those who realize that and those who don't.

Kierkegaard points to the three main fears as the fear of God, the fear of death, and the fear of marriage.

The fear of God may be coming back to me, as I have indicated. It may be that He is there, at the end, patiently knowing that the last laugh will be His.

As for the fear of death, if that is different from the fear of God, naturally it is much worse with me than it was when I was young. I mean I keep thinking that every minute is bringing me, screaming and kicking, nearer to my grave (which is not to say that I *enjoy* life), and that there aren't many minutes left. I have a feeling of acceleration. I'm not a scientist, and I've never owned an hourglass, but it seems to me that as the grains of sand get fewer they run out faster. (An analogy with my hair.) "No young man believes that he shall ever die." Well, hardly any. But middle-aged people sense that Someone has his foot on the gas. Which accounts for their odd behavior.

I look around at whoever's there, and I keep thinking that he—or she—no matter how young and fresh of skin, will also be shoveled under and moldering, worms crawling in and out, fifty years from now or next week. And sometimes I shrink from them, as if they were dead already, just as I am horrified by my wrinkling face, my death mask, in the mirror. I visited yesterday, in the way of business, a woman in her sixties who had the smell of death on her. It made a funeral parlor out of her living room. She didn't know it, just as people who had the plague didn't know it until they dropped. But my friends and acquaintances and passersby needn't be old to receive this special forevision from me. I suppose it is my form of adjustment to imagine them dead now and get it over with. It saves—what shall I say?—time. There's our pretty secretary, the possibly not original blonde, at the home office, with whom I exchange pleasantries. She has high cheekbones, like a Slav, though her name is Miss Miriam Connell. What Miss Miriam Connell is unaware of is that my x-ray eyes really see her bones, the skull beneath the cosmetized flesh. I used to undress women in my mind; now I wolf up their dermis. As my soul-brother said apropos of Yorick, "Now get you to my lady's chamber, and tell her, let her paint an inch thick, to this favour she must come; make her laugh at that." The annotators never tell you—you know how they let you down when it comes to something both relevant and exciting—but this may be a topical allusion to Queen Elizabeth's keeping Essex's skull in her chamber, a story mentioned by Camden. I keep a skull in my chamber, every time *I* enter it. I palpate my ever-more-exposed scalp, as well as my flabby jowls.

Now we come to the third fear, marriage. I never did. I may be crazy, but I was never crazy enough to get married. Like Hamlet, I've seen enough of marriages. In fact I've known intimately much of other people's marriages. The outsider, I become the insider, by way of adultery. I may never see the husband, but I learn a lot about him. I have had adulterous relations with seventeen women. Victor Hugo said that adultery is curiosity about another person's pleasure. I count it a much wider curiosity, wondering what it would be like to be married to *her,* and trying her on for size, without too much responsibility. It is also a way of having more lives than one. We, whoever we two are, lead a double life, so "they"—spiteful, envious—would call it. But two lives are better than one.

Wives are ridiculously easy to seduce, which is a sufficient commentary on marriage. If they've been married six months, they're already dissatisfied with their husband and their lot. The couple are lucky if they don't quarrel on their honeymoon. I, a stranger and, for once, unafraid, have entered on business the home of a housewife who was alone, and been in bed with her twenty minutes later. Maybe the Boston Strangler did better, but I don't do badly. Of course I pick and choose, and those I can see I don't attract don't attract me. There's no fighting chemistry. But, caught in the right mood and sure the opportunity is safe, any housewife is likely to open herself to a man she knows less well than her husband, and for exactly that reason. She'll do anything for a change, to get out of the boring—or irritating—rut. The sociologists blame modern society. I blame marriage.

The most persistent obstacles are children. You go to a house, and there's a little Leslie (either sex) running around, at least one. Between twenty and forty they're bringing up children, and after forty they're undesirable. It's a problem. It must have been a problem for my mother. What a handicap Sis must have been, first, and then accidental I. I feel almost sorry for her, as I've felt sorry for mothers I couldn't seduce—though we'd both been glad of it—because some four-year-old was tugging at her apron strings. We'd exchange significant glances (like Henry James characters), and that was all we could do. Locking children up—I've not seen that since Katharine and Dickens. (How many houses have inside doors with keys, anyway?) And if the mothers are, perchance, affluent, then the telltale maid is a problem. She opens the door; she answers the phone. You have no protection from her. You can escape to a motel in your second car, but how is the stage of agreeing upon that ever reached? You have no idea what a rough time I've had with mothers, and yet, somehow, I prefer them to the childless. I suppose I'm busy reenacting again. I get this funny feeling that a woman who's never had a child won't treat *me* right. Still less do I go for the unmarried, not since that peculiar experience with Maureen.

In the first place, they may expect you to marry them. As for college girls, I agree with Humbert Humbert that they're the biggest fright of all, not that I resent education in a mature woman. No, I've got a thing for—and only for (sorry all you desolate others!)—mothers in their thirties, regardless of whether I'm in my twenties or my forties.

My business the past eighteen years has been favorable for the pursuit of adultery. I am a door-to-door salesman, my current territory being Bergen County, New Jersey, a hotbed of dissatisfied wives, if ever I saw one. My letter-writing business petered out after four years. Its demise was hastened by a jealous Bar Association that accused me of practicing law without a license. Admittedly, many of my letters were those that you might apply to a lawyer for, if he knew how to write intelligibly, which of course a lawyer doesn't. Anyway, I had to give that up. And the piano playing at parties dwindled too. They wanted me one year but not the next: that was all the culture they could take. No doubt they're having guitarists now, the plunk-plunk of politics. I had a spell of playing and accompanying in a singing restaurant in Greenwich Village, but gave that up, in fact gave New York as a possible residence up, after I was mugged.

Have you ever been mugged? If you haven't you will be, if you don't get the hell out. Manhattan used to frighten me just on account of the police. I have a chronic fear of committing a traffic violation. When I come in sight of the man in blue or their patrol car, my driving instantly worsens, and I start backing up illegally (to get away from them) or hurry through a changing light or charge up a one-way street the wrong way. Every time I have to go into town, I find they've added a new one-way street, just for me. Just about everything you can do with a car in New York is illegal. I haven't seen a legal parking place since I was eleven. Even abandoning your car, just junking the impossible fear-tank forever on some cross street that you were growing old trying to wriggle through—*that* is illegal. And are pedestrians happier—or safer? It was completely predictable that

New York's Traffic Commissioner, if not run over, would die of a heart attack.

If I *were* a criminal—as distinguished from a breaker of the Seventh Commandment—I would dye my hair. I've long considered that anyway. Not to erase gray, but just to stop being singled out. I walk down the suburban street: everybody notices me. I'm the rusty stranger. It is a violation of privacy to be so conspicuous. But hats give me headaches. If there's a group disturbance, no one remembers any of the people, except that one with my complexion was on the scene. Freckles in the summertime. Slow fading in the fall. I want to fade out, phase out myself, all seasons. I have wanted to be noticed only by a choice few of available women.

I was telling about the mugging. There's painfully little to tell. My neck was snapped back and I crashed to the pavement and blacked out. I never saw who did it. I never saw the hand. It just came out from behind and flattened me. It could even have been an athletic woman, for all I know, with a big hand, one that could stretch twelve notes. I awoke to an Italian cop bending over me, not looking at all like my mother. For a moment I thought I was handcuffed, the culprit instead of the victim, because I could not move or even find my arms. The greatest pain came from the fourth finger of my left hand, from which my mother's gold seal ring had been ripped off. The crime occurred within a short distance of the police station. Most crimes in New York City do, either because there are, of necessity, so many police stations, or because it's fun to give a final fig, fillip, nose-thumbing that way. I had thought I would cross Central Park as a pedestrian, just to see what it would be like—in broad daylight, of course. Whatever broad daylight means—daylight of broads? There had been one yards ahead of me, with a tight skirt that her split rear was working to split. Was she the decoy? Then there was another irony: I wasn't following her, in the intentional sense. I just happened to be behind her. It was at Ninety-sixth Street, and drivers must have seen it—I mean me being laid out—and hurried on their way. Which is exactly what I would have done. I lost eleven dollars and some change. Sometimes they kill you for not having enough.

When the cop mentioned the ambulance I sat up, as I had done at the beach when Sis put a snail in my hamburger. The prospect of Bellevue was all I needed to help me decide my neck or head wasn't broken. But Death, ever since, has been The Hand, blacking me out, the tie that binds.

So severe was the sprain (worse than a break) in my finger that it looked permanent. It still swells. I feared that, as with Robert Schumann, I would be unable to play the piano properly again, not that it mattered financially any more. I reflect also, in my spare time, on the symbolism—sexual, matrimonial, genealogical. You can call me a man injured in his—or his mother's —wedding-ring finger, and not recovering. The fourth finger, that's the weakest, as all we players know.

My worries, you see, are personal. I don't have much time for the atomic bomb or Red China. People who give themselves to that are neglecting their immediate family. I have to worry about making love and not being discovered, and getting down the street safely, and my health and my job. First things first. I bend over backward to count right on my income tax form: so much for politics. I wouldn't want to think the G-men were after me, the way Hemingway did. My income is of a very uninteresting size.

Adulterers and adulteresses have enough on their minds. They can be betrayed by one little thing, such as Lady Windermere's fan, or an upraised toilet seat. Leaving the fan to the nineteenth-century dramatist, let us consider the latter, for the housewife may not. Besides her husband, there are only females in the household: she has only girl children. Her husband, a careful man, left the bathroom in the morning with the seat down. During the day her lover comes for a pleasant time, but in the course of it goes to the bathroom and leaves the seat up. It is still up, looking erectly at him, when the husband comes home.

His wife has been too busy attending to the sheets to notice that. What can she say when slapped with the question, what man has been there? The faces of those who are slapped turn red. She stammers that she had been cleaning the toilet and forgot to put the lid back down. A manifest lie. It doesn't look particularly clean. I, my dear, can prove that it has not been scrubbed. Well, she was about to clean it when the phone rang. And who was on the phone? And whatever she invents about the phone call (which can be checked, unless she's quick-witted enough to say it was a wrong number), there's still the problem that she was nowhere near the toilet—had she completely forgotten the unfinished task (which she at first claimed was finished)?—when hubby walked through the door to his sweet little *lying* tart, whom of course he will never trust again, if he did before. He will either set a detective on her or be his own, or go merrily on his own.

It would have been better if she had frankly admitted that a salesman came and had to pee. (Never mind what *came* means.) My mother trained me always to put down the seat. I have never smoked: no cancer of the lungs for me. So husbands don't find my aroma. Besides, I saw at the old Met the Wolf-Ferrari opera, *The Secret of Susanne*. I have to worry about the wife's purchased odors—perfume, toilet water (gosh, I used to think it came from the toilet—I put my head in once), bath salts, even the stronger mouth washs. They cling to me for hours. I have to warn, "Please be your own unvarnished self next time." You come as an early dinner guest, do some embracing, and when the husband arrives all too soon, he sniffs first his wife (kissing) and then you (shaking hands), and both smell of *Ma Griffe*, which he well remembers cost him fifty dollars for 8.002 fluid ounces. The average husband just isn't a voluntary sharer.

It is a twist of life that I, shy as I am, should have ended up as a salesman, risking doors slammed in my face by hostile or suspicious strangers. Do I *want* to be rejected? Is that how I got into this line? I *think* I want to be accepted, and the housewives and barking dogs present a challenge that I *take pleasure* in overcoming. (You know *that* joke, don't you? The suitor says to the father, "Thank you for being the father of such a lovely daughter." The father answers, "Don't mention it. It was a pleasure.") Anyway, my daily routine is simple enough, though fatiguing. After securing the permit or permission of the police, I park my car conveniently on the suburban street, get out with my little satchel, and ring at the first door. If and when someone appears (sometimes only at a window) I explain cheerfully, "I sell knowledge."

For what I am the salesman of is an encyclopedia. It's not the best encyclopedia on the market, but it's not the worst either. I always have a sample volume with me, as you'd expect, and a knowledge of some of the contents that you wouldn't expect. Like a metaphysical poet I enjoy bringing together seemingly unrelated facts. Just yesterday, when a Jewish housewife in Englewood Cliffs let drop the boast that her son went to Horace Mann and thus might have some use for my product, I reeled on her with the remark, "Did you know that Wallingford, Connecticut, where the Choate School (800 wooded acres) is, was settled in 1667, which is the year that Milton published *Paradise Lost?*" You see, I wanted to give her a sense of higher things—Choate rather than Horace Mann, Connecticut rather than New Jersey, Eve instead of Marjorie Morningstar (Morgenstern), my thirty-volume encyclopedia (315 dollars in the plain buckram binding) instead of the *World Almanac*. In the old days a mention of *Paradise Lost* would have been a plant on my part to get her thinking of nude shapes, one of each sex. But I haven't wandered down those Edenic paths since Florence, my last love.

It's been nine months since it happened. I haven't had a woman since. And I find I don't even want to talk about any other woman except Florence, who summed up my hopes and my fears. If I'd been conceived when it happened, I don't think I'd care to emerge now, knowing what I know.

She lived in Ridgefield, New Jersey. (She told me that she

spent much of her life explaining to persons just encountered that *her* Ridgefield was not the Connecticut one, that there really was another Ridgefield, which nobody had ever heard of, though as a matter of fact it is conveniently near the George Washington Bridge. They would say to her, these strangers, "Oh, you have that beautiful wide avenue," and she'd say, "No, but we do have Broad Avenue." People in New Jersey are terribly defensive about Connecticut, which, as noted, I've taken advantage of. And even Bergen County residents gave Florence trouble, by assuming that by Ridgefield she must mean Ridgefield Park. Or possibly Ridgewood? Or Woodridge?)

Her house was in the northern part, on Maple Avenue, called Morsemere (that used to be the telephone exchange—"Morsemere 6"), a romantic name if ever I heard one, conjuring up far-off places and times, the meres of Anglo-Saxon poetry, where heroes fought with monsters, with the first syllable suggesting *moss* and therefore relaxing on it after a day's labors. Never mind the Morse code man: I'm going to have my fantasy and you're not going to spoil it with a fact. This is free, they call it free fantasy, free association, don't they, not what I'm selling. My love is free. So was hers.

Her house was friendly white clapboard, not brick (cold and discouraging to wolves). It was old enough to have a porch, like the one we had in Philipse Manor. I much regret the modern truncation, the naked house without a front porch, a circumcision of comfort. You could watch the world go by, in the old—what shall we call them?—Booth Tarkington days. You watched openly and honestly, not slinking at a window, as now. Or worse, not caring, not having human interest. I always say for Peeping Tom, he cared enough to look his very best. I don't mean you have to use the front porch for copulation, as my sister did.

It was a sunny morning in May, my birthday month. As I mounted the porch steps with my satchel, there came, haltingly, through the screen door (the front door was already open, which is half the battle), the strains of Chopin's familiar Nocturne in E-Flat Major, the piece that every third-year pianist tiptoes into (and in some cases it might just as well *be* the toes) because it's languorously slow and sentimental. The shallow tones were unmistakably those of a spinet, which the housewife who values a pretty little trashy piece of walnut more than music always has a cute alcove for, having discarded—or failed to purchase for the same price—a good instrument because it was big and second-hand, like a Guarneri cello. I could have thought it was a child playing, if it had not been a school day.

The tinkling broke off. She hurried (boredom? eagerness?) to the door without my having knocked or rung. Black tresses on shoulders, svelte, slenderizing blue slacks, man's pink shirt, late twenties or early thirties. Possibly Jewish. Certainly pretty.

"Good morning." Having gone to an Ivy League college, I never added "Madam," like common salesmen. "Good morning. I sell knowledge."

She drew back her head in that quizzical way I came to know so well. It was a little like an inquisitive bird, reacting to some puzzling crumb. Except that I never loved a bird.

It got me in, as it often does. That's a great line, if I do say so myself. Did Dr. Faustus ever use it? "I sell knowledge." It at once separates the sheep from the goats. The intelligent ones want to know more, and the stupid ones, unless filthy rich, aren't likely to buy an encyclopedia, no matter how much I talk about our generous deferred payment plan (that works out to 22 percent interest per annum, which, after all, is fairer than 22 percent interest per volume).

"I planted knowledge and life's tree in thee," as the poet said. But the same poet also said, "I run to death, and death meets me as fast, / And all my pleasures are like yesterday."

"You don't have enough legato," I commented, walking past her beckoning bare-footed form (her toes weren't painted—I can't endure painted toes) and seating myself at the instrument, which was in the near corner of her living room under a print of a Klee fish. It proclaimed itself "Melodigrand Spinet," and was the hypocritical kind. That is, it had three pedals, not two, but the middle pedal was just a dummy. My hand, though it trembles, has never lost its skill; I have kept it in, all these years, though unpaid. Without pretending to look at the music, I trickled through the piece dolcissimo in approximately four minutes and ten seconds.

"Great," she remarked. "I should take lessons from you."

"That's not what I do," I said. Her slacks enclosed long legs with scarcely any hips. She sent my thoughts spinning back to the boy high jumpers at camp. I also connected her with Egypt, though I soon learned that Florence was a genuine Jewish Bergen County product. Her nose was wonderfully straight, as on an old frieze or fresco—Cleopatra must have had such a nose, and with her dark ringlets and complexion, and sensuous, bare-ankled walk, I thought of Sargent's painting, his *only* painting, of the ruddy-bodied Egyptian girl—a slave, or purchasable, or so one hoped. Florence's liquid black eyes were unbearably affecting, when turned directly on—well, on me. They were like the fishpools in Heshbon.

I use that simile advisedly, because it turned out that Florence was herself fond of quoting from the Song of Songs. This was part of her oriental sensuality. Not everyone can quote, unblushingly, "Thy belly is like a heap of wheat set about with lilies." But she could, and did (without reference to anyone in particular). I'm a bit of a Puritan in my speech, having trouble getting further down than "Thy neck is as a tower of ivory," which is what I had silently applied to Marjory, who, if alive, is old.

Now you overanalytical people will argue that my penchant for women with long necks is evidence of my latent homosexuality, because a long neck puts me in mind of the erect phallus. And indeed it does, mine, not someone else's. You would make as much sense by saying that, if I were an author, I should be published by New Directions: because that slips into Nude Erections.

"Those sixteenth-notes at the end," she was musing, not taking her eyes off me, drawing me deeper into her fishpools in Heshbon, "they're real sensual."

"It takes control," I insisted, feeling that I was advertising myself as a lover. "You can't just be sloppy, spill it all over the place."

I moved over with my satchel to her sofa, took out my display. Naturally she sat beside me. I wasn't long in learning that she had two children, a boy and a girl, which is what I like to hear. "And the older is eleven already? Impossible!" I exclaimed. That brought out that she was thirty-two, a very nice age.

You know how it is when you're pointing to things, and the other body has to get closer to see the print or the picture. Arms brush arms. Hairs on same quiveringly recognize the opposite sex. A palm may glide past a knee or the back of a hand, indented, undaunted. I point with my left forefinger, boldly. I think it's overtimid—and doesn't make a good impression on a healthy woman—to employ the pinky, that smaller erection. I had the "B to Birds Foot" volume with me that day, and our cheeks nearly grazed over, in color, "A typical Bermuda beach scene. Towering cumulus clouds roll majestically over a purple sea which changes to turquoise in the shoal water along the coast. Gray coral cliffs are crowned with verdure the year round."

"My honeymoon," she said. "I was there." She frowned.

"It's better to read about it," I said. "For $315 you can go to a thousand places with no trouble at all."

She held me with her eyes just the way I wanted to be held. Like Paolo and Francesca, that day we read no further, and the book was a pander to us. With my pianistic fingers I touched her hair, her cheeks, her mouth. She bit my forefinger laterally, in

247

foretaste of intensities to come, and a sigh or shudder went through her. I reached for her fly, which was not on the side.

"Not here," she said, and staggered up and shut and bolted the front door. "What will you think of me?" she went on, from the hall. I still sat, for good reason.

"I will think everything of you," I promised, "everything good. We're being instinctively right, and we both know it."

"What is your sperm count?"

"My God, are you an astrologer?" I demanded, getting up, willy-nilly, and facing her across the newel. I felt I had a good chance to herd her upstairs. She already had one bare foot on the first step.

And, with just one nudge to her elbow and without further words, we did proceed to the master bedroom, which had its own bathroom, and on the threshold of that she explained. "It's my diaphragm. My husband is a laboratory technician, and suspicious. He just might put it under a microscope."

"What's *his* sperm count?"

"I don't know."

"Well, I'd suggest having two diaphragms."

She nodded understandingly. We were old conspirators already. "But now?"

"Live in the present. Sufficient unto the day is the diaphragm thereof. One of us will go to the drugstore afterward. The pill is better."

"I'm afraid of swollen legs. I've always used a diaphragm."

"What's your size?"

She didn't answer, which made us even, because I hadn't given my sperm count, which of course I didn't know, though I could have offered up a nice normal figure from the Merck Manual ("Office Laboratory Procedures"). The last thing I'm interested in is fertility. But what size diaphragm a woman has, now that's interesting. Say two inches, and a prospective lover will stay; say four inches, and he'll flee. I know men who shun all mothers on what they regard as sound anatomical principles, but this is very narrow of them.

I was still sitting on the bed in my underwear (always the hesitation, no matter how much experience, to expose my lower half, or even my upper half), when she emerged from the bathroom in smiling nakedness and stood beside me. I darted with my tongue to her black target. She moaned, and clasped the back of my head. My hands kneaded the pillows of her upper legs. Less pillowy was my thinning hair: my scalp felt her wedding ring.

I had learned this three women before, from a pseudo-blonde in Secaucus, learned what a good many women really like. They like the tongue; some like the hand. But, for many, copulation is beside the point. You may as well use your hose for wetting the bed. You may as well not have it, as far as they're concerned. Which is all to the good if you're a wee bit worried about it.

Of course I don't invite them to "kiss" me. That would smack too much of homosexuality. Besides, I have a fear of being bitten.

I started to maneuver her onto the bed, but she admonished, again, "Not here." We disengaged long enough to patter into what she identified as the guest room. One must give her credit for delicacy. I'm crude. I prefer to wallow in the marriage bed.

But we got along spasmodically well, in that other double bed, for a few minutes. I've reached the point of liking to be appreciated, of requiring for my own enjoyment visible or audible reaction from my partner. Is this an advance in unselfishness, or egotism? Are my doubts calmed only by *her* excitement? Well, it was like touching her with a hot iron. I worried about open windows somewhere in the house. I did not think the brass bedstead would endure our frantic weights. She was tickle o' the sear, if ever I saw, heard, touched, tasted, and smelt it. I'd have felt more secure on the floor, where we nearly ended up a number of times. In my opinion, the best place is a mat, but what do interior decorators care about heterosexual love?

I was on top, the position I like best (the Turks don't allow the woman on top, because that would signify the subjection of man), and engaged in an activity that at that juncture was more mine than hers when suddenly her dark beautifully Hebrew eyes widened in alarm.

"What time is it?"

I paused. My wristwatch was on a table a thousand miles away.

"What's the matter?"

"I forgot. He'll be home for lunch. It's his half-day."

That shriveled me. I rolled to her side. She bounded up, her lovely buttocks all aquiver, and darted for my watch. Then she sat down and lit a cigarette, which is the quickest way I know to create distance, even if the man isn't nervous about getting burnt. I guess that's one reason I don't smoke. It messes up a lot of things, including the sheets: and that's just not the way I think sheets should be messed. I did once, in my sundry adventures, receive a hot ash in a tender hypogastric spot. I also dislike smoky breath. That was one thing my mother never had.

I caressed her with the back of my hand above the knee. I made physiological experiments on myself with the aim of being a better lover, and found that the hairs gave a frictional, fractional advantage over the palm. You, my wives, if you only knew—but of course I never told—the lengths I went to, in the way of rehearsal, alone in my bed at night, imagining myself a woman, so that I could feel what you would feel and heighten your joys.

"If there's time," I said, "tell me about him." She had pitched me into a sort of *Decameron* nervousness. I saw myself fleeing naked out the back door (where was it?), while the husband entered the front. It just wouldn't be funny (except to read about or see in an Italian film) to be caught there. I recalled the fate of Peter Abelard. This lab man, he probably carried a scalpel on him.

She had replaced my watch with the dial turned from me. Even if she thought we had time, was she right?—and she didn't know that my watch ran slow. Women can be more reckless than men, even when they have more to lose. I tried to calculate what time it must be. If the husband started work at eight, his half-day would be over at twelve. Wasn't it twelve already? How far away was he? He might be nearer than either of us thought. He could have gotten sick and quit early. There might well be such a thing as telepathy. I hated to be the first to start dressing—it's ungallant—but I reached for my red-striped, my peppermint candy, shorts (the older we get the sportier we get: I used to be content with white) and started twirling them. Would she follow my banner?

Smoke came from her nostrils, like Fafnir. I really was tempted to point out (this is not just an afterthought)—but it would have sounded self-serving—that smoking is bad for the heart. Which is probably why all the dragons have died out.

"He weighs a thousand pounds, and he gets on me for thirty seconds, and that's it."

"You mean that's all that ever happens."

"That's all that *he* does."

"You're still waiting for the Second Coming?" blasphemed the ex-Presbyterian.

Being Jewish, I doubt if she got it. As a matter of fact, I had been moving towards *my* second coming when she threw her husband's lunch-coming at me.

Now I just wanted to get out. But she reached—not for my watch or her undies—but for a pretty chapbook (you know the kind that goes on Special for $1.98, with a cover like wallpaper) that I hadn't noticed before, and handed it to me in such a way that it nearly got very wet.

"You play beautifully, you make love, you must read beautifully. Read me No. 22."

It was Shakespeare's Sonnets. My God, she wanted culture! First the bed, then the lecture. *La lecture.* If I had been a teacher it would be first the lecture, then the bed. But I thought we *had* had the lecture first, downstairs.

I cast my eye over the first line. "My glass shall not persuade me I am old." Then the word "death" leapt out, Cerberus unkenneled. I snapped the book shut.

"I doubt if there's time to do a proper job," I observed, slipping on my shorts at last. "By the way, don't you find No. 20 interesting? Line 12 proves that Oscar Wilde and Frank Harris were wrong in claiming the Bard was homosexual. But he was careless in having the first child only six months after marriage. But worse was then going on to twins. Hamnet and Judith. 'Judith' is an attack on his wife, who did him in. 'Hamnet' is a variant of 'Hamlet.' Which is much better to have begotten, as Plato would have said. Hamnet, symbolically, quickly proved his mortality by comparison with Hamlet, dying August 11, 1596, if memory serves. Science should find a way to prevent twins, anyway. Robert Burns was the only well-known poet to have *illegitimate* twins."

I was dressed now, except for coat and tie, and my watch said 11:18. I don't know what her husband would have made of her, if he had loomed at the threshold of the guest room at that moment. She could have been convicted of exhibitionism, at least, elbowed back on the edge of the bed in shameless nudity, without even her legs crossed. Wanton provocation? Soliciting to adultery? Powerless to keep my eyes off favorite areas, and, more than remembering—reexperiencing—how they had felt, I softened—or hardened—and had to rein in the impulse to unbutton again, come hell or husband. "My dear temptation," I said, and stooped to her lips. It was the usual tug-of-war between love and fear that any reasonably conscientious adulterer will know as intimately as Laocoön knew the serpents. I knew it with Florence for eight months and six days.

The problems we had to review, when finally she was

covered—except, again, for those alluring bare feet that had, as it were, prostrated me, walked all over me, when I entered the house (Donne makes some sort of connection between the foot and the vulva: is it the charming indentations between the toes?). (It's curious that I shouldn't like clams: still, there are important differences.) (I told Florence I wanted to nibble her toes, but in the time that we had I never got around to it. Her reply was that she could "live without it." But that turned out not to be true.) First there was the diaphragm. Would Leonard —and he was really imminent, he was employed at the Pfitzer Chemical Works in Ridgefield—put it under a microscope that afternoon? We decided she would keep it in her (she was supposed to, anyway, sperm speaking, for how many hours?), the safest place in the world (Hans Carvel's ring) unless Lenny got amorous. Then, at night, if he did demand his thirty seconds (I suggested it might be better to pick a quarrel with him: was *I* jealous?), she would go through the usual motions of visiting the bathroom and preparing. But he knew where she kept it; might he not look first, right after lunch, or even, if hunger wasn't what was bothering him, before? There wasn't time for me to go to the drugstore. She would go and have a new one—same brand, of course—snuggled in her powdered bag. Or did she need a gynecologist's prescription—she couldn't remember. Well, suppose he put the new one—if she did succeed in getting one—under a microscope, looking for traces of his own past sperm? She could say the old one split and had to be replaced. Where, by the way, could she hide the old one, which was mine now exclusively, and which I ought to pocket, but, again, it was too soon for safe removal. Abortion, that's one problem I've always done without. Was it a fertile time with her? She hadn't the smallest idea. (It is I who am an arithmetician.) If Lenny became aware of *two* diaphragms, he would instantly draw the correct conclusion.

She wanted to give me a check for the encyclopedia (they had a joint checking account). "You've really made a sale," she smiled from her desk, her dark ringlets down on her cheek. "Do you always make sales this way?"

I demurred. I wasn't sure it would be prudent to take the check. That would be admitting having been alone with a salesman. Keen-scented Lenny would start barking up a tree, the right tree.

No, she argued. On the contrary, flaunting the sale (and the salesman) would point to her innocence; otherwise she would have kept me secret. Besides, the whole family of four needed and wanted the encyclopedia.

Well, needing the sale, I let her coax me into accepting the check. I had my serious doubts as to whether she was any better than I was at figuring out how her husband would reason. (Was he reasonable?) Sometimes we toil so hard and with such ingenuity to make jealous people think such and such: and they don't follow our leads. Ignoring all plausibility, they twistingly land on the truth—and it's you, you cunning two, who are squashed. Cleverness is frequently wasted on stupid people.

"You should stay, maybe, and meet Lenny. *Be* the salesman."

"No, thanks. No identifications."

It goes without saying that, in the way of business, I frequently had to return, in the evening, to push or confirm a sale with the so-called master of the house. But naturally my preference—and I may say my aptitude—was to deal with the women alone, and just hear about their husbands. It often didn't take much to trigger some remarkably intimate revelations, even if we didn't go to bed. Moreover, I have my sensitivities, and encountering a husband in the flesh, after being carnal with the wife, gave me an uncomfortably bigamous feeling that mere subjective description of him spared me. Like an analyst, I strive to confine myself to a one-to-one relationship. I'm good at whatever has two sides, but triangles—that's geometry, which I nearly flunked. The next-to-last thing I want is to identify with (you know, sympathetically) that third angle, the poor dope or dupe. Now suppose I saw Lenny and didn't find him fat at all. That would really bother me.

The *last* thing I want is to be identified by him. I could see Lenny taking one look at me, my amorous red hair, and rushing up to the guest room and sniffing. He would know me the second time he saw me, which would probably be when his wife and I were turning in to the motel. For we had already decided we couldn't meet there again, with him at work just a few blocks away.

"The rendezvous could be the Grand Union lot. It's big enough, and I'm not known there—I don't shop there."

"Maybe you should start shopping there," I replied. "That would make it more normal. The parking. But, on the other hand, when you brought the groceries home, your husband would notice where they came from, and I'm not sure we'd want that. Problems, problems. Grand union. How sexy!"

This was over the phone the next morning. I had fled, apparently successfully. "Are you sure you want to see me again," I said jestingly. When the answer is in doubt I don't ask.

"Dearest, as Cassius Clay said, you're the greatest."

And her husband was fourteen years younger than I! Well, as Hedy Lamarr pointed out (or was it Marlene Dietrich?), the best lovers are from thirty-five to fifty-five.

I would prearrange the motel. I had already used two on nearby Route 4 that I couldn't return to. I mean, there's a decorum—you don't go back to the same motel, no matter how satisfactory it's been, with another woman.

So I would have to go through the trouble again of checking as best I could for bugging devices, knotholes, and one-way mirrors. I'm not about to give a free show, accommodate mixoscopia, which is one big reason some motel-owners are in the business. Maybe I'm lacking in vanity. Even real mirrors around the bed I find disturbing and would prefer to cover them.

I must be the world's greatest authority on New York-area

motels. As used for illicit love. Of course there's one I've never been to—the No-Tell Motel. I don't see how they can have any business at all. If you're married to each other, it's an insult; if you're not, it's an admission.

I can remember when I was a neophyte, and went to my first. I appeared first, as became my delicate custom, by myself, to get the key. I deemed it the height of prudence to order a single, not a double. Then the wife and I—nice brown hair and stunning figure, from Stamford, expensive leather clothes but drank too much—wheeled up to the room and were cosily in bed when there came a knocking on the door as terrifying and unexpected as Milton's two-handed engine. "God help me, it's John!" whispered Beverly, and bobbed up and flew to the little bathroom and locked herself in. The second knock was even more urgent. I found my voice. "Yes?"

"Hate to bother you, sir, but you only paid for a single. That will be two dollars more, sir."

And he actually stood there, that slovenly Irishman, till I had clothed my arm sufficiently to be able to thrust it out with money. And I only had a fiver. So my first beloved stayed in the bathroom until the proprietor had gone to the office and shuffled back with three filthy ones. I certainly wasn't going to say to *him*, "Keep the change." He never saw us again, but I did learn the hard panicky way that the signs—that trappy place hadn't one—about *no visitors allowed to singles,* meant it.

At the places I went to, you did not have to sign in the lady. You just filled in the number of occupants as 2. But you had to give your own name, besides (which they could see) your correct license plate. It is a misdemeanor to supply a hotel register with a false name. That, the first time, gave me pause: I am timid about breaking the law. I compromised by writing my last name backwards: K. Mloh. If ever indicted, I could say I was confused: there is a mental disturbance whereby you write backwards. K. Mloh sounds rather interestingly European. With a name like that I'd have been widely acclaimed in this country, had I toured as a concert pianist.

You never knew who was seeing you and suspecting you. I always arrived before Florence (key in my pocket) at the parking lot: a Dartmouth man is never late, except for classes. I'd sit there wondering if other people were wondering why I didn't get out and shop. That clerk wheeling the shopping cart my way, wasn't he about to accuse me of coming every week, or nearly every week, and using space that was for patrons only? Could I say, "I'm waiting for the wife"? (I love these ambiguous truths.) Dare I rapturize, "Oh, I swear by grand union: I really do."

Then her purple Catalina would sidle up to my green Corvair. Without a word we'd both look around like international spies to see what was the best moment for her to get out and transfer to my front seat. That would strike any spectator as a bit odd, despite the prevalence in Bergen County of two-car families. All a suspicious clerk—or private detective—had to do was jot down license numbers. (I raised the question of whether she would—or wouldn't—be more inconspicuous riding in the back seat. Or possibly even crouching on the floor. During the perilous four-mile trip to and from the motel. I could get a chauffeur's cap, blotting out my culprit's hair, doffing it at the last minute only. But a chauffeur in a Chevy? Well, that's how the wealthy are, eccentric, spending and saving at the same time.) She'd dangle a little paper bag containing sandwiches, made by her own sweet hands. Once her husband returned in the morning, having forgotten something, and caught her boiling two eggs. (Two boiled eggs. Testicles being transferred. The sight of a boiled egg leaves me uncomfortable. Mutilation.) He said nothing, which was worse than if he'd made a joke, like "Eating for two again, Flo? Why didn't you tell me?"

Which reminds me how often I worried over whether we'd had an "accident." In fact I even had to worry about *his* accidents. Well, you know, the thing could slip, couldn't it? Rubber is slippery, isn't it, and worse with jelly on it, which is supposed to make it safer. And just one time, she might not put it in right. She had longer nails than I—mightn't she scratch a hole in it? I would hold it up to the light, like a jeweler searching for flaws in a moonstone. That's all we needed—a baby looking exactly like me. Hadn't I seen a cover in one of the women's magazines: "Is What You're Using Defective? Survey Shows Women Are Paying the Price for Manufacturer's Holes."

Her menstruation was quite irregular, defying all the books and my calculations. Her cycles ranged from twenty-six to twenty-nine days. That meant we had to be extra careful from the eighth day (twenty-six days minus eighteen) to the eighteenth day (twenty-nine days minus eleven). But it took time to find this out—she never knew it, and I'd be anxiously phoning: "Has it come?" "No." "My God, it's the twenty-eighth day! I thought surely it would have come yesterday. Try jumping down some steps. I saw a French film in which the woman sat in hot water for an hour." "That must have been a very boring picture. Who made it—Andy Warhol?" "Very funny. All right. It's your baby. You deserve to be a Roman Catholic."

Midway in our relationship Lenny started talking about wanting another child. He was asking her not to use the pessary, but she was resisting and would resort to deceit, if necessary (letting him think she didn't have it in when she did).

Around then I had a nightmare in which my mother came to me in a red bathrobe and said, "Sorry, son. I didn't mean it. You were just a slip of my pessary."

22

My dark demonic Flo, my water of life, what a
contrast there was—as with the ocean—between your storm and
your calm! Or rather, the difference was between your physical
stimulation and your mental, for you were always ready, in your
abounding energy, for the one or the other. I think it is a charac-
teristic of Jewish girls. Besides the bag of lunch, there was a
good chance you would be carrying one of your slim pretty
chapbooks—Shakespeare's Sonnets, *Sonnets from the Portu-
guese,* or the invert A. E. Housman with all those dead lads of
his. During part of our six or seven hours together in the Sunny
Crest Motel you would, as often as not, ask me to read. There
being no piano, I tried to be musical that way, just for you, and
you said I was. I hadn't read out loud since camp. Sometimes
you seemed to want a lecture on Beethoven or Shostakovich.
When I wanted to stop, all I had to do was touch you, almost
anywhere.

You loved my tongue that way, and you loved my tongue
the other way. How you needed it, down below. Your husband
never gave it to you, that sanitary man in the white coat. I
thought you would go out of your mind, or your body, in your
extreme illustration of orgasm, as defined by Kinsey, measured
and registered and filmed by Masters and Johnson, and called
by the French "the little death." You would groan, shudder, roll
up your eyes, cry "No, no" and "I can't stand it," and scissor-lock
my head. If I had been an infant your thighs would have gone
right through my soft cranium.

No more symbolic action for me, no more temporary entering of wombs. My situation is comparable to that of the infant of
Saguntum, in Pliny's anecdote that Ben Jonson began a poem

259

with. Hannibal was devastating that city in Spain when the infant was being born; it took one long wail and went right back into the womb. "Womb: tomb": shortest life, shortest poem.

In a love affair there is always the problem of how confiding to be. Perfect love, perfect confidence, but where is that to be found? No doubt, the ultimate is *no doubt,* never having to be tactful, to be so sure of each other and each other's mutual understanding that you can say whatever pops into your head, knowing you won't hurt or be hurt. I can't say we were together long enough for that, quite. I don't know what she held back. I do remember distinctly when I did. She told me her husband had gone to a dermatologist to have an excrescence removed from his forehead. This put me in mind—but apparently not her—of the cuckold's horns. In fact there *is* a thickening of the human skin that may take place above the brows, known to dermatologists as keratosis. That may have been what Lenny was treated for.

I did hint darkly about my uncertainty as to who my father was. I described—without identifications—previous carnal encounters. About San Toy I reminisced very frankly. Indeed the nearest we ever came to a quarrel was in that connection. I had come up for air from below, from the nether region (by Jupiter, it sounds like Aeneas or Dante emerging from hell), and when I was in a conversational position vis-à-vis my mistress, I blurted: "Pekingese dogs were bred by Chinese ladies to serve as lickers. That's how we have them, if now no longer why."

"How disgusting! What a disgusting thing to say!"

She actually got out of bed. I reached for her departing hand. "Come on, Flo. I was just being encyclopedic, free associating."

"Yes, me with your damn San Toy. Did *she* lick *you?*"

"I'm sorry. If anything, I was demeaning myself—not you, comparing myself to a dog."

"You cur, if that's what you want to be called. You demean us both. And I didn't like that crack of yours the other day about

260

an electric vibrator being better than a man. *Are* you a man or not? *If* you are, shut up."

Our reconciliation was silent. As you see, there tend to be limits. There just isn't anybody you can say everything to, unless you pay fifty dollars for fifty minutes.

But we came close. We were getting there. We needed time, only. I'm being honest. I've reported the worst. What's *your* worst?

She was quite free of guilt feelings, as wives go. It is likely that our mutual sense of the forbidden heightened our pleasure, in accordance with the truth enunciated by my favorite Pope (which Pope? Pope Alexander), "How glowing guilt exalts the keen delight!"

I never suspected her of psychogenic illness. All I ever noticed was colds. She'd bring a box of Kleenex and lay it beside the pillow. "I know it's not very romantic." I told her when she was older she'd have fewer colds. I didn't tell her she'd have other things instead.

Let me be given full credit for braving her germs: greater love hath no hypochondriac. (If she loves me, I romantically reasoned, there will be nothing hostile in her body.)

The day she died was without portent, except for a nebulous sky in the morning and an hour's snow in the late afternoon. While fully aware that light snow can be much more dangerous, on account of slick, than inches of it that give you traction, I don't recall worrying about it any more than usual. We did peek out on the cold world from our well-heated cocoon ("A womb with a view"), naked arm on naked shoulder, and say something about allowing some extra time in case of trouble getting home. It is true that my attitude toward snow has changed since I was a boy and afraid merely of sleds. I would prefer to see it confined to Christmas cards, if I weren't also weary of Christmas cards. But I belong to the AAA, I had new expensive snow tires, I had a bag of sand and a shovel in my trunk: I even had a tow chain. Everything foreseeable had been provided for. We had spoken, long before, of the necessity of not having a minor accident on the way to or from the Sunny Crest, with the police taking all names and our being summoned into court. I invariably drove with fanatic care and painful slowness those four miles. This took self-restraint, when I was urged the one way by eagerness to join and on the way back by zeal to separate safely. The return way was not at all the *triste animal post coitum* situation, but the simple wish to finish another day without mishap, get back to the parking lot and go unnoticed our separate ways. Speed naturally had its strong temptation as presumably decreasing the chances of our being noticed by some curious party. While I slow-poked at the wheel, she served as lookout. "That car's been behind us quite a while, though you're only doing twenty-five." "All right, I'll signal a right turn, and if he follows I'll keep going around the block, which ought to embarrass him, if anything can." Any disaster of discovery *she* would bear the brunt of: which made it imperative for me to be cool, if not jocular. I didn't worry about character assassination for myself: just assassination.

Minor accidents? I could have told her I don't have *minor* accidents.

On the other hand, *her* favorite quotation, from the Song of Songs, was, "Love is strong as death." She repeated it, in purple ink, in an unsigned Christmas card she mailed me. "Did you like it, dearest? If you knew the trouble I had to find one without snow, without Santa Claus, without bad poetry, and all the other things you can't stand."

I also can't stand being asked to believe what isn't so. I'll leave it to the Atheist Society to compile the long list of things in the Bible that science has disproved.

After looking at the snow, we scrambled back to bed, *enfants du paradis*. Soon I was kneeling on the carpet, as if at the Communion rail, and she, on the bed, was clamping my head between her thighs and the Oh's and the No's that I loved to elicit began coming. In the midst of what I took to be the final paroxysm, the final groan, I hurriedly mounted her and rammed myself home. I wanted some share, visually, tactilely, of her last pleasure.

Her eyes widened in distress as they had done that first morning in her house. I thought maybe I was hurting her. There was a gasp, I didn't know whether of the ecstasy of pleasure or the ecstasy of pain. Abruptly she was quiet. Her eyes remained open.

When you faint, aren't you supposed to close your eyes? I drew away from her, extricated myself, got out of the range of her vitreous black stare. Would water help?

I do not know how many minutes I sat beside her on the double bed, not holding her hand, not touching her. She wasn't breathing: with a naked person you can tell beyond any doubt. Her mouth was slightly open. I didn't know whether to use my one handkerchief to bind her jaw or to protect myself from her eyes, which I tried not to look at.

My heart beat twice as fast to make up for her stillness. A heart attack, that's what she must have had. But there'd never been any hint of this weakness, except maybe that early reference of hers to the pill possibly swelling her legs. She smoked too much, but she seemed as strong as she was young, and under her influence I had been getting stronger, scarcely ever giving a thought to *my* health anymore.

At last I eased myself off the bed and dressed, even to my fur-lined gloves. I picked up the red-tagged key from the vanity table and stepped out into the neon-lit snow and closed the door behind me. I inserted the key into the spring lock, left it dangling there, the way I always did, the way I was supposed to at that motel. This indicated to the owner or the maid that you were going away and not coming back. It regularly made me uneasy, driving off and leaving the key and the room accessible like that. I did not see why someone might not sneak by and in and make off with the TV set—and I be accused. In the driver's seat I sat staring through the windshield at the key. Anyone could go in now and find her lying naked on the double bed.

As I sat there in my enclosure, thinking about her in hers, my loss hit me as it had not before. I not only realized how much I missed her but how much I was going to miss her, alone in my car, alone wherever I went. And I couldn't then do what I had never done before, drive off without her. There was the usual mixture of selfishness and unselfishness: panic no longer blinded me to the fact that I would be convicting myself by driving away. The proprietor had my name backwards, but he also had my correct license plate and could identify me and my green Corvair. Her, on the other hand, I believe he had never clearly seen: we always took No. 28, the outermost room, the room farthest from the office and the traffic ("I like quiet").

There was nothing to do but go back to her, and I did. With the light back on, but not looking at her, I dropped into the maple armchair that had more than once been our experimental seat of love.

Would I be charged with murder? I enacted an explanation in which the hysteria was real. "Officer, I'm a compulsive adulterer, on account of a delicate situation having to do with my mother. Now she, there, is—or was—Florence. Florence who no longer flowers. Flo who suddenly stopped flowing. I had been meeting with her—without the least coercion, two consenting adults, or adulterers, if you insist. And she's gone and died on me at the Sunny Crest Motel. On me? Not exactly. Under me. Her sunny crest wilted. The woman who used to moan as she pressed my head, 'Oh, I can't stand it.' And finally she couldn't. *Liebestod.* The last chord, the last shudder.

"You want her last name? Can't you just write down X? I swear to God I was going to get her to change it. I'm almost ashamed to admit it—it's against everything I have ever lain for—but two weeks ago I spoke of marrying her. That's how much she had grown on me."

We had been having one of our contented chattering interludes, lying naked side by side. I mused over the mistake that motels were making in not having rockers. "Assume certain postures in a rocker with your mistress, and start rocking, and if you're not careful—so intense is the pleasure—she'll go off her rocker." She had read something about dildos and swings in Japan. Then we got off on traveling. She asked me if I ever wanted to visit South America, and I said no, it was too buggy. "Beetles in the coffee—jumping coffee beans!" Chile was in the news on account of some border incident. She confessed to not having any clear idea as to where that country was.

I propped my head on an elbow and surveyed her.

"That would be Volume Six, and our Information Service would even prepare you a pamphlet, if you sent in your numbered coupon. Well, let's say your lovely body is South America. Your left leg—though it would have to be fat—would be Argentina. Your right leg—which I'm glad to say isn't that thin—would be Chile. And up here, on the border of Argentina and Paraguay, is Resistencia."

I laid my hand on her dark vital center. No resistance, except that she put her hand over mine. "Or maybe we're at Concepción, in the center of Paraguay," I went on, wiggling a finger.

Conception. "We might get married," I said.

She drew back her head on the pillow, in that way she had. "Now you're piling up distractions. You don't believe in marriage. Remember?"

"There are exceptions, or so I hope."

She stilled my hand. "None of your tricks, just to take me at a disadvantage. We'd have to do a lot of cool thinking. Isn't it the part-timeness of a love affair that makes it work?"

And that was all that was said on that subject. But I would have come back to it—I know I would, O my America, my New-Found-Land!

One leg was still arched upward, almost coyly. About that I at last did something. Standing alongside the bed in my overcoat, I pressed it down with both gloved hands.

Not helped in my sweat by removal of overcoat and gloves, I

next arranged her black hair over her eyes, sufficiently so that all that part might have passed for the back of her head. I didn't touch the eyes or the eyelids, just shoveled them under with hair, hair which, as the medical counsellor had taught me at camp, is the first thing about us that's dead, dead skin. Fortunately her hair came to her shoulders, the kind I have always gone for, and so by catching it under her scarf, which I tied tightly around her neck, I had a fairly eye-proof bundle. At least as long as she wasn't moved.

But she'd have to be moved. She'd have to be dressed.

I sat that out a long while. I had never dressed a woman. I had never carried a woman, either. Once, as I was running my hand over her curves, I had asked her her weight. I told her in my encyclopedic way about the Roman custom of the husband's carrying the bride over the threshold, for good luck. "Did Lenny carry you in Bermuda?" "No, he didn't. Is that why we had bad luck? But suppose the husband stumbles. What then?"

I got up and looked out from under the drapes. It was long past the time we were supposed to go home. Now there would be a delay till the middle of the night. The proprietor, who was used to having us depart at 4:45, would be surprised. I expected that he rented the room all over again at night to people who merely wanted to sleep. But I was entitled to it without further payment till 11 A.M.

I made a mess of dressing the corpse. I pulled and I pushed and got out of breath and sank back in the armchair for frequent rest. I ripped a stocking. Both stayed wrinkled at the knees. I didn't attach to the garter belt, keeping contact with her skin to a minimum. That ridiculous thing, I had a momentary uncertainty as to whether it went over the panties or under. I got the brassiere through her arms but didn't clasp that either. The main point was to leave nothing at the motel.

In George Eliot's *Middlemarch* a romantic young man says of the heroine, "I would rather touch her hand if it were dead,

266

than I would touch any other woman's living." What a blissfully ignorant statement.

It took hours before I had her laid out, wrinkled, ruffled, but complete even to her cloche hat. But, though dark, it was much too early to go. The traveling salesmen, the truckers, the people who really intended to sleep that night—were beginning to fill the place up. We had a tenant on the one side now. I had jumped at the rattle of the lock. Television pulsated with all too perfect clarity through the wall. It was a musical comedy program and must have been full of visual jokes, for the audience kept going into loud convulsions without audible reason, without a word said. I was tempted to turn on our own set, in self-defense. Act normal, or rather, average: it's usually the safest thing to do. But, no, if anyone was going to disturb me at my door I wanted to be sure to hear.

It was ten minutes after midnight before all around me had been quiet long enough for me to feel that I could venture out with you, Florence, in my arms. I had your cloche hat well down over what didn't look at all like your face. But you were watching behind your hair—I knew you were. I nearly did stumble over the threshold with my borrowed bride (going sideways through the narrow door), on account of the slick and the—to put it mildly—unaccustomed weight. I wondered whether a scientific detective could figure out by measuring the footsteps that whoever made them had been carrying a body, 138 pounds added to 155 pounds. I don't know where I found the strength. My childhood minister preached that you don't know what strength you have until the trial comes.

That night there was not the moon's evil eye, but there was more neon light by the car than I wanted—the puke-colored curse of modern civilization. I just had to assume that no one was peering out, or, if so, thought I was handling a stiff—by which I mean a drunk.

No, you hadn't become stiff, but I had every intention of

not dallying. I did not see your face. I understand it starts with the face.

I did not follow the dictate of melodrama by attempting to stuff you into the trunk. I laid you on the floor of the back seat where I had once, more than half seriously, suggested that you crouch on our trips to and fro. I covered you with two blankets that I carry around in winter to keep from freezing in case my car breaks down. I was planning to drive correctly but inconspicuously, as usual, so that there would be no excuse for stopping me. Besides, they've seen the same films I have, read the same newspapers, and the trunk would be the first place they'd search.

Moreover, a Corvair (now on its way out, like me) has the trunk in front. Thus Florence would have *preceded me to the grave* in a double sense, me the unnerved driver (drive her). No thanks, Demonic Jester.

I'm not one to gaze at cemeteries as I drive past them, but there's a big one on River Street in Hackensack that I couldn't help but be aware of. Automobiles and trucks used to make long lines there waiting to pass through the State Inspection Station. You'd inch along (if you didn't stall) in a process that could consume several hours, worrying about whether they'd give your car the OK sticker, and meanwhile on your right was the invitation to wonder about the OK—or the KO—of the Eternal Judgment. It was a situation that I got into only once; subsequent times I hired the garage man to take my car. I wouldn't have faced that again for a hundred dollars; he did it for five. Shows how different people are.

Churches boast that they are open day and night. Was it true of cemeteries? The big gates of Heaven-Hell (we Protestants are decisive, no middle ground of Purgatory for us) were closed, but I gave them a nudge with my bumper and they creaked open. And I dragged her out onto one of the nearest graves, leaving her propped up against the tombstone, her handbag (for identification) beside her. I loosened her hair before I fled.

I guess that night, Lenny, you didn't sleep any more than I did. What did you do when you came home for dinner and your wife wasn't there? Did you bound up the stairs two at a time and check on the diaphragm? It was there, one was there, right there in the powdered bag depending from the hook on the bathroom door. She used to keep it in the medicine chest, but we made the decision—after the usual doubt-laden discussion (wouldn't a change make him wonder why it was made?)—that she should flaunt it.

"Th' other, let it sleep with death."

Did you at last call the police, Lenny? Or are you the type that waits a long, long while before making public private trouble? Well, in the morning they'd phone you.

If I killed her, I killed her with joy. Which is more (is that good or is that bad?) than you would ever have done, Lenny. What a way to go! Or would you rather die as Vespasian did (according to Sir Francis Bacon's essay "Of Death"), while squatting on the toilet (that is, the Roman imperial equivalent of a toilet)? "Ut puto Deus fio," were the Emperor's last words, the emperor upon his throne. "As I think, I am becoming a god." Only, my theory is that Vespasian was punning with the verb from which we get "putrescent": "As I stink, I am becoming a god."

I was forty-six then. Nothing has happened since except that I'm forty-seven. ("By the way, Holm, is your health good?" "No, MacSwain, it isn't.") My troubles and fears this morning may owe something to last night's reading. Just as you have to be careful what you eat before going to bed, your choice of literature may undo you. I went back for the first time to that Shakespeare Sonnet 22 that was the first thing that Florence asked me to read her. I never did read that one to her: and you know how it is, you do something when it's too late, or even *because* it's too late. So I looked at it in bed last night and got stabbed for my trouble by the line, "Presume not on thy heart when mine is slain." That clearly—as if Flo were looking down and speaking through a medium—promises me a heart attack.

And the dizzy spell was another circulatory warning, and I don't see how I can get up and go to New York as scheduled and face my boss Harvey-Garvey, who is never satisfied with the number of encyclopedias I have sold, or trees of knowledge I have planted.

If I knock on the wall, Sis will eventually get up and bring me coffee. That I am living with her, here in a small rented house in Little Ferry, may surprise you, after all that I have said against her. We bumped into each other on Broadway six years ago, and she looked terrible. Her grocery clerk husband had disappeared ages ago, and I don't know what she had been living on: very little. I was perfectly ready to suspect prostitution in her younger days, but now she couldn't even pass as a madam. Anyway, I took her in, which was why (apart from curious neighbors) I had to go to motels. When she doesn't tipple too much (like Miss Warren), she is capable of preparing for me good balanced meals without spices. She never looks cross-eyed at me and I got her a headphone for her TV. Since she knows which side her bread is buttered on, we get along quite well. The only trouble, which I can't altogether blame her for, is that, as she looks a little like me in a grotesque sort of half-sister way, I see myself in fat caricature seven years from now, seven years nearer the grave, should I not be in it.

So much for my next-to-last embarrassing revelation, the last being my nightmare. Much as I hate to go into that, I'm not going to forget it by not setting it down.

But let me mention also that increasingly of late I fear the coming of a condition that will cause me to long for nightmares. I fear getting blind. (If I become blind, dreams, no matter how horrible, will be welcome as the only times when I can see.) After three hours of sleep I wake up to darkness, the victim of some morbid summons. I blink my eyes and roll my head and when there is nothing—black nothing—everywhere I turn my sightless orbs—for the book of knowledge fair presented with a universal blank—I press the panic button of my night-table lamp, by which San Toy squats in a picture taken before she suffered cataracts. During my troubled sleep an iritis or the sudden thrust of a brain tumor could, with terrible ease, have rendered me permanently blind. I would go down the street with my cane, frightening little children. I would *want* to have nightmares rather than nothing and would eat indigestible foods to induce them. . . . About eight nights ago I pushed the button and no light came. I screamed "Sis! Sis!" and stumbled into her room and was a maniac until she put her light on and we discovered that my bulb had blown out. I now keep a lamp on both sides of my bed, and a flashlight on the floor.

In my dream I wandered out in a transparent garment of uncertain sex, like a nightgown, made of whatever a fish's eye is made of. Bodies that might or might not have been alive stood lined up looking at me as I paraded past. A thousand pairs of unmoving eyes were fixed on me. They took in my hairless chest, my potbelly, my membrum virile that wasn't very large and didn't look good for much of anything except squirting the bed. I was exposed to everybody. Every body. My arms were paralyzed but I tried to fend off the starers by shouting, "You're dead." They shouted back, like the voice from the whirlwind: "Peek-a-boo. We see you. You're dead, too."

> *Thou, looking then about,*
> *Ere thou wert half got out,*
> *Wise child, didst hastily return,*
> *And madst thy mother's womb thine urn.*

The infant of Saguntum. O rare Ben: rarer if never born. Ken Holm. (Know home.) K. Mloh. In my end is my beginning. In my beginning is my end. Tomorrow never knows.

271

Le Comte, Edward
The man who was afraid.